PRAISE FOR **THE SCATTERING**

"Wylie's compelling first-person narration, tough conflicts with others, and her courage against formidable odds make this an un-put-downable thriller."
—*Kirkus Reviews*

"As was the case in the series starter, it is action-packed and fast-paced. There is some backstory for readers new to the series, but those who have not read the first book may feel overwhelmed by the many characters and their shifting allegiances. Fans of the first book will dive into this second entry with gusto, as Wylie's journey continues in a compelling fashion."
—*VOYA*

"Another twisty-turny psychological thriller from a master."
—ALA *Booklist*

"*The Scattering* is breathlessly fast-paced and enticingly suspenseful."
—Associated Press

Also by Kimberly McCreight

The Outliers

For Adult Readers
Reconstructing Amelia
Where They Found Her

THE SCATTERING

THE SECOND BOOK IN THE OUTLIERS TRILOGY

KIMBERLY McCREIGHT

HARPER
An Imprint of HarperCollinsPublishers

The Scattering

Copyright © 2017 by Kimberly McCreight

All rights reserved. Printed in the United States of America.

No part of this book may be used or reproduced in any manner whatsoever without written permission except in the case of brief quotations embodied in critical articles and reviews. For information address HarperCollins Children's Books, a division of HarperCollins Publishers, 195 Broadway, New York, NY 10007.

www.epicreads.com

Library of Congress Control Number: 2016950348
ISBN 978-0-06-235913-1

Typography by Sarah Nichole Kaufman
18 19 20 21 22   PC/LSCH   10 9 8 7 6 5 4 3 2 1
❖
First paperback edition, 2018

For every girl who's been told she's too sensitive.
For every woman who's taught herself not to be.

Life is a dream. 'Tis waking that kills us.
—Virginia Woolf, *Orlando*

AUTHOR'S NOTE

This is a work of fiction. The things that you read here did not happen. At least, not yet.

THE SCATTERING

PROLOGUE

I STAND IN THE DARK, BAREFOOT AND COLD ON THE EDGE OF THE SHARP ROCKS, staring out over the long stretch of black water in front of me. And I wonder if I really can make it all the way to that small light on the dock in the distance. It seems so impossibly far away, the water so frighteningly still like it's just waiting for someone fool enough to try.

I am not a very strong swimmer, or not nearly strong enough. I've never made it that kind of distance. Not fully clothed, not in the darkness. Across unfamiliar water, with all the tricks a pin-prick of light on the horizon can play, who knows what could go wrong? But we have no choice. They are coming for us. For me, actually. They are already here. Voices in the distance, creeping closer. It's only a matter of time.

But the real crazy thing? These bad facts notwithstanding, deep down I do believe I can swim the mile or more to that dock. I know it, actually. Maybe that's all that matters. Because if I have learned anything in these past weeks, it's that strength is just another word for faith. And true courage lies in holding out hope.

And right now, it's just me and my doubt at the water's edge anyway. I know not to let that get the better of me. Instead, I need to trust my instincts.

So I take one last deep breath before I step forward and set my gaze on that faraway horizon. And then I start to swim.

1

I AM IN OUR FOYER STARING AT THE TEXT FROM JASPER. AT THAT ONE WORD:
Run.

For a minute. For an hour. Forever.

My heart drums against my rib cage as my eyes stay down.
The six agents say things. Their names—Agent Klute and Agent
Johansen and Agent something else and something else. *Run.
Don't run. Run. Don't run.* They say other things: Department of
Homeland Security. Ruling out a domestic security threat. The
rest is just buzzing.

Run. Don't run. Run. Don't run.

Run.

I spin toward the steps, phone gripped like a hand grenade.
Run first. Questions later. Quentin taught me that.

"Wylie?" my dad shouts after me. Stunned. Confused. Worried. "Wylie, what are you—"

Voices, jostling behind me as I pound toward the steps. Don't look back. Don't slow down. On and up the stairs. On and up. That's what I need to do.

But why up? Shouldn't I run out the back door and not deeper into the house? The upstairs bathroom and the slanted, notched part of the roof. That must be it. A way out. I grab the banister when my feet slip.

"Ms. Lang!" one of them calls. So close I can almost feel his breath.

"Stop! Leave her alone!" My dad sounds so angry I barely recognize his voice. Many more voices shout back at him. Gasping, thudding, a struggle. "You can't just barge into our house!"

"Dr. Lang, calm down!"

"Hey! Stop!" The voice behind me again. Even closer now. I lunge forward as I hit the upstairs hall.

The bathroom. That's where I need to go. *Focus. Focus. Faster. Faster.* Before he grabs me. The door isn't far. And I'll only need a second to open the window and crawl out. After a quick slide to the ground, I'll do then what I have done before. Run. Like. Hell.

Down the hallway I pound, loud feet still just a stride behind me. "Wylie!" the man calls out, but stiff like he doesn't want to admit that I even have a name.

"This is our house!" my dad shouts again. He sounds closer to the steps.

"Dr. Lang, you need to stay here!"

My eyes are locked on the bathroom door at the end of the hall. It seems so far away. The hallway endless. But I need to get to that door. Window up. Slide out. One step at a time. As fast as I possibly can.

"Ms. Lang!" The voice again, much closer. Too close. And nervous. He is near enough to grab me but is too afraid of hurting me. "Come on! Stop! What are you doing?"

Past the first door on the right. Two more left to go.

But then my foot catches on the carpet. I manage to get my hands up at the very last second so that it's my wrist that cracks hard against the wall, and then my shoulder instead of my face. Still, the shooting pain makes me feel dizzy as I hit the ground. I think I might vomit as I roll into myself, cradling my arm against my stomach. I'm afraid to look down. Terrified the bone might be poking through.

"Jesus, are you okay?" The agent has stopped in front of me. I can now see he's the short one with the overly muscular arms that stick out stiffly from his sides. And he is definitely as nervous as he sounded. But also annoyed. He looks up and down the hall like he's checking for witnesses. "Damn it. I told you not to run."

A FEW MINUTES later, I am sitting on the slouched couch in our small living room as my dad wraps an ice pack around my throbbing wrist. The pain is making my brain vibrate. The men have silently positioned themselves so that they now block the door and the stairs and the hallway toward the back. Each and every one of the possible exits. They look even bigger inside the compact frame of our old Victorian home than they did outside. There is definitely no way out now.

"I don't think it's broken," Agent Klute announces, peering at my arm. But not nearly close enough to make that kind of assessment.

My dad, on his feet in front of me, turns around and gets right in Agent Klute's face. He looks so tiny by comparison, like a little boy.

"Get the hell out of my house," he snaps, pointing toward the door. "Now, I mean it. All of you out."

Like he will try to remove Klute by force if he has to. My dad's fury has made him blind to their difference in size. He would die trying to protect me, I can see that so clearly now. I wish I had known it before. I'm not sure what it would have changed about what happened at the camp. Everything maybe.

"I'm afraid we can't leave, Dr. Lang." Klute lowers his head. "Not until Wylie answers our questions."

He is trying to appear unthreatening. Apologetic. It doesn't work. Especially because he doesn't *feel* sorry. I can tell. I can read his feelings well enough to have no doubt. Actually, Agent Klute feels so very little. It's chilling. My dad steps closer, his anger rising.

"You can't just barge into my home and *chase* after my daughter. She is the *victim* here," my dad says. "Even if she *was* a criminal, you need a warrant to be in someone's home. It's not legal. God help you if her wrist is broken."

"To be clear, Dr. Lang, your daughter ran from federal agents. Do you have any idea how dangerous that is?"

My dad almost laughs. Then he presses his fingertips to his mouth, as if in prayer. I have never seen him this angry before. Rage has changed the shape of his face. But I can feel him trying so hard to stay calm. To do what needs to be done.

"Get out. Get out. Get out," my dad says—slow and quiet and steady. Like a drumbeat. "Right now. Or so help me God—"

"As I said, we can't do that." Agent Klute is still so freakishly calm. "Wylie is a material witness to a multiple homicide that could be linked to domestic terrorism. We need her to come with us now and answer some questions. That's all."

"Ha!" my dad huffs. "I'm calling a lawyer."

What lawyer? I think as my dad grabs for his phone and dials. And yet he seems so confident as he puts the phone to his ear. Time stretches out as we stand there, waiting for someone to answer his call, for my dad to speak. I can feel Agent Klute staring at me. I try not to look back at him, but I cannot help myself.

Sure enough, his cold, black eyes are locked on me, his mouth hanging open a little so that I can see his huge white teeth. I imagine them biting into me. But I don't sense any of the hostile feelings I would expect to be coming from him—no annoyance or suspicion or aggravation. There is only one thing: pity. And, it turns out, that is so much more terrifying.

I cross my arms tight as my stomach balls up. Maybe I should just answer their questions. Maybe that would make this all go away faster. Except I also have the most awful sense that—no matter what I say—this is the beginning of something and not the end.

Breathe, I remind myself. *Breathe.* Because the room is narrowing, the floor beginning to shift underfoot. And this is definitely not the time to black out. I've been an Outlier for thirty-six hours, but I know I am still capable of totally losing it.

"Hi, Rachel, it's Ben," my dad finally says into the phone. "I need you to call me back as soon as you can. It's an emergency."

Rachel. Right. Of course my dad would call her. Rachel was my mom's friend. Or ex–best friend. After years of her and my mom being out of touch, Rachel appeared out of nowhere at my mom's funeral. Ever since, she's been like some kind of rash we can't get rid of. She wants to help. Or so she claims. My dad says it's probably her way of coping with her grief. If you ask me, what—or who—she actually wants is my dad. Regardless, the whole thing is weird. *She* is weird, and I don't trust her.

But like her or not, Rachel is a criminal defense attorney. She would know what to do in a situation like this. And Rachel might be a totally shitty person—the details of their falling-out were never something my mom would share, but even she always said that Rachel was the person she'd call if she ever found herself in real trouble, because "Rachel could keep a bragging serial killer out of prison." And my mom didn't mean it as a compliment.

"Dr. Lang, if Wylie has nothing to hide, it shouldn't be a problem for her to talk to us," Agent Klute says when my dad hangs up.

"Maybe it would be less of a problem if you hadn't tackled me," I say, because it seems like my dad could use some help.

"Hey, you fell!" the short agent pipes up. "I didn't touch you."

That's true, of course, but it hardly feels like the important point.

Agent Klute frowns at me. None of this is going the way it was supposed to. And now he is aggravated, but only a little. Like he's just gotten a small drop of soup on an otherwise dark shirt. "I can assure you, Dr. Lang, we have *extremely* broad authority to question witnesses in cases of suspected terrorism. And we don't need a warrant. Wylie is not under arrest. At least not yet."

"After that"—my dad points to me, my arm specifically—"the only way we're answering your questions is if our lawyer tells us we have to."

Agent Klute takes a breath. "Fine. When will she be here?"

"I don't know," my dad says, trying to sound like this gives him the upper hand. Though he knows that it does not. And he's worried about where this situation is headed. I can feel that loud and clear.

Agent Klute stares blankly at my dad. "We'll just wait for your lawyer then. For as long as it takes."

FOR A WHILE after, a half hour maybe, my dad and I sit in silence, side by side on the couch. The agents stand as still as statues in each corner. Agent Klute is the only one who moves, pacing as he sends texts. He's getting more agitated with each one, our floor creaking eerily under his heavy feet.

I want to text Jasper, but who knows what he will say? And if the agents do bring me in for questioning, they could easily take my phone. It's safer to wait to talk to Jasper until after they are gone.

My dad calls Rachel two more times, but both calls go to voice mail. And so we wait some more. Thirty more minutes go by. Then an hour. I cannot believe how uncomfortable our living room couch is. I don't think anyone has ever sat on it that long, definitely not me. Eventually, I need to use the bathroom, but I can't bear the thought of someone going with me. And I am sure they will.

I'm just beginning to think I'll have no choice but to bear bathroom babysitters when Agent Klute's phone vibrates loudly in his hand. "Excuse me, I need to take this call," he says, nodding at the other agents, letting them know they are temporarily in charge before stepping outside the house.

As the front door closes behind Agent Klute, my dad's phone finally rings. "Rachel," he answers, desperate and relieved. He's quiet, listening for a minute. "Well, not great to be honest. Could you come over? It's kind of an emergency. No, no, nothing like that." He pauses and takes a deep breath as he stands. But he doesn't actually go anywhere. He just hovers there in front of the couch. On his feet, he seems so unsteady, like part of him is disintegrating. "There are some federal agents here, and they want to interview Wylie and I'm just—she's been through a lot, and I want to schedule it for another time." Silence again as Rachel responds. "I did. They refused. They said because this has to do with domestic terrorism and Wylie's not a suspect . . ." More silence. "Yeah, okay. Okay. Thank you, Rachel."

He seems better, more hopeful when he turns back to me. "What did she say?" I ask.

"That we're doing the right thing," he says. "We should just wait here. She's on her way."

MY DAD STILL has the phone in his hand when Agent Klute steps back inside the house. "We'll be in touch soon, Dr. Lang," Klute says matter-of-factly. As if this is an extension of a conversation we were already having. As if this was already agreed upon. "We'll schedule another time for that interview."

But why? Because I am not buying that Agent Klute is taking off because he's afraid of some lawyer he's never met. He doesn't even know Rachel finally called back. Klute nods in the direction of his men. No, they are leaving for their own reasons. Bad ones.

"Where are you going?" I ask though I would probably be much better off not saying a word. It's not as if I want them to stay.

When Agent Klute looks at me, I feel it again: pity. And it's worse this time. So definitive and deep. He nods again. "We'll be in touch."

I watch as Klute and his men gather together and disappear out the door. And I imagine it like that eerily quiet moment when the tide gets pulled out to sea, right before a tsunami crashes back to shore. Silent and astonishing and totally terrifying.

2

Six weeks later

I OPEN MY EYES TO DARKNESS. MY BEDROOM. THE MIDDLE OF THE NIGHT. JASPER calling. Without checking, I already know it is him. But I don't reach for my phone. Sometimes he only calls once and hangs up. And tonight, for the first time in a long time, all I want to do is sleep.

Ever since we got back from Maine six weeks ago, Jasper's late-night calls have become an everyday thing. Jasper is on his new phone, of course. Because it hadn't been him who sent the text telling me to run that day all those weeks ago when the agents were standing at my door.

As soon as Agent Klute and his friends had left our house, I called Jasper back—wanting to be sure he was okay, wanting to know why exactly he had told me to run. But he hadn't answered his phone. After two more hours of calling and being unable to track down a landline number for Jasper's family, I'd insisted—over my dad's strong objection—that we drive over to Jasper's house and check on him.

Jasper had been completely fine when he'd finally answered the door—sleepy and confused, but fine. He didn't even have his phone, hadn't seen it since Quentin had taken it from him at the camp.

The local police had found my phone in the main cabin and had returned it to me that morning during one of the many interviews at the rest stop. But Jasper and I were being questioned separately then. I had just assumed he had gotten his back, too. Actually, I hadn't thought about it at all. But the officers had never found Jasper's phone.

Someone had told me to run at the exact right moment, though. And to what terrible end I could only imagine. Maybe they had been hoping that running would get me killed.

My dad did contact Agent Klute later when we realized the message hadn't come from Jasper. Klute had agreed to look into the text and then sometime later proclaimed the whole thing to be some kind of prank. We did press him for details. A prank didn't make sense. But Agent Klute stopped returning our calls. And it was hard to object to that when we also never wanted to hear from him again.

My phone chirps again now and I feel around for it on the nightstand. Think again about how I should change it to some less jarring ringtone. But then, I'll stay jumpy regardless of my ringtone.

It's a big achievement that I was asleep at all. Neither Jasper nor I have slept much since we got back from Maine—too much regret, too much guilt. Instead, we survive the endless nights on the phone, talking about everything and nothing. And I lie on my bed, staring at the old photos that line my bedroom walls, thinking I should take them down because they remind me of my mom. Knowing that is the reason I never will.

Jasper and I try to keep our conversations light, to help blot out the darkness. Maybe that's exactly why it doesn't work. The "what-ifs" of the choices we made that night as we drove north— "what if" we'd told Cassie's mom right away, "what if" we'd ignored Cassie and had gone to different police earlier—are way too loud and angry by comparison. But all the talking has made Jasper and me closer. Sometimes I wonder how long it will last or how real it can be, this friendship born out of so much awfulness. Other times, I don't want to think about that. I don't want to think too hard about anything. There are too many questions I don't know how to answer.

In her usual therapist way, Dr. Shepard has said she doesn't think it's a good idea for us to rehash too much, and neither do I. Jasper can't help himself, though. We both have our what-ifs, sure, but it was Jasper who straight-out blamed Cassie for getting us locked in the camp. I say the same thing every time he brings it up: No, it is not *your* fault, Jasper. Cassie is dead because of Quentin, not you. And that is what I think.

Jasper doesn't believe me, though. Sometimes when I look in his eyes, I feel like I am watching someone slowly starve to death. And I am standing right there, my arms filled with food.

Not that I am totally fine now by comparison. I still have

horrible nightmares, and every day I cry at least once. Normal signs of grief and trauma, Dr. Shepard says. My anxiety didn't disappear the second I was told I was an Outlier, either.

But these days there is less oxygen fanning the flames. I am working on separating out other people's emotions from my own anxiety. There are little differences, it turns out, in the way each feels. My own anxiety is colder, deeper in my gut, while other people's feelings sit higher in my chest. And now Dr. Shepard's breathing exercises and her mindfulness meditations and her positive self-talk—things she has always advised—are actually starting to work, probably because I am more willing to believe they will.

Finally, I lay my hands on my phone, almost knocking it to the ground before I answer.

"Hey," comes out garbled. I clear my throat. "What's up?"

"Shit, were you sleeping?" Jasper asks. He sounds almost hurt, betrayed by my lack of insomnia.

"Um, not really," I lie. "I was just—what's up?" Then I remember why he's probably called so late. Because this is late, even for him. "Oh, wait, the dinner with your mom. How was it?"

Jasper was supposed to tell her that he's having second thoughts about playing hockey for Boston College. And by second thoughts, I mean he's totally changed his mind. The summer camp for incoming freshmen starts in a few days, and he doesn't plan on going. And BC isn't going to pay his way on an athletic scholarship if he isn't playing hockey. No hockey, no Boston College.

But Jasper is *totally* okay with this. Completely. He isn't even sure he wants to go to college anymore. In fact, talking about bagging Boston College is the only time Jasper sounds remotely happy these days. Though I am fairly sure that's because never playing hockey again is his own punishment for what happened to Cassie. Because as much as Jasper's mom pushed him into the sport, he also loves it. Turning his back on it is a way to make himself suffer.

"Dinner was okay," Jasper says. But he sounds distracted, like this isn't at all why he called.

"What did she say?" I push myself up in bed and turn on the light.

"Say? About what?"

"Um, the hockey?" I ask, hoping my tone will bring him back around. "Are you okay? You sound really out of it."

"Yeah, yeah. I'm fine." It's totally unconvincing. "The thing with my mom didn't go well. But, I mean, it's not like I thought it would." He doesn't sound upset either, just totally flat. I wait for him to get into details, but he stays quiet.

"Is she going to let you drop out?" I ask as my eyes settle on my photograph of the old woman and her plaid bag and all those crumbs. The one that Jasper called depressing that first time he was in my house, the day we raced off in search of Cassie. I wonder if he'd see it the same way now.

"Define 'let,'" he says, and then tries to laugh, but it's wheezy and hollow.

My body tightens. "Jasper, come on, what happened?"

"Oh, you know, kind of what I expected," he says. He's trying to rally, but I can hear the effort in his voice. I can feel it, too, even over the phone. "Except worse, I guess."

"Worse how?" I ask, though maybe I should be distracting him instead of pressing for details. As usual with Jasper these days, I feel totally out of my depth.

"My mom said if I don't play hockey—go to the camp and whatever—I can't live under her roof." He pauses and sighs. "Listen, it's not like she was going to change into this totally different person because I almost died." I'm not sure if he means this as a joke. But the weird tightness in his voice is pure sadness. It makes my own chest ache.

"I'm sorry." I want there to be something else to say. But anything more would be a lie and I know what those feel like. Jasper deserves better.

"Maybe she's got a point."

"So you're thinking of playing after all?" I sound too hopeful. I can't help it. I don't like Jasper's mother, but I agree that he should go to Boston College and play hockey. He's too lost right now to cut himself free from the one thing that still brings him joy.

"No way," he says, like that's the most absurd suggestion ever. "I'm definitely not playing."

My heart has picked up speed. Yes, there is a line between me reading Jasper's bad feelings and me being anxious, but it is still super blurry. All I can say for sure is that this conversation is making me *really* worried.

Whether that's because of my feelings or Jasper's feelings is still up for debate.

"SO I MADE it to your actual office," I said to Dr. Shepard in our first face-to-face meeting a week after the camp. I was fishing for praise. All that trauma and there I was, getting myself out of the house.

She nodded at me and almost smiled, looking as pretty and petite as she always did in her big red chair. Still like Alice in Wonderland shrunk down to nothing. I was relieved that hadn't changed.

"I'm glad you're here," Dr. Shepard said.

It wasn't exactly the job-well-done parade I was hoping for. But that was Dr. Shepard's style: don't make too much out of anything. Not the good or the bad. She wanted me to have expectations for myself, but she wanted to be sure I knew she didn't have any of her own.

We chatted then for a while: how was I spending my days, how were things at home? But there was only so much dancing around what had happened at the camp that we could do.

"You know, I felt *less* anxious while I was going after Cassie," I said, finally diving into the middle, probably a little too aggressively. "Shouldn't that have made me *more* anxious? I was having a hard time leaving the house. Wasn't leaving the house actually."

"Anxiety is variable, Wylie. No two people manifest it in exactly the same way. There are no 'shoulds.' Even for one person anxiety can change over time depending on life events—your mother's accident certainly made your anxiety worse to the point that you were unable to go outside for a brief period. The adrenaline of being called upon to help Cassie likely camouflaged your own anxiety temporarily," she said. "For once the alarm bells going off inside you matched the actual danger of your situation. It's not surprising that your anxiety would be less noticeable."

"So that's my cure? To be in some crazy emergency all the time?"

Dr. Shepard's mouth turned down. She was never a fan of sarcasm. "People do go through intensely anxious periods and come out the other side. Others have good and bad periods cyclically throughout their lives. With anxiety, there are no one-size-fits-all explanations or predictions, Wylie. No absolutes. The unknown can be frustrating, but also encouraging. You're here now. Perhaps we should start there."

"Do you believe my 'Heightened Emotional Perception,' this 'Outlier' thing"—I hooked quotes around the word and rolled my eyes in a totally transparent attempt to show I wasn't taking it very seriously—"could be the whole explanation for what's wrong with me?"

My dad had called ahead to explain to Dr. Shepard what had happened at the camp and its link to his research, including his newly coined "Heightened Emotional Perception," or "HEP," which I think he felt had the benefit of heading off any eventual comparison to ESP. He had also told her I was an Outlier and what that meant. It was a relief not to have to go into the details, especially about me being an Outlier, which I found one part thrilling, one part confusing, and two thousand parts terrifying. It was like learning that for years you'd been carrying around some kind of enormous benign tumor in your belly. Sure there was good news: you weren't sick *and* you'd lose eight pounds when the watermelon-sized thing was removed. But you still had to contend with the daunting sense that you'd been invaded, occupied. Worse yet, you'd had absolutely no idea.

"Wrong with you?" Dr. Shepard asked. "Right and wrong is not an effective way to frame a discussion about anxiety."

"You know what I mean," I said, though how could she? I wasn't even sure what I meant. I wanted certain answers (how anxious was I really?), but wanted to avoid others (what did being an Outlier really mean?). I wanted to off-load my anxiety without taking on being an Outlier, to cherry-pick my truth. "Do you think it's possible that I'm not actually anxious at all?"

Dr. Shepard stared at me and I felt with troubling clarity the moment she decided to play it straight, instead of opting for the good old therapy bob and weave. It wasn't necessarily comforting, this being able to see through people so easily. It made everyone so much weaker, their gifts so much more ordinary.

"I believe awareness is a powerful thing, Wylie. Do you understand?"

I nodded. But then reconsidered. "No, actually, I don't understand at all."

"This Heightened Emotional Perception could have exacerbated your anxiety, certainly. It's possible that in some instances you have mistaken the emotions of others for your own. However, I'd say that it is highly unlikely that being an Outlier is the explanation for all your anxiety. Let me ask you this. Do you feel anxious now?"

I tried to pull in some air. It wasn't easy. And there was that cold heaviness in my stomach for sure. "Yes, definitely."

Though my anxiety did feel a little more separate now that I could pick out its peculiar chill. More like a backpack I was wearing than one of my internal organs.

"I can at least assure you that the anxiety you are feeling right now is yours, not mine, Wylie. Bottom line: I think the answer is yes, you are anxious, *and*, yes, you have this Heightened Emotional Perception. Where the line is will be something for you to figure out."

But that was the problem. In those first hours after Jasper and I escaped, still reeling from what had happened to Cassie, being an Outlier felt like it might be the answer to everything that had ever been wrong with me. The secret to my freedom. But so quickly "being an Outlier" turned into a bottomless box filled with questions and more questions. So far I had decided to close the lid and lock it up tight. Knowing that I alone reserved the right to use the key.

Not yet, though. I had politely declined to engage in any of my dad's "follow-up testing" and had taken a pass on him teaching me to "do more" with my Heightened Emotional Perception or "reading" ability. I'd even intentionally avoided learning where my dad's research was headed. I knew only his two main questions: the "scope" of the Outlier ability (what could we do if we practiced) and the "source" of the Outlier ability (where did it come from).

After he had accidentally discovered the three original Outliers—me and the other two girls—my dad had done additional "exploratory" studies using a handful of volunteers, but nothing that could have been published. It was during these exploratory studies that he had noticed the Outliers were all girls, and only teenagers. All of that was before what had happened up at the camp. Now, my dad had been spending most of his time on applications and proposals to get the money he needed for a proper, peer-reviewed study that would prove the existence of the Outliers. Then, and only then, would he be able to move on to the more complex issues of source and scope. For now, as far as the scientific community was concerned, it was like nothing had even happened.

"And what if I don't want to be an Outlier," I said to Dr. Shepard, my throat pinching unexpectedly tight.

"You may not be able to choose whether or not you

are an Outlier, Wylie. Or, for that matter, whether or not you are anxious." Dr. Shepard leaned forward and looked at me intently. "But you can decide what you do with who you are."

I BREATHE IN to the count of four, trying not to exhale into the phone still pressed hard to my ear. "Jasper, what do you mean, that your mom 'has a point?' A point about what?"

"About the not living with her," he says. "Maybe I'll just hit the road or something. You know, freedom and all that. Figure it out as I go along."

"Figure what out?" I snap, my fear rising.

"Figure out everything," he says. "I'm sorry I woke you, Wylie. It was good you were asleep. We can talk about my mom and everything later, or tomorrow. Or whatever. That wasn't even why I called. I was awake and wanted to say hi. That's all."

This is a lie. Even through the phone I can feel it.

"I'm up now. You don't have to go."

We are silent then in a way that I hate.

"You were right, you know," Jasper finally goes on. "When you said it was my fault that Cassie got so out of control."

I wince. I did say that—before we even got to Maine—maybe more than once. And, my God, did I mean it at the time. It's hard now to even remember how much I had blamed Jasper for everything.

"I never should have said that, Jasper. I was afraid it was *my* fault for being a bad friend. Cassie getting messed up wasn't your fault. It wasn't my fault."

"Even if I liked that Cassie was so messed up?" Jasper says. And I can see now how deep his guilt is. He doesn't even need to blame himself for what happened in those last moments in the cabin to make himself responsible for Cassie being gone. He sees himself as the one who set the train loose down the tracks. "That way I could keep on saving her over and over again."

My stomach twists, deep and cold. My feelings, not Jasper's.

"Who doesn't like being the hero?" I offer, scrambling for the right thing.

"Yeah," Jasper says. "But people don't usually end up dead because of it."

The awful flatness to his voice is back.

"Why don't I come over?" I say. "You don't sound like you should be alone."

"No, it's okay."

"It's no big deal. I don't mind." Already, I'm getting out of bed. My dad will take me to Jasper's even if he's not going to be thrilled.

"No, Wylie," Jasper says, louder this time. "I'm serious. Don't come. I don't want you to." He takes a breath. "I—it's my mom. She was on a double shift at the hospital, and she just got home. She'll freak out if anything wakes her up, and she's already pissed enough at me."

"Are you sure?" I ask. "Because I feel like—"

"Yeah, I'm sure. If you come here right now, it will make everything worse," he says firmly. "Listen, come over in the morning. We can take a walk or something. Talk it out." His voice is softer, warmer. More convincing. Sort of.

"A walk, yeah," I say.

"Listen, I'm fine. When my mom works second shift, she usually gets up around ten. You want to come by then?"

"Only if you promise me one thing."

"What's that?"

"That you will be okay."

My throat tightens around the words and I have to swallow hard. Jasper is so broken. And he isn't supposed to be. Despite his messed-up dad and a mom who loves him only for what he can do, he is still the optimist. I'm supposed to be the broken one.

"Definitely," Jasper says, the flicker of brightness in his voice an obvious cover for how he agreed too quickly. "Now, you have to promise me something."

"Definitely."

"Don't come over without calling first."

3

I WAKE TO THE SMELL OF SATURDAY PANCAKES AND BACON, AND A FEW SWEET
seconds of amnesia. Then it all comes rushing back: Jasper, his
house, ten a.m. The pit in my stomach from the night before. I
turn to look at my clock; not even seven thirty a.m. Going back
to sleep will be the best way to pass the time without letting my
mind twist about Jasper.

But then I hear voices downstairs. Gideon and my dad. And
they are not happy. I put a pillow over my head to muffle their
voices, but it's no use.

WHEN I GET downstairs, my dad is standing over the stove. His
jaw is clenching and unclenching like he's trying to eat his
teeth.

"So that's it?" Gideon snaps, rocking back in his stool at the kitchen island. My twin brother is once again ready for a fight. He's hungry for it.

I can read that loud and clear. I might have avoided my dad's follow-up testing and training, but since that first post-camp session with Dr. Shepard, I have made strides at perfecting my Outlier skills on my own. It was my box. My key.

I started practicing at home, reading Gideon's and my dad's feelings until I could do it with near-perfect precision. It wasn't pleasant. Gideon's anger can be so toxic that it feels like my skin is being burned and my dad's sadness is totally smothering. It was also pretty much all they felt. Eventually, I knew I needed to branch out: more people, more practice.

At the Newton Public Library I learned that it's hard to read people's feelings when they're mixed up with the characters in the books they're reading. So I moved on to restaurants, which is where crap gets real—people break up, they confess, they promise, they argue, they apologize. And they stick around long enough that you can watch the fallout. It was there I learned **Outlier Rule #1**: Eye contact helps in reading people. And **Outlier Rule #2**: Crowds make it harder to read people. And before long there came **Outlier Rule #3**: You get better at reading with practice. Because when I started at the restaurants, all I could make out were the basics—happy, sad, angry. Five weeks later and I can now divide shame from regret, joy from contentment.

The better I've gotten at reading, though, the less I want anyone to know. And the fact that my dad has worked so hard to respect my boundaries, not to push or interrogate, has come as a shock.

But then again, maybe it's not such a surprise to him that I have to learn this whole Outlier thing on my own. I learned to swim in the same stubborn, lonely way. Gideon ran right up to the pool and jumped in. He almost drowned before my dad rescued him and then showed him how. Meanwhile, it took me weeks of walking back and forth across the shallow end until I could catch even a few strokes. But swim I did, eventually. And all by myself.

"Hi, Wylie," my dad says when he notices me in the doorway. He smiles, relieved that I have appeared. "Do you want some pancakes?"

Gideon huffs in disgust.

Disgusted that my dad is trying to change the subject. Disgusted by the sight of me. No, that's not right. Disgusted is too mild. Gideon is enraged by me this morning. It rocks me back on my heels.

And this is partly why I still have not embraced this whole Outlier thing. Who wants to risk knowing what anyone is *truly* feeling about them? Also, I'm aiming for normal at the moment. Being an Outlier means accepting the fact that I am never going to fit in.

My dad puts a huge plate of pancakes down in front of me as I climb up on a stool next to Gideon, trying to ignore the anger pulsing my way. I wish I hadn't come downstairs.

"Good news! Looks like the NIH might fund Dad's official Outlier study!" Gideon shouts. As if this is the final comeback in some long argument we've been having.

And in a way maybe it is. Gideon's own test results were

average. My dad couldn't lie about that. Which means his non-visual, nonauditory emotional perception was normal and fine when the auditory and visual limitations were each tested separately, but he—like the vast majority of people—has no HEP. He's not an Outlier. And Gideon might have been able to accept that *if* there'd been some hope of changing it. But my dad insists that Gideon cannot be an Outlier because the Outliers are only girls. He may not know *why* yet, but that has not made him any less certain of this crucial fact.

At first, Gideon outright rejected the whole "only girls" thing, convinced that my dad had made some small but critical miscalculation. But when my dad refused to waste energy confirming the gender disparity, it sent Gideon into a rage spiral. Like how dare all males be denied.

It makes me want to point out all the other things boys get the better part of the deal on: like height for instance or running speed or being able to procreate without their bodies being ripped apart. Or, I don't know, having only the most remote chance of getting raped when girls have to think about it every time they walk out the door.

But I know how Gideon would take that: as a declaration of war. And who wants to go to battle with a lunatic?

"The NIH response to our funding proposal has been encouraging," my dad says. "But nothing is guaranteed."

"Aren't you going to tell her the rest, Dad?" Gideon goes on. "I mean, it is her brain after all."

My eyes fly wide open. "Tell me what?"

My dad takes a loud breath, then looks up at me and forces a totally unconvincing smile. "Everything else is very preliminary. But there is a neuroscientist from UCLA who thinks she might be onto something on the source question. It sounds promising, but it is very early days."

Already, my heart has picked up speed. Here it is, sooner than I thought: the dread final diagnosis. I am not prepared. I can maybe accept that I am an Outlier, and I can almost have a little fun learning what that means. But I am still afraid to know why. There is something too permanent about that. I have the urge to put my hands over my ears. It's only the thought of how much this would please Gideon that keeps them balled at my sides.

"So tell her," Gideon says. "Tell her what the neuroscientist thinks."

"Gideon, if Wylie wants to know those kinds of details she can ask me," he says sharply. My dad turns to me. "And you should take your time."

"Spoiler: your brain isn't normal," Gideon hisses in my ear.

"Gideon, that is not helpful!" my dad shouts. He takes a breath, trying to calm himself down. "It's also not true. 'Normal' is a meaningless word."

"Meaningless?" Gideon shouts, pushing away his plate and jumping off his chair. "Oh, wait, I get it! The more *messed up* Wylie is, *the better* she is. Wow, and here I am trying to do the things I'm supposed to do, and all the while what you want is a freak show like her." Gideon shakes his head. "Except you and I both know, Dad, if *I* was the Outlier, that would make me damaged, not special."

"Gideon." My dad clenches his jaw tighter and stares down

at the counter. "You are special exactly as you are." My dad is trying, but he is so mad it doesn't even sound believable. "And Wylie, Gideon is upset at me so he's taking it out on you. There is nothing wrong with you."

"Unless that other guy is right, and it's some kind of illness," Gideon says, resting a hand on the back of his chair like all of a sudden he has no plans to go anywhere. "Then, technically, there would be something wrong with her."

My dad closes his eyes as his nostrils flare—he is *really* angry now. It's obvious he told Gideon something, probably offhandedly, that he now is regretting.

"What illness?" I ask. I have no choice. My anxiety isn't going to let a whole "illness" thing just go.

"I've spoken with numerous experts," my dad does on, all calm rationality now. "And I'm glad because I think it has given me a more complete picture. However, there is one very persistent immunologist who seems set on convincing me that HEP is the result of a disorder that is itself the result of an infection."

"What? What do you mean?"

"There are a few viruses that could theoretically cause psychological symptoms, and in my exploratory studies some of the Outliers I found had various mood disorders. Not only anxiety, but a whole range of issues: addiction, anorexia, cutting, depression, antisocial and criminal behavior."

"You've finally found your tribe, Wylie," Gideon says, pointedly eyeing the remnants of my hacked hair. It's grown out, but not completely. "Sick, and sick in the head. And by the way, this immunologist Dad is trying to blow off is a professor at *Cornell*."

"Yes, Dr. Cornelia has been associated with Cornell and he is on staff at Metropolitan Hospital in New York," my dad says. "But, to be clear, his entire premise is suspect. It was by no means *all* of the Outliers in my exploratory study who exhibited behavioral or psychological difficulties. Not to mention that the other two original Outliers had no such issues whatsoever. So there may be some relationship between mood disorders such as anxiety and being an Outlier, but that relationship is certainly not straightforward cause and effect."

I think this is supposed to make me feel better. It does not.

"Dr. Cornelia from Cornell?" is all I can think to say.

"Yes, it is a bit ridiculous. Dr. Cornelia from *Cornell* also has a very controversial book out about bioterrorism that he is actively trying to promote as well as a career in dire need of a restart."

"Bioterrorism?" I ask, but Gideon and my dad are fixated on each other now.

"Still, it's not like Dr. Cornelia is some random guy." Gideon turns and looks at me. "And unlikely isn't the same thing as impossible. Right, Dad? She could still just be *sick*, right?"

Gideon is trying to hurt me. The stupid part is how much it is working.

"No, not right. Dr. Cornelia's theory does not adequately explain the HEP." My dad slides the last pancakes off the griddle and onto a spare plate. Then he holds his spatula upright against the counter like some kind of staff. "Would you rather I lie and pretend that you are an Outlier, Gideon? Or that you could be? Because that seems insulting to your intelligence." My dad exhales, hard. "Wylie is an Outlier, and you are not. Period.

This does not mean that I love you any less. Or that you are any less special. You are simply special in a different way than Wylie is. That's the truth, Gideon. What else do you want?"

"I want you to admit that she's the only thing that matters to you now." Gideon's pointing at me. But at least he's not looking at me, so I don't have to feel the full force of his hatred. "Your kid and your research all in one place. What do you even need me for anymore?"

My dad winces. "Gideon, you know that's not the way I feel."

"No, Dad, I don't know anything about the way you *feel*." Gideon's voice is quiet now, devastated. "That's Wylie's specialty, remember?"

My dad closes his eyes and lowers his head. As he passes out of the room, Gideon knocks hard into my shoulder, almost shoving me off the chair. I push myself back up as he storms to the foyer. My dad and I both flinch as the front door slams shut behind him.

4

WHEN MY DAD FINALLY OPENS HIS EYES, HE TRIES AGAIN TO SMILE. IT'S NO
more convincing than it was before.

"That went well," he says quietly, then motions to the dozen
pancakes now stacked on the plate in front of him. "Please tell
me you're hungry."

Without waiting for me to answer, he picks up the plate,
walks to the garbage can, and presses the trash open with his
foot. He reconsiders, though, letting the lid slam shut. Instead,
he pulls out some plastic wrap and sets to covering each pan-
cake, then stashing them in small groups inside the freezer. It's
amazing how fast this seems to buoy him. He may have no idea
how to fix things with Gideon, but we now have enough pancakes to survive a nuclear winter.

"So this guy from Cornell who thinks being an Outlier is a

sickness . . ." I begin, and then stop. Open-ended is more likely to get an honest answer.

My dad looks me right in the eye. I can feel him willing me to know that he is telling the truth.

"Dr. Cornelia is just looking to inject himself into something that he thinks will get him attention from the press."

"What press?"

Despite all of us bracing for an onslaught of reporters and television cameras after what happened at the camp, the only real coverage was a thumbnail of an article in the *Boston Globe*, mostly about Cassie's violent death at the hands of a cult. (The police had also officially deemed Cassie's death a homicide, not that there was anyone around to prosecute anyway.) The article mentioned my dad's research only vis-à-vis its connection to Quentin, who was described only as a "cult leader," associated with The Collective, which—it turned out—was a national organization with various beliefs and branches, most of which did not appreciate being called a cult. They made that pretty clear in the online comments on the article. No one seemed to care about the Outliers or HEP, maybe because there had been no official, peer-reviewed study on the topic yet, maybe because science wasn't as sexy as the word "cult."

The only actual interest in my dad's research came from one blogger—EndOfDays.com—who identified himself only as a "centrist" member of The Collective and who laid the blame for the deaths at the camp squarely at my dad's feet. EndOfDays had decided that the Collective members were innocent victims caught in the deadly crossfire of scientific recklessness. My dad didn't want us reading the blog. And so I hadn't. Gideon, of course, couldn't get enough.

"IT IS ONLY the maniacally egotistical who believe that they should insert themselves between man and the will of God," Gideon was reading from his laptop at the dining room table. "It is an abomination to interfere with this sacred covenant."

"What the hell is that?" Rachel asked. She was in the kitchen with my dad, helping with the dinner dishes. Since what happened at the camp, she'd been glued to us even tighter. It was aggravating, no matter how genuine her intentions (and I still wasn't convinced). "Actually, forget I asked. I don't care what it is—stop reading it."

Rachel often used that overly familiar way with us like she was a member of our loud, no-holds-barred family and she was allowed to shout because it was all out of love anyway. Except we were not loud, and whenever she used that tone, it set my teeth on edge. As annoyed as I was at Gideon for torturing my dad by reading that blog, I was even more annoyed at Rachel for talking to him that way. I had a hard time imagining she ever could have been my mom's friend.

Rachel and my mom had met in the third grade in Park Slope, Brooklyn, and somehow had managed to stay best friends for years, through different high schools, separate colleges, and then different graduate programs. When they finally got their first jobs, they had been thrilled to land in Boston together. Rachel was my mom's maid of honor, and there were countless pictures of Rachel holding Gideon and me as babies.

Then, suddenly, Rachel was gone. Out of our life. Once, when my mom had been trying to comfort me about the distance between Cassie and me, she had said that she and Rachel had grown apart, too. But their separation had been so sudden and complete. I could tell even then—long before I knew that I was an Outlier— that my mom was leaving out important details. When Rachel reappeared after my mom's funeral I had thought about asking my dad what had really happened between them, but he'd been so overwhelmed and sad that it had felt stupid and wrong to care. And there was a tiny part of me that had felt comforted being around someone who had even once upon a time been so close to my mom.

"It's Dad's stalker," Gideon said of the passage, obviously enjoying Rachel's reaction. "EndOfDays. He's in The Collective, and he blames Dad for basically everything."

"What?" Rachel asked as she handed my dad another rinsed plate for the dishwasher, then dried her hands on a towel. "What is Gideon talking about, Ben? What stalker?"

"A guy with too much time on his hands. To be honest, I don't think he knows what he wants. He's angry, that's all. No one reads it anyway."

"You mean, except the 3,523 people who commented," Gideon said. "But who's counting?"

"Ben?!" Rachel shouted. "Have you talked to the police? That doesn't sound like something you should ignore."

"They did look into it. The guy lives in Florida somewhere," my dad said, waving a hand. As though Florida was the same thing as Mars. "Anyway, Agent Klute is not concerned."

"The same Agent Klute that ran Wylie down?" Rachel asked, eyes wide. "No offense, Ben, but I think you better wake up a little here. You need to protect yourselves."

I watched my dad's nostrils flare. "Don't you think I know that?" He was angry but hurt, too. He turned and dumped his glass of water into the sink. "Thank you for coming by and bringing dinner, Rachel. But I'm tired," he said. "I think it's time for you to go."

"I'm sorry, Ben. I didn't mean to—I'm just, I'm trying to help." Rachel smiled at him apologetically as she crossed the room. Her mouth was stiff, and I could feel how badly she wanted to cry. "I promise next time I'll keep my mouth shut."

"YES, WYLIE, THINGS have been quiet in the press so far," my dad goes on. "But if I can convince the NIH to fund a full-scale study of the Outliers and get peer-reviewed publication that will change, and quickly. There's already some Senator Russo, from Arizona. He's on the Intelligence Subcommittee and he's insisting on a meeting. Somehow he got wind of my funding application. My guess is he's worried about protecting some secret research the military has been doing."

"Secret research?" Fear surely shows on my face.

My dad grimaces, then holds up his hands. "I just mean, in the way everything the military does is secret. They've been looking into how to use emotional perception in combat for decades," he says. "They haven't succeeded, but I'm sure they're not thrilled about competition, or about not being able to control the flow of information."

My dad's phone pings then with a text. I feel worry jolt through him as he looks down at the screen.

"What is it?" I ask. "What's wrong?"

"No, no, nothing—it's not about the research," he says.

He hands me his phone. I look down at the text: **Accident file for Hope Lang will be available for review at 9 a.m. today. Sincerely, Detective Oshiro.**

I have to read the message three times before I fully understand its meaning, like it's coming out of nowhere, even though I am the one who has called Detective Oshiro pretty much every day since I got back from Maine, asking to see my mom's accident file. I feel surprisingly foolish, too, now that I have gotten what I wanted. It's because of what Quentin said—that my mom's death wasn't an accident—that I got so obsessed. It's not as if anything else that Quentin claimed up at the camp turned out to be true, but knowing that hasn't loosened my grip. Even my dad admitted that he had considered the possibility that my mom's death hadn't been an accident, though he backpedaled hard as soon as he could tell I was fixating.

"I am only going to say this once, Wylie." My dad's voice is quiet and firm. "And I am saying this as your father, but also as a psychologist and because I don't want to see you hurt any more than you already have been. Looking in your mom's accident file could be extremely traumatic for you. *Extremely.* There might be photographs or details that are far more upsetting than you can possibly anticipate."

It is true that I have thought a lot more about getting my hands on the file than about what it would be like to actually look in it. It seemed so unlikely I ever would. Detective Oshiro had said that he needed clearance, higher-up approval, permission. Case closed or not, they didn't ordinarily have the families of victims coming by to rifle through their files.

Jasper. I want to talk to him about this. Maybe I need to, the way the thought of him just popped into my head. He has listened to me go on and on about my mom's accident ever since we got back from the camp. He gets how much I have wanted to look in that file. But he will also understand how not sure I feel about finally getting what I want. Jasper's single best quality, I have learned, is his ability not to judge. But it's not as if I can have that conversation in front of my dad.

"If I can't handle it," I say. Because I can't show doubt, not to my dad. "I'll stop."

My dad's shoulders sag. "Okay," he says quietly as he turns around, head hanging low as he starts to clean up the dishes.

"Dad," I begin, though I don't even know what it is I want to say. "If you don't want me to go . . ." I can't even get myself to fully make the offer though. I'm too afraid he might take me up on it.

Instead, he turns to look at me. He crosses his arms and presses his mouth tight. All I feel now is love, his love for me—so pure and simple and complete. And for the first time ever—being able to feel *that* so clearly—I am grateful for being an Outlier.

"Well, you shouldn't go down there on an empty stomach," he says, motioning to my plate. "Eat something and I'll drive you." He looks at his watch. "It's not long until nine."

I look up at the little clock over the stove: 8:34 a.m. I'll try to call Jasper on the way, see if I can come earlier if I finish up with the file before ten. It's not the same as talking to him now, but it's something. The station isn't far from his house. If I can't reach him, I'll go to his house at ten a.m. like we agreed.

And maybe after we're done gluing his loose pieces back into place, we can spend a little time on mine.

"Can we just go, um, now?" I ask.

My dad nods slowly.

"Yes," he says finally and with some effort. "We can go now."

5

THE POLICE STATION IN THE CENTER OF DOWNTOWN NEWTON IS A TIDY REDBRICK
and white stone cube on a block next to several other municipal
buildings and a bunch of trees. I've never had a reason to be
inside. Even after the camp, they drove us straight home, then the
agents arrived. But looking at the building from the outside now,
it looks a lot like a brick version of the Seneca police station—if
the Seneca police station had taken up the entire building.

But once we're inside, any similarities disappear. The Newton
station is much larger and more modern, not to mention busier
than the one in Seneca. It's actually way busier than I would
have imagined. With the low crime rate in Newton, I can't imagine why so many people are at the police station.

There are a dozen desks lined up in a large room behind
a railing to the left. At a tall desk in front sits a tired-looking

uniformed officer doing intake. He has thinning gray hair and rumpled eyes and he is dismissively sorting people into a second set of lines: complaints to be filed, summonses to be paid. It all seems seriously bureaucratic and super boring.

My dad and I take our places at the back of the line, and I listen as people register their complaints. One man's apartment was broken into, a woman's car was vandalized. And on and on. It's 9:05 a.m. by the time we are next in line. I called Jasper twice on our way to the police station and he didn't answer. And now, not only do I want to talk to him, but I've also got a bad feeling about him not answering.

"Yes. Hello!?!" It takes me a minute to realize that the officer behind the tall desk is finally talking to us.

"Wylie?" My dad puts a concerned hand on my arm. He's taken my hesitation as a sign. "You don't need to do this."

"Yeah. I do," I say, meeting my dad's stare as firmly as I can.

Reluctantly, he nods and we step forward. "We're here to see Detective Oshiro," my dad says. "We have an appointment."

"Wait over there." The old guy points toward the railing in front of the desks without looking up at us, then picks up the phone.

We aren't waiting long when I see Detective Oshiro heading our way. I've only met him once, and I'd forgotten how tall and imposing he is. Broad shoulders, crisply pressed shirt, and fashionable tie. Good-looking and young. Not too young, but younger than my dad. And way younger than the rumpled old detective I had in mind before he turned up on our steps the day after the accident.

That day, Detective Oshiro was calm and kind and exceedingly competent. Firm, too, in laying out the facts of my mom's accident. That it *was* an accident. He never wavered on that—there was nothing to lead investigators to suspect otherwise. It was simply the way the car had impacted the railing in the area of the gas tank that had caused it to burst into flames. There was no evidence of foul play.

"There is something you should know, Wylie," my dad says suddenly. His voice is rushed and tight, like this is his very last chance to make something right. "They think your mom had been drinking the night of the accident. She was upset and I take responsibility for that," he says. "Anyway, it doesn't change anything. I just didn't want you to be surprised if you saw some mention of it in the file."

"Drinking?" He actually feels relieved confessing this. Me? I'm furious. "What the hell are you talking about?"

And here I thought he'd been trying to protect me from grief. Was this—this thing that makes *no* sense whatsoever—what he was trying to avoid me knowing? My mom had the occasional glass of wine and that was it.

"Wylie, I know—"

"That is not true," I snap. But I sound like a ridiculous little kid, refusing to accept that the tooth fairy isn't real.

"Dr. Lang, it's nice to see you," Detective Oshiro says before my dad can respond, but he is wounded. I can feel that much. And I am glad. My dad and Detective Oshiro shake hands and then the detective turns to shake mine. "If you want to come back through here, I've got you guys set up in a conference room in the back. That way you can take as much time as you need."

Detective Oshiro has made peace with this. He didn't want us coming down and going through the file in the first place, but now that we are here, he's not going to be anything but professional.

I expect the other detectives in the room to stare at my dad and me as Detective Oshiro leads us toward the conference room, for some kind of hush to descend. *They're here. They're about to find out everything.* But they don't even look up from their desks. Because they do not care. Because there is no great secret about to be revealed. At least not one that is going to turn back time and bring my mom back, not something that will make all this Outliers nonsense go away. Is that why I'm actually here? Am I putting my dad through this trauma for *that*, a distraction?

"I can go in myself," I say to my dad as Detective Oshiro stops about halfway down a row of doors. I am still pissed at him for dropping this whole "drinking" bomb on me, but now I feel ashamed, too. "I feel bad I even made you come down here."

My dad turns and smiles at me, sad but also grateful. "I'm not sure I can handle looking through anything myself, but I'll stay in the room with you." He reaches down and squeezes my hand. "I know that none of this has been easy on you, Wylie." And he means *all* of it—the Outliers, the camp, Quentin, my mom's accident. "I want you to know that the way you're handling all of it—I am so proud of you."

THE ROOM IS plain and windowless, but clean, with floor-to-ceiling glass between it and the main room where all of the detectives are seated. It is surprisingly quiet inside, like maybe it's sound-proofed. There is a small table against the wall, two chairs on one side, a single chair on the other. A rectangular cardboard box—long, about the size of three regular book boxes—sits in the center of the table. Looking at it, I feel my heart catch.

"I'll be right outside if you need me." Detective Oshiro points to a desk that is only a couple steps away. "Please don't remove anything from the evidence bags, and nothing can be taken from the room. If you see anything of value in your mother's personal effects, let me know. I'll make sure you leave here with it today."

"Okay, thanks," I say, checking my watch: 9:15 a.m. "I'll be fast."

Detective Oshiro nods and then closes the door after he leaves. I take a deep breath as I stare down at the box. Suddenly, this feels like a mistake. And I may not know exactly where that feeling is coming from, but that doesn't make it any less real.

"You should take your time, Wylie," my dad says. "We're here now, and I don't think you're going to get another chance."

He's right. As much as I want to get this over with, I need to be thorough. It's now or never.

I keep my eyes on the box itself for a minute. It looks brand-new, the top crisp, the label clean and clear. *Name: Hope Lang. Date: February 8. Description of Matter: Automobile Accident.* The ordinariness is both a relief and a disappointment. A tiny part of me did hope it might say *Murder* somewhere. Another part of me was dreading that, too.

As I lift the long lid from the box, I turn my head away, allowing a moment for the most awful of the ghosts to escape.

I rub my palms against my jeans then to dry them and suck in some air as I turn back to the open box, bracing myself to see something truly horrifying, like my mom's charred bones. But it's just an ordinary box divided into two sections, one with hanging file folders, the second with a stack of evidence bags.

The bag on top holds something small and black and silver, like a hardened lump of mixed clay. It isn't until I look closer that I realize it is a car key. Or what was once a car key, melted now beyond recognition. My stomach inches up into my throat. My dad was right—this is more awful than I thought it would be. Because now all I can think about is my mom liquefied. And Cassie, too. Everything and everyone I have ever loved reduced to a puddle—and then hardened into a shapeless rock.

I turn away from the evidence bags and toward the files, glancing over at my dad to see if he is watching me. I have a faint hope that something in his face will give me a real reason to stop. But his eyes are on his phone, reading something, an email or a text. His brow is furrowed as he begins to type. He is not going to rescue me from my own terrible idea.

I turn back to the box. I wanted to come here. I need to trust that I had a good reason. And I need to get it over with, fast. The first file contains an accident investigator's report, notes from the interviews that Detective Oshiro conducted with my dad, Gideon, and me. I pull out the notes from my dad's. They go on for several pages that I have no stomach to read but for this: "Husband reports Lang departed the home in a state of agitation, though husband has no reason to suspect self-harm."

Gideon's interview is much shorter. I can remember him

sitting there on the steps that night. No tears, only stunned and silent. But in its few lines the report contains: "Son states his mother left the house at approximately nine p.m. He does not have a specific recollection of her mental state."

I can remember they asked me something like that, too. They were so focused on my mom's mood. Because they thought there was a chance she'd killed herself, I realize now. One car, a fatal accident. Ruling out suicide is probably standard. I don't recall how I answered, but when I scan the notes from my interview, I discover that apparently I decided to lie: "Daughter reports that mother went out for milk. Mother was in a good mood."

I wonder who I'd been trying to protect: My dad? My mom? Myself?

The next thing I pull out is the autopsy report. It's a single page that shakes in my hand as I try to keep my eyes toward the top of the page, likely home of the most innocuous details. Name, height, weight. But even that is not entirely safe. There is the word "estimated" behind both my mom's height and weight. After all, a fractured and scorched skeleton hardly reveals such details. I squint down the page until I get to the notes at the bottom, to the cause of death: *Blunt-force trauma*. Manner of death: *Accidental*. I let go of the breath I've been holding. At least she was already dead when her car caught on fire. It is such a pathetic relief.

The next folder looks empty until I tilt it and an envelope slides out. I peer inside with my head pulled back and catch a glimpse of photos of the blackened and mangled front of my mom's car. I close my eyes and swallow hard, hoping that will keep me from throwing up as I jam the envelope back in the file.

"Are you okay?" my dad asks. When I look up, he is watching me.

"Are you?" I ask, deflecting. "You've been tapping on your phone nonstop."

"Oh, yeah, sorry." He always falls for distraction mixed with guilt. "The assistant from Senator Russo's office emailed a minute ago. Apparently if I go right now to DC, I can meet him and someone from the NIH this afternoon." His tone is dismissive as he shakes his head. "And this meeting is now a prerequisite before they'll even consider my funding. And if I don't go to this meeting I will now have to wait until September for anything to happen because the senator is off for summer recess. Feels like they're trying to create a situation where I'm the one who can't make it. I'm not even sure a senator is allowed to get involved in NIH funding."

"There's no way you can get there?" As much as I've been avoiding information myself, I don't want his pride to be the reason he doesn't find out something important.

He checks the time. "If I go right now to the airport, I guess I could be down there in time for a late afternoon meeting and then back home for bed." He thinks doing this would be kind of absurd, though. I can feel it. Insulting to snap to it because they've told him to. But hesitation is also tugging at him like he is afraid of something slipping through his fingers.

"But maybe you should go?" I ask. Because that seems to be the way he feels.

"There are other ways to get the research funded, Wylie." He frowns as he stares at the floor. Then he nods. "But I suppose I should go, yes. I've never been willing to play this politics game, which is probably why it's taken me so long to get my research this far. But it's too important now not to be willing to put up with some politics."

And I know what he means by "now." He means with me so directly involved.

I nod. "Then you should go." Though I feel a deep pang of regret once I've said it out loud. I just wish I knew what it was exactly that I regretted.

"I don't want to leave you here." He motions to the box. "Doing this."

"I'll be fine," I say, and while this does not feel entirely true, it also does not feel like a complete lie. It's a reason for him to go—a good one. He should take it. It's bad enough that I've put him through this whole thing with the file when I'm not even entirely sure why I'm doing it. "I'm supposed to see Jasper when I'm done anyway. I promised him I'd come by his place. I can walk from here."

"Oh," my dad says, failing to hide his concern. "'Promised' sounds serious."

He likes Jasper well enough, but he worries about the same thing Dr. Shepard does: Jasper pulling me down. And it's much harder to argue with my dad. He's seen the state that Jasper is in—the circles under his eyes, his way of staring off into space randomly when you're right in the middle of a conversation. I get why my dad is worried. *I'm* worried. But ever since my dad said his piece about Jasper shortly before Cassie's funeral, he's tried hard to keep his mouth shut about our friendship. Rachel, on the other hand, took the funeral as an invitation to jump right into the fray.

///////////////////////////

"HALF THOSE GIRLS will end up pregnant by the end of college, *if* they go to college," Rachel muttered to me, motioning to Maia and the others. We were at the reception at Cassie's house, which followed her funeral. Maia and her friends had been buzzing around Jasper from the start, "attending" to him in a way that was gross and also pointless because he was so out of it. "And, I mean, are they serious with the short skirts and the shaking their butts in his face? It's his girlfriend's *funeral*."

I turned to look at Rachel, not sure whether to be pissed or grateful—for her being there in the first place, for weighing in on Maia and her friends, for trying to act like my mom. Because that's what she was doing. That's what she had been doing ever since I got back from Maine. And maybe that's what made me angriest: her pretending that she could ever live up to who my mom had been.

"They are serious," I said flatly, trying not to watch. Trying even harder not to care. I already knew enough about Jasper to know that their attention was making him feel worse. Like less of a person. Or more like a terrible one.

Maia and her friends had sniffled at Cassie's service, and there'd been some running mascara. But I had been near enough to feel that underneath all of that, there wasn't much more than a collective: *ugh, crap, that totally sucks, but Cassie was kind of a disaster.*

"Well, I think you should stay away from Jasper, too. I mean, look at him," Rachel went on. "He's a total mess. And this is exactly the kind of situation where—well, I could see how things between the two of you could—"

"Stop it," I snapped at her. "I mean it."

How dare Rachel pretend she had some special insight into Jasper and me? After everything we'd been through, Jasper and I were friends, but that was all. Of course, I would have much preferred if Rachel hinting otherwise didn't bother me quite as much as it did.

Maybe I didn't want a reminder about how someone "normal" would be feeling in this situation. Maybe normal was like Maia and her friends: ready to turn Jasper from friend into *boy*friend at the first hint of the light turning green. I cared about Jasper. I cared about what happened to him. But not like that. No. I did not.

I was much better off steering way clear of all those kind of complications—and that wasn't denial or whatever Rachel might think. It was what I *wanted*: none of it. Trevor—my one real foray into the world of romance a year ago—had been right to dodge the responsibility that was me. I would definitely never wish *me* on Jasper. Not now. Everyone was so worried about him dragging me down, but who knew how far or how fast I might fall?

Or how deep I'd take him with me.

"Sorry." Rachel held up her hands, then tucked them under her armpits. She wasn't sorry, though. I could feel how badly she wanted to say more about Jasper and our "relationship."

"Why are you even here, Rachel?" My face went hot as the floodgates opened. "I mean, seriously?" My voice was too loud; people were starting to stare. "You were my mom's friend. And she's *dead*. If you think you're helping me, you're not. So why don't you go find something else that will make *you* feel better?"

Rachel blinked at me, stunned. But instead of storming off or telling me I was being rude, she nodded. "You're right."

Then she stepped closer and wrapped her arm around me. And, of course, I started to bawl. Couldn't help myself. I didn't stop until I felt someone's hand on my back. My dad, I assumed.

"I'm so sorry, Wylie. I know how much she meant to you." A man's voice, not my dad. And from the look on Rachel's face, she did not approve of his hand on me.

When I turned, it was Cassie's dad, Vince. His hair was chin length now, his face softer with his new beard. This was the hippie Key West version of Vince. Sober for nearly a year, he had opened a kayak rental place and otherwise totally cleaned up his act. He had also gotten super New Agey weird, Cassie had told me once, but with a kind of pride. At least he wasn't drinking anymore.

Vince had delivered the eulogy and it had been beautiful—moving and eloquent and thoughtful. It managed to bring out all the best qualities of Cassie while putting her death in a meaningful context. So perfect I would have expected to feel differently about Vince the next time I talked to him. But here he was—and there I was—thinking what I always did: that he was totally full of shit.

"I'm sorry about what happened," I said.

He smiled then in a way that looked kindly and spiritual, but *felt*, in every way, the complete and total opposite. "Well," he said, and that was all.

I waited for him to go on. To say all those things people do: it was no one's fault, we all know how much you loved Cassie, blah, blah. But he stared at me instead. Like he was waiting not so much to hear whether I blamed myself, but to enjoy how much I did.

"Um, take care," Rachel said finally, dismissing him.

But he just smiled at her. "It is both a tragedy and a gift that Cassie will be missed by so many." He turned back to me. "Be sure to tell your dad that I'm sorry for his loss, too."

Then he squeezed my arm in a way that should have been warm, but felt creepy. And what loss? My mom? He'd seen my dad so many times since then, hadn't he?

"What a dick that guy is," Rachel said when Vince had gone. "I know he lost his daughter and all, but I bet he was a dick way before that."

"He's a minister now," I said. "Or something like that."

"He can still be a jerk."

"Is there anybody here that you do like?" I asked, even though I couldn't argue with her assessment of Vince.

She smiled. "You."

BY THE TIME my dad finally leaves—after much hemming and hawing and him saying that he's worried about me, and me saying he doesn't need to be, and lots and lots of details about where he'll leave his itinerary—it is almost 9:40 a.m. I try Jasper again, but once again the call rings and rings before finally heading to voice mail.

My stomach has officially started to churn.

I move fast through the rest of what's in the box, turning to the evidence bags. Luckily, there isn't much that survived the fire, which is why we never received anything in the way of personal effects. Nothing my dad had wanted, anyway. The things in the evidence bags must have been thrown from the car when it hit the guardrail. A set of headphones I imagine tangled in a nearby tree. There's one of my mom's blue clogs, too. I always hated those shoes. I'd been trying to convince her to throw them out instead of getting them fixed again. The force it must have taken to rip the shoe off her foot and hurl it away from the car. What was she doing wearing clogs in the middle of winter anyway? I lift the shoe, only a tiny bit. But as soon as my hands are on it, I know it's a mistake. *Don't touch the shoe. It will make you cry.* When I drop it, there is an odd, hollow thump.

I move the plastic bags around until my hand lands on what's under the shoe. Smooth and hard and kind of flat inside its bag. When I pull it from the very bottom of the box, it's a bottle. An empty vodka bottle. A small one, the kind you'd hide in your purse, or even in a big-pocketed jacket.

"Your dad says that it would have been out of character for her to have been drinking in the car," Detective Oshiro says from the doorway.

My cheeks burn. "How about fucking impossible?"

I look down. I shouldn't be swearing at a police officer, not like that. But Detective Oshiro is unfazed.

"It's possible that it was on the road where she had the accident and got mixed with—well, the scene was chaotic. There were no fingerprints on it."

But I can tell he is only saying that to make me feel better. Or not to make me feel worse. I squeeze the cool glass tighter as I peer at the label. Vodka? There is no way. My mom only drank wine and only occasionally. Cassie's dad, Vince, and vodka? Definitely. Even Karen, Cassie's mom, liked her martinis. My mom? Never.

"It wasn't hers," I say, but it only makes me feel worse.

"Yes, that's possible," Detective Oshiro says.

I turn and look straight at him. The wave of sympathy that greets me when our eyes meet unleashes tears. I blink and look down before they can make their way out. Was my mother somebody entirely different from who I believed her to be? Maybe she was lying to me about much more than me being an Outlier.

"It's not hers," I say again.

This time when I look up, the tears are streaming down my cheeks. But I no longer care. And Detective Oshiro looks right at me and lies, just the way I need him to.

"I'm sure you're right, Wylie. I'm sure you're right."

6

OUTSIDE THE POLICE STATION, I PULL OUT MY PHONE AND TRY JASPER. I'M losing count of how many times I've called. It just rings and rings. At least his house isn't far, a three-minute walk, but a million miles away from the fancy shops and restaurants of downtown Newton.

"Jasper," I say when his voice mail finally picks up. "This isn't funny anymore. Where the hell are you? I need to talk to you."

I shove my phone back in my pocket, hating how completely and totally true those words feel. As I make my way up Crescent Hill Road—one block down and over from the station—the sun is warm on my face and the air smells of cut grass. I'm almost hot in my jeans and T-shirt. It's the first day it seems like summer. And I want so much for that to feel good, but the vodka bottle is lodged too deep in my stomach, right next to all my unreturned calls to Jasper.

When I round the corner onto Main Street, I close my eyes so that I don't have to see Holy Cow, the ice cream shop where Cassie used to work. The one where she met Quentin for the first time. There are some things I will never again be able to bear, like the sight of Holy Cow, or the smell of strawberries, which reminds me too much of the lip gloss Cassie always used to wear.

I set my eyes instead on Gallagher's Deli up ahead. It's one of the few not-so-nice places in town—dusty with cramped aisles that smell faintly of cat pee. I've only been in there once to buy cigarettes with Cassie during the week and a half she smoked. I can still remember how the smell seemed to cling to me for hours afterward. Gallagher's means that I am almost there.

To ease the pain in my feet, I slide them back a little in my vicious, toe-gouging yellow flip-flops. I never would have put them on if I had known that I was going to have to walk so far. I dial Jasper's number one more time, but this time the call goes straight to voice mail. Like he's turned it off, or his phone has died between this and my last call.

I can't wait anymore to speak to him before going to his house. No matter what I promised.

I HAVEN'T SEEN Jasper's house much in the light of day. His mother is always on night shifts, so that's when Jasper has me over. This is not a coincidence. Jasper's mother blames me for everything that happened in Maine. He hasn't said that outright, but there have been clues.

"It doesn't have a face," Jasper had said once about his house, sounding sad. "Most houses have the windows on either side and the door in the middle. Like it's a person looking at you or something. The way mine is, it's like the front is just . . . empty."

He's right, and it is depressing. I start up the concrete area that is part driveway, part "front yard." Jasper's brother's Jeep is parked there and, as usual, seeing it makes the hairs on my arms lift. When the police went looking for it, the car was right there at the gas station where we'd left it, the starter purposely ripped out by Doug. Looking at it now is like seeing a ghost. Cassie's ghost. I wrap my arms around myself and shudder hard. Luckily, I know Jasper's brother is out of town visiting his "girlfriend," which Jasper is pretty sure is code for buying pot. I'm relieved that at least I won't have to deal with him. I have met Jasper's brother and—like Jasper said—he is bigger than Jasper and also a total asshole.

I climb the rickety steps to the narrow porch, hold myself tight as I knock. The door sounds hollow beneath my hand. I wait. Nothing. Check the time. Ten a.m. exactly. I knock again, harder this time, then lean back to look in the window for signs of life.

My face is pressed to the glass when the door swings open.

"Can I help you?" a woman snaps.

I jerk back and turn. Jasper's mom is glaring at me. At least I'm assuming it's her. Her short black hair is pulled back in a low, no-nonsense ponytail. Her skin has a grayish undertone and she has puffy bags under her eyes. Still, you can see how she might have been quite beautiful once. How she still could be if she got some rest. She's wearing green hospital scrubs and has her nurse's ID badge looped around her neck.

"Sorry," I say. Opening with an apology seems wise. "Is Jasper here?"

"Good Lord," she huffs, but mildly. Like she's too tired to even care. "That kid will be a picked-over carcass, and one of you girls will still be coming around, trying to drag him home."

"He was expecting me." My voice rises at the end like a question. But instead of that making me sound sweet and polite, it kind of makes me sound like a stalker.

"Well then, I guess he changed his mind," she says, face pinched. Then her eyes shoot up to my hair. A headband is the only thing that makes my hacked hair look okay, even now. I jammed an elastic one in my pocket on the way out of the house, but it's too late for that. Her eyebrows draw tight. "Yes, well, I can't tell you why he's not here because I haven't seen him. But Jasper's been changing his mind a lot lately."

And then I feel it—even without her looking at me—the full weight of her heartbreak. She isn't angry at Jasper, or hoping to get rich off of him playing professional hockey. She isn't worried about money. She's afraid she is going to lose her son. That something awful is going to happen to him.

And Jasper has absolutely no idea she feels this way. It makes me so sad for the both of them.

"Are you sure he's not here?" I ask.

"Jesus, you are a persistent thing." She looks me up and down. And then I feel a momentary twinge of pity. She knows what desperation feels like. "Come on in if you want. I am going to take my shoes off, but you can go look for him yourself if you think I'm hiding him."

I step inside the dim entryway with its two sagging arm-chairs and worn wooden bench against the wall. Jasper's mom winces as she sits down to take off her shoes. It isn't until then that it occurs to me: she just got *home* from work. She is not just up from being asleep after a double shift like Jasper said. He lied to keep me away. And now he is gone.

"Can I look in his room?"

"Will it make you go away?" she asks. I nod. "Then go ahead, but be quick."

She flaps a hand in the direction of Jasper's room, though I already know where it is.

THE LIGHTS IN Jasper's room are off, but the curtains are open. Twin bed, dark comforter, a desk and some bookshelves along one wall. As usual, it is freakishly neat, the bed made with military precision. Full of promise, but tinged with sadness—like everything about Jasper. I'm still surveying how tidy everything is when something on Jasper's nightstand catches my eye. As I get closer, I can see that it's a stack of clipped-together envelopes, each already torn open. I look over my shoulder before picking them up. Jasper's mom said I could come in his room to check for him. I'm pretty sure that wasn't an invitation to rummage through his things.

There's no return address on the envelopes, only Jasper's name and address printed on the label. When I pull out the note inside the top envelope, I recognize Cassie's curly script right away.

It's not that he's better than Jasper. He's different. Which I guess, in this case, is the same as better. Jasper is nice and

smart and sweet, but with him I can't breathe. I always have to
pretend to be someone I'm not . . .

My eyes move to the top. There's no "dear" anybody, only a
date. And only days before the camp. And the lined paper is rag-
ged at the side as though it's been torn from something. Some
sick asshole has been sending Jasper excerpts from Cassie's
diary? There's so many of them, too. Jasper has been getting
bits and pieces of Cassie's journal ever since we got back from
Maine, probably convincing himself more and more that he was
the reason she got mixed up with Quentin in the first place. No
wonder he's been getting worse.

Then I see one more envelope, this one on the floor. Dropped
there or maybe it slid from the stack. I pick it up. Postmarked
yesterday. I slide the page out.

I'm not saying that it's Jasper's fault that I'm spending time
with Quentin. It's more complicated than that. But I do think that
Jasper being so perfect made me want to get even more messed
up. I wanted to prove to him that not everyone is worth saving.

I swallow hard. Poor Jasper. The thing he was most afraid
of—that he drove Cassie to Quentin and drinking and all of it—
written right there, in Cassie's own words.

I COME BACK out into the foyer, holding the stack of envelopes.

"I didn't say you could take anything." Jasper's mom glances
at me.

"Do you have any idea where Jasper might have gone?" I press on. "I think he might be really upset."

"I have no goddamn idea where he is!" She shouts, so loud I flinch. But then she hangs her head and bites down on her lip hard—guilt and sadness. That's all. The anger is just easier. I wonder what I would think if I couldn't read her so well, if I were Jasper. "I don't know why you're here or what you want with my son. But Jasper is not in any condition to be anyone's boyfriend."

"I'm a friend, that's all," I say. "A friend who's worried about him." Though for the first time, that feels like a lot less than the truth.

"Maybe he went for a walk," she says, motioning toward the door. Her voice is quiet now, unsteady. "He does that these days. A lot. He likes to go to the Bernham Bridge to watch for canoes. We used to do that when he was little."

Bridge. Bridge. Bridge. It's the most awful alarm ringing in my brain. A bridge you can jump from? I do not want it to stick in my head the way it does, but it already has. My heart is racing as I clutch Cassie's letters tight in my hand and head for the door.

"I'll go look for him," I say. "But I also think you should call the police."

"The police?" Worried still, yes, but also suspicious. "The last thing Jasper needs is trouble with the police. We've had enough of that with his brother."

"I know, but—all I can say is that I have a *really* bad feeling. Like he could be in danger. We were talking on the phone last night and—"

"Danger? What are you—oh no. Wait one second here." Her

eyes flash hard in my direction. Then they move again up to my hair. Finally, she has realized, and when she looks me in the eye again, the blast of anger burns. "*You*," she growls, pushing herself to her feet. "You're *her*. The one that almost got my son killed."

She steps forward. And I take another couple steps back toward the door. I toss the envelopes addressed to Jasper into a nearby chair. This feels like a peace offering.

"I'm sorry about—but right now—" My foot catches on a chair.

"Oh, so *now* you're worried about him? You know what, you *should* be worried. You know what you cost him? What you took from your so-called friend? How hard he's worked since he was a teeny-tiny kid to get that opportunity at Boston College? The hours and hours at that ice rink freezing his ass off? And now—" She makes an exploding motion with her hands. "You destroyed everything."

I am finally at the door, fumbling with the knob behind me as she steps closer. I turn my face, bracing for her to slap me.

"I just—I'm worried about him," I say again as I get the door open. It scrapes hard against my back. "I'm sorry."

"You should be sorry!" she shouts after me as I rush outside.

7

I STUMBLE DOWN THE STEPS AND RUN AWAY FROM JASPER'S HOUSE. *Bernham Bridge. You should be sorry. Bernham Bridge. You should be sorry.* The bridge is not far, I don't think, maybe less than a half mile. Only a couple of quick turns. But I need to get there *now.* I can feel it. And that isn't about reading anybody's feelings, not about simple Heightened Emotional Perception. There is no one there to read. This feeling is something more.

But I have never been more certain of anything in my life: Jasper needs me, and he needs me *right now.*

I look around for a taxi, a car, some other option, over-whelmed by the sense of the time I have already wasted. The things I should have realized. Should have said. But there is no one around to help. I have no choice but to run on. I look down at my stupid, useless flip-flops, tugging them off and sprinting barefoot, one gripped in each hand.

My legs feel wiry and taut as I turn down Juniper toward Sullivan. Soon my feet go numb against the sharp, hot pavement as I race past the bigger, more beautiful houses. The only sounds are the rough heaving of my breath, and the slapping of my bare feet against the concrete. *Don't do it, Jasper. Don't do it.* Because I am thinking that he has gone there to jump. And I pray that I am wrong.

Finally, I reach the place where the road curves and ends in a cluster of trees. After that, there is the bridge.

I am running so fast now. I can barely feel the ground.

Jasper.

A bridge.

And all that emptiness below.

But I will be in time. I have to be. And somehow I will say exactly the right thing. And he will realize that he's not thinking clearly. Because he may not care about what happens to him right now. At this moment. But he will—tomorrow, the next day. And I care now. So much more than I realized.

I am almost at the bridge now, the span in clear view. My eyes scan the length of it, searching up and down. But there is nothing. There is no one to convince. No one to save. Maybe I was wrong. Wrong, and not late.

I have to be.

But then I spot something on the ground about halfway down, along the railing. A small, dark pile. I race ahead to see what it is.

I am shaking when I finally stop in front of it. It isn't until I crouch down that I realize it's a sweatshirt. Blue and green. Any other colors would be better. Because blue and green are the ones worn by all the Newton Regional High School sports teams. I have to put a hand on the railing to steady myself as I pick it up. Before it's even in the air I can see the arc of the words on the back: *NRHS Hockey Team.*

No. No. No.

This is not the way it ends. It can't be. I should have—no. It's not. Jasper is okay. He has to be. I press myself hard against the railing and over the water below, scanning for any sign of him.

I need to calm down. Focus. Even if he jumped, there's still time to get him out. It couldn't have happened that long ago. My hips press against the railing like a gymnast propped up on uneven bars. Looking for signs of life. Praying I find something.

There's a loud sound behind me then. Wheels screeching to a stop, doors opening. Footsteps. I am afraid to peel my eyes from the water. Afraid I will miss some glimpse of Jasper.

"Stop!" a man shouts behind me. Not quite angry. But very, very firm. "Come away from the railing."

The police? Jasper's mom must have called them. Thank God.

But I do not turn. I do not take my eyes off that water. I will spot Jasper if he surfaces—no matter what anyone says. "He's down there!" I shout back instead.

"Come away from the edge!" Even louder now. But a woman this time. "Miss, get off the railing now!"

"But my friend Jasper—"

"We aren't listening until you come away from there!"

I glance over my shoulder and see the two police officers

coming slowly closer from either side of a stopped police car.

"Someone has to go after him. Do you have a boat or scuba people or something?"

"We can talk about that after you step over here, miss." When I look quickly again, I see the female officer has curly hair pulled back in a ponytail. And she's waving me toward her. "Take a step or two away from the edge, hon. Toward me."

The way she says "hon" has a warm ring to it, but she's nervous. I can feel it. I see her look down at my shoeless, possibly bloody feet. I get it: I look unhinged. But she is trying to be patient, to give me the benefit of the doubt. Her partner, on the other hand—young and jumpy and overmuscular—seems like he is going to pounce. They are focused only on me, too. They don't understand what's going on. They've been misinformed.

"You're wasting time! It's not me, it's my friend! *He* jumped!" I shout back at them as I turn again to the water. "He is going to die down there if you don't hurry!"

"We want to help you," the female officer says. She is calmer now, like she's hit her stride. "But we can't until you step away from the railing."

Help *you*. They are *still* not listening. I am just going to have to make them.

"If you want me away from the railing, then send somebody down there!" I scream, jabbing a finger toward the water.

I whip around and lean way back on purpose over the railing. The female officer stops, but her partner is still inching toward me, off to the side. His right hand is at his hip, reaching for something. I don't think they would actually shoot me, but there are other options. She raises a hand again, telling him to hold. He does, but he's pissed about it.

"We'll see about your friend," she says, forcing her voice higher. "As soon as—"

When I press even farther back over the railing, she stops talking.

"Now! Go look for him now!"

God, why didn't I go over to Jasper's house last night? Because I had believed him, that's why. Maybe he'd even been telling the truth last night when he said he'd be okay.

"Wylie, hon?" The female officer knows my name? Jasper's mom might have told them. So why does her using it seem so off? "Are you listening to me?"

No, I am not. What I am listening to is this terrible feeling I am having. I am listening to the way she feels, which is completely and totally focused on me and not listening to a word I am saying, the worst combination imaginable.

"They didn't send you for me. They sent you for my friend Jasper." I push up and actually sit on the railing. I feel queasy when I glance down toward the water and see nothing—no boat, no search party, no flashing lights on shore. No Jasper. And being suspended so far over the water is totally terrifying. "Get people to look for him. Now!"

She holds up a hand. "Okay, okay." Now she is pissed. Worried, too, but in a mostly pissed-off way. She hates that this situation has gotten away from her. Her nostrils flare as she dials her phone. A second later she is asking for a marine unit. "Possible male teenage victim in water. Fall from Bernham Bridge." She pauses, gives some more details. It is like she is actually talking to someone, and not pretending. "They're on their way," she says when she's done. "Now, Wylie, we had a deal. Come down."

I still have the most awful feeling. Different now, though. Like I am missing an essential detail. The most important one.

"What's going on here?" I ask.

"You've got yourself leaning over the side of a bridge, which is *extremely* dangerous. And you're scaring the hell out of us."

The girl with the knife has become the girl sitting on top of a bridge railing. Threatening to jump. A danger to myself, no doubt. Shit. How did that happen? How did I become exactly who I didn't want to be?

"Everyone wants to help you," she goes on. "We want you to be okay."

"But it's not me," I whisper. I do want to come down, though. It's scary hanging over that railing. And she has done what I wanted—sent people looking for Jasper. "Okay, okay."

I grip the metal tighter as I push myself back to the ground. As soon as my feet touch down, something knocks me hard from the side, throwing me off balance and also away from the water. I'm yanked up by my arms right before I hit the concrete.

"Let go!"

"Calm down." A man's voice. A new one, behind me. "Or we'll have to restrain you."

Here it is, at long last. People coming to take me away. But I hadn't pictured it like this. Being so obviously unjust. No. I won't let it happen. I won't go quietly. I won't behave, not the way they want me to. They are wrong about me.

And so I nod, like I have heard them. Like I am listening. "Okay," I say quietly. "But you're hurting my arms. Please, let me go."

They loosen their grip, a little and then a little more. It's my chance. Maybe the last one. I lunge forward. *Run. Run. Run.* One step, two steps.

"Stop!" Loud. Right in my ear. That same man, the one who was holding me. And now he is furious.

Run. Run. Run. But he is so close. Like I haven't gone a single step. And there are more voices. Lots of shouting. The sounds of stomping feet. I am knocked down again, much harder this time.

"Careful! Don't hurt her!" the woman shouts.

My hands burn against the pavement. And there are so many hands on me. I try to slap them away. But there are too many. There are way too—

"AND THEN WHAT happened?" Dr. Shepard asked.

I'd gotten to *that* part of the dream: the important part. That was why I'd stopped talking. I was a good patient that way: not easy to fix, but so obviously broken.

"I pushed her," I said finally, after the silence grew too awkward to bear. "Into the fire."

I'd been having the dream nightly since Jasper and I had gotten back from the camp. But it was the first time I'd told Dr. Shepard. The dream was so transparent it was almost embarrassing: I felt guilty about what had happened to Cassie so I was having dreams that I had *literally* caused her death.

"I see," Dr. Shepard said, in that totally annoying therapist way that I thought we'd evolved past.

"Seriously?" I asked. "You're not going to say anything about what the dream *really* means. Me feeling guilty and all that?"

"I don't know." She shrugged. "It seems like it's *about* you pushing Cassie into the fire." She shifted a little in her big red chair. "I mean, did you?"

It was a real question.

"Of course not!" I snapped back.

"Well, don't blame me. It was *your* dream," Dr. Shepard said, and in the taunting voice of a five-year-old. It didn't seem very professional.

Also, couldn't she at least *try* to make me feel better, after everything I had been through? I jumped to my feet and started to pace the room.

"I tried to stop her, you know. I did everything I could." I pointed hard at my own chest.

Dr. Shepard blinked her pretty brown eyes at me, repositioned her small body once again.

"I don't know why, Wylie, but you did do it. It's been decided. There is no doubt."

"I did not!" I shouted, charging closer. I wanted to hit her. I was afraid I might even do it.

But then there was a noise behind me. A cough?

Someone clearing their throat. There was someone else *in* Dr. Shepard's office with us? But how could that be? That's when I notice the room has turned orange, and Dr. Shepard's red chair is blue. I go to tell Dr. Shepard, but she has disappeared.

"Are you going to do it?" A voice from behind me.

I try to turn, but I can't move my feet. The floor has turned to tar. Instead, I twist to look over my shoulder.

My mother is sitting in Dr. Shepard's big, red-again chair. She is wearing the outfit she had on the night she died. Her left foot is bare. On her right is a single blue clog. Her skin is smudged and black like it is covered in ash.

"Mom?" I whisper.

"So are you going to?" she demands.

"Am I going to do what?" I ask.

"Come on, Wylie. First me, then Cassie—are you going to kill Dr. Shepard, too?"

I GASP AWAKE like I'm breaking through the surface of water. I squint my swollen eyes open. A bright, white room. Fluorescent lights hum overhead. Like an office building.

I try to take a breath but can hardly suck in any air.

It comes back then. Like the bangs of a hammer. The bridge. Jasper. The police. I tried to get away.

A mistake.

Oh, Jasper. My chest clenches.

I try to push myself up, but I cannot. My head is too large and weighed down like it's encased in plaster. I try again and this time, my head lifts. But I am still stuck. It's not my head that's pinned down. It's my arms.

Strapped down. To a hospital bed.

8

STAY CALM. KEEP IT TOGETHER. FOCUS. BUT THAT IS SO MUCH EASIER SAID THAN done. My head is so foggy, too. It must be from whatever they used to knock me out. That was always part of the nightmare: being kept so doped up on the wrong drugs that I never got better. And then I died sad and alone in a mental hospital—exactly like my grandmother. I pull again against the straps around my arms, but it is no use.

And Jasper? Did they find him? Did he actually go off that bridge? Oh God, I did everything wrong. I was supposed to save him, and instead I got myself locked up here. I start to cry. Hard. I can't help it. Soon my sobbing has made my stomach hurt and my face is covered in tears and goo.

The door opens then, and a woman with long, very straight brown hair and a white doctor coat steps inside. She is young and pretty but in an aggressively earthy way—no makeup, no jewelry, square bangs. Like she was once told that she was quite beautiful and has worked hard to hide it ever since. I try to stop crying. But that only makes it worse.

"Jeez, are you okay?" She rushes over to grab some tissues off a nearby table. And then there's the awkward moment when she realizes I cannot wipe my own face because I am restrained—she looks so surprised. Like she's new to this. She hesitates for a second, then starts to undo my wrists. "Here, I'm sorry about these . . ." Her voice drifts like she doesn't even want to say out loud what they are.

Once my hands are free, I take the tissues and dry my face.

"Did you find my friend?" I ask. "His name is Jasper. I was on the bridge looking for him. *I* wasn't going to jump or any-thing. But the police came, and I think maybe they thought I *was* him—or I don't know. But they were definitely confused." I close my mouth tight, hope that when I speak again my words will slow. "They said they would look for Jasper. I need to know that he's okay."

Because he has to be.

"That's awful." She looks confused, then sympathetic—maybe even a little appalled on my behalf. "I'm sorry, I'm Dr. Alvarez. I'm afraid I don't know anything about your friend. But I will try to find out. Let me quickly take your vitals first."

I nod. Cooperative, that's the way to go, at least for now. I am glad for the tranquilizers that are still in my system because they're keeping my pulse in check even though I am terrified. And staying calm will make it easier to prove there is nothing wrong with me. This Dr. Alvarez does genuinely want to help. I can feel it. She is easy to read with my own anxiety sidelined—even if it is only by medication. And there is no deception, no hesitation. It would be good to keep her on my side. Because this is a mistake, a mix-up, a totally messed up and terrible one—not to mention ironic. But—as Dr. Shepard has reminded me time and again over the years—coincidence is not the same as causation. And the saner I can act, the faster all of this is going to get sorted out.

Dr. Alvarez lifts my wrist to take my pulse, clips a small device to my finger, and sticks a thermometer in my mouth. It's all finished and recorded on her clipboard within a minute, maybe two. Then she puts a hand on my arm. Kindness and concern, and again that hint of outrage on my behalf, that's all I feel. I cannot be sure yet whether or not I can completely trust Dr. Alvarez, but God knows I want to.

"Your vitals are good," she says with a reserved smile. "Now let me try to find out about your friend. My supervisor, Dr. Haddox, will be in to explain things to you."

"I just—I want to go home. I wasn't going to jump. I'm okay, truly. I swear." I sound desperate. Like I am lying. Maybe I should keep my mouth shut.

I feel sorrow rise in her chest as she looks at me. "I want to help if I can." She nods, but she has her doubts. I'm not sure if they are about me or her own ability. "What's your friend's full name?"

"Jasper Salt."

"Okay," she says as she steps toward the door. "Let me see what I can do."

I WAIT UNTIL Dr. Alvarez is gone before I get out of bed. I spot my flip-flops lined up against the far wall; the only personal belonging of mine anywhere in sight. My phone is what I really want. I need to call my dad. At a minimum, he can get Dr. Shepard to call and vouch for me. I have no idea what time it is, but hopefully he's not on that plane to DC yet.

I don't see my phone anywhere. I get out of bed, hoping it might be stashed somewhere in a drawer. It isn't until my feet are on the floor that I look down and notice that I have a gray sweat suit on. I feel embarrassed and exposed thinking of my clothes being changed while I was passed out. Worse yet is the sense that they've already readied me for a longer stay.

Now, my heart is wide awake, pumping faster than it should be.

I make my way around the room, opening and closing the smooth, brand-new drawers, checking the closet, too. All empty. All immaculately clean. There's nothing in the gleaming, white tile bathroom either except a little set of travel-sized toiletries. Not a set of manicure scissors or tweezers in sight. Nothing sharp. And definitely no phone.

I step over and press my ear to the door, listening. That's always been the thing I have dreaded most about an imagined commitment: the sounds of a psychiatric unit. But I can't hear anything. Either the hallway is silent or the door is too thick. And it doesn't seem wise to open it. I can't afford to look like I am trying to escape again.

Instead, I head to the window and push open the heavy curtains. It's light still, the same day. Hopefully. Maybe only a couple of hours gone. Maybe. I force myself to take a breath.

Across the way is a shiny glass-and-steel building, modern and brand-new. Its polished front reflects the building we are in. Much the same: tall and polished, windowpane after windowpane. Nice, as hospitals go, which I am glad about. But also maybe a little too nice. From the window, I can see a parking lot. At the far end is an old, white stone building with a set of steps leading up to a grand but crumbling entryway, a small dome perched on top. A haunted-looking leftover from what the hospital used to be.

My chest is tightening. A legitimate panic attack coming on. Apparently an emergency where I am trapped alone in a room isn't enough to neutralize my anxiety the way chasing after Cassie did. I try to use the deep breathing Dr. Shepard taught me, try to talk myself through. It helps a little. But not as much as it has been. And if I legitimately start panicking, it will only help prove their point. Then again, maybe I need to kick up a fuss. Demand to talk to my dad, immediately. Be the squeakiest wheel. I'm still staring out the window when the door opens behind me.

"Not a great view, but not terrible either. At least it's not a brick wall."

When I turn, there's a man standing in the doorway. A little older than Alvarez, a little younger than my dad. He has kind blue eyes and sandy-colored hair, good-looking without being off-puttingly handsome. He has a folder in one hand.

"I'm Dr. Haddox," he says, smiling as he steps forward with his free hand outstretched. Close up, I can feel that he is nervous or uncomfortable or something, but he's trying to cover that up by acting exceptionally calm and confident. It's not working. At least not on me.

Because I may be beginning to panic, but that is a distinct

feeling—deeper in my gut and colder like before—than what I am feeling from him. His unease is of a higher frequency, hotter somehow, and coursing instead through my chest. The contrast is becoming more and more clear. This Dr. Haddox may be the one in charge, but he's not at all sure he wants to be.

I hesitate before reaching out my own hand. His face softens, relieved when I finally do.

"How long have I been here?"

"Oh, a few hours, I think."

"Where's my phone?" I ask—and from the way Dr. Haddox twitches, probably too aggressively.

"Um." He looks around like he genuinely thinks we're going to see it sitting somewhere. "I'm not exactly sure. But I do know that we are holding phones—different parents, different rules. Just trying to avoid any problems. Did you have it when you came in?"

And I sense not a trace of deception as he steps over to the bureau and pulls open a drawer to look for it himself the same way I did only moments ago.

"I have no idea if I had it or not," I say. I remember that it was in my back pocket when I got to the bridge. For all I know it fell into the water. Or it could have easily gotten knocked from my pocket when I hit the ground. "I was unconscious when you dragged me in here. I don't have any idea what I had."

He closes his eyes momentarily. "Right," he says quietly. "About that—I'm very sorry. I don't know what the mix-up was, but that never should have happened."

Mix-up. Finally, someone gets it.

"So I can go then?" I ask, looking around again for my personal belongings, which I will gladly leave behind if it means I can get out of here.

Dr. Haddox's eyebrows bunch as he tilts his head to the side. "Oh no," he says, uncomfortable. "By mix-up, I mean there was a whole procedure they were supposed to follow, none of which happened. Starting with the fact that they were supposed to go to your house."

"Not *my* house," I say. "Jasper's house."

"Jasper is your friend, right?" he asks. "The one you were on the bridge for."

"The one *they* were there for," I say, wishing this doctor was altogether a little faster on the uptake. "Jasper's mom called the police because I told her to. I was worried Jasper might, I don't know, do something stupid. Things somehow got confused because they thought it was me they wanted." I wait for some reaction, some sense that I am persuading him. But his confusion is still the only thing I can read. "Anyway, I'm here because they thought *I* was Jasper."

"No," the doctor says, quietly, gently. "You're here, Wylie, because an ambulance and officers were sent to your house. And"—he consults the folder in his hand—"it looks like it was your brother maybe who—?"

"My brother?"

"Yes, your brother Gideon? Oh no, wait, it says he didn't know where you were. I think it was your friend's mother who said that you were on the bridge," he offers then with a quick, satisfied nod.

Something new—apart from all the obvious of this being a messed-up situation—is not adding up. "Gideon didn't know I was at Jasper's house," I say.

"I'm sorry, I don't know. The details aren't here." And I suppose it is possible that Gideon could have guessed and sent them to the house of the only friend I still have. "Regardless, none of it should have happened the way it did. There is no—" He shakes his head and takes a breath. "It shouldn't have happened. And I'm sorry. But it's not a mistake that you are here. You're supposed to be."

"What are you talking about?" I ask. "Why?"

The worst part is that I can feel that he's telling the truth—at least the truth as he believes it to be. My hands have started to shake.

"I know this is hard to understand. And I promise I will explain. But if you could first just—"

"No!"

I shout so loud it echoes. And I am glad. Even if shouting has made the air feel thin.

I fell for this kind of crap once before. With Quentin at the camp—*wait one second and we'll explain everything.* I am not going to do it again. I am not going to go around trusting a bunch a people who have me locked up somewhere. You grab me off the street, I am going to assume that every single word out of your mouth is a lie. Even if you don't realize it.

"I understand that you're upset, Wylie, and confused, and under the circumstances you have every right to be," Dr. Haddox goes on, and his eyes flick toward the door. He's wondering if he should call someone. Maybe even someone with a syringe who can help control me. And I do have to be careful. Strategic at the very least. They are the ones with the tranquilizers. But I also feel guilt from Dr. Haddox. He doesn't like keeping me in the dark. If I keep pushing, I think his conscience will get the better of him. "I promise I will explain everything in a—"

"Now," I say, quiet and calm. I can do this. I can demand the answers I deserve without them being able to say I am "irrational" or "overemotional." I can use what I know about Dr. Haddox—that he has his own doubts about this situation—to get him to tell me the truth. I may not want this whole Outlier thing, but I am sure as hell going to use it to my advantage. "Listen, you people cornered me and *drugged* me. I think the fact that I want an explanation makes me the most sane person ever." I cross my arms. "Otherwise, I guess you'll have to drug me again."

Dr. Haddox winces, then brings a hand to his forehead and rubs his temples. The drugging thing bothers him the most. It's a card I might have to keep on playing.

"Okay," he says, motioning to the guest chair as he leans back against the bed. But I make no move to sit. "We think there is a chance that you—that all of you here—have something called PANDAS."

"PANDAS? What's that?"

"It's a disorder that results from untreated strep. It can cause a whole range of psychological symptoms, primarily OCD and anxiety, though we suspect there may be a variation in this instance or that the symptoms of PANDAS may be broader than

we realized previously, encompassing additional mood distur-
bances. Have you experienced heightened anxiety recently?"

That's not a question it's in my best interest to answer.

"I don't have strep. I don't even have a sore throat," I say
instead.

"Strep is often asymptomatic. And in this instance it might
have even been food borne. It wouldn't have the usual symptoms
you associate with strep, like a sore throat."

"What are you talking about?" I ask. "What the hell do you
mean, food-borne?"

"I know this is a lot to take in," he says with a lopsided smile
that is closer to a grimace. "It would be easier if they had explained things to your parents the way they were supposed to."

"Yeah, because you can't keep me here without my dad's con-
sent." Of this much I am 100 percent sure. Assuming that they
aren't going with the whole "danger to yourself" approach,
which they don't seem to be. "That's illegal."

Rachel was just talking about this the last time she was over,
how it amounts to false imprisonment if the government holds
you.

"Not in a situation like this, I don't think," Dr. Haddox says,
and almost like he feels bad about that. "Listen, I'm a doctor
here to evaluate the likelihood of PANDAS. I don't have all the
information. I don't even know exactly how they isolated all of
you. But I am pretty sure they are acting within their discretion
legally. The NIH has done this kind of thing before with measles
and Ebola."

"Ebola?" I ask.

"Don't worry, PANDAS is nothing like Ebola. It was just another example of something that the NIH has dealt with."

The NIH. Someone called my dad to meet with the NIH in DC on the same day the NIH puts me in some hospital? *That* is definitely not a coincidence.

"I need to talk to my dad."

"Absolutely. We already have called him more than once and haven't been able to reach him," Dr. Haddox says. "Do you know where he might be?"

Washington, DC. The airplane. That's probably where he is.

"What time is it?"

"Almost one, I think."

"He's on an airplane," I say. "But he should be in DC soon. With his phone on again."

"We'll keep trying him definitely," Dr. Haddox says. And then his face gets tight. "But there is broad authority in potentially infectious situations like this for the government—the NIH in this case, though I suspect the CDC, too, eventually—to act in the interests of public safety." That line isn't his own. This doctor was given it to use. "Again, that doesn't excuse the specifics of your situation. I suspect, honestly, the officers and EMTs panicked. They haven't been told much. This is an unusual situation, and we've all been told to keep information flow to a minimum. They were trying to do their jobs. I'm not excusing what they did—"

"Except you are," I say, but matter-of-fact. "That's exactly what you're doing."

"I'm sorry," he says, turning to look at the ground. "My

understanding is that we're only keeping you here so we can run some tests. We'll need to do a simple blood draw, conduct an interview, make sure that nothing gets worse. We'll give you all a course of antibiotics to treat the strep and that should be that. If this is PANDAS, the psychological symptoms generally resolve on their own fairly quickly." Dr. Haddox looks up finally, meeting my eyes. Determination, that's the emotion. He is determined to do his job right, to be trustworthy. And I do believe that *he* believes what he's saying. I also know that is not the same thing as him being right. "It is strange to see so many people fall ill in a small geographical area, and PANDAS is a relatively rare, noncontagious condition. At least up until now. It's raised questions about how you all might have contracted it. That's why the NIH got involved, and they got us involved."

"So *you* don't work for the NIH?"

"Oh no, I'm just a fellow. I work for a research professor. My boss is an expert so the NIH reached out to him. And now we're here," he says like he's still not sure how it happened. And is not happy about it.

"And you don't know why they think I have this?"

"No," he says. "They haven't told us that. Just that they have reason to suspect you all do."

You all. I am afraid to ask how many of us there are. And I'm not sure if it should be making me feel better or worse than when I thought I was being committed.

"Someone from the NIH is supposed to be here soon to go over all the details. I'm sure it sounds ridiculous that I don't know, but I honestly don't."

"And what if I want to leave?" I ask. "What if I don't want the treatment or the tests? Can I walk out that door?"

Dr. Haddox takes a breath. I feel him consider dodging the question, then decide instead to play it straight.

"No, you can't leave," he says. "Not yet. But if you come with me, I can introduce you to the others and schedule your blood draw. That will at least—well, move things along."

"I need to know if Jasper's okay first," I say. "My friend from the bridge? Dr. Alvarez said she was going to check on him."

He nods. "Of course, she was headed to make the call when I came in here. We can find her on the way."

9

THE HALLWAY IS EMPTY. NOT A HUMAN BEING IN SIGHT. THOUGH IN ALL OTHER respects, it looks like a normal hospital: a nurses' station with expandable racks full of manila folders, assorted medical equipment scattered nearby, and open rooms lining the hall, even an unoccupied stretcher at the far end. But there is something deeply unnerving about the hollow silence. Like we've stumbled upon a place that has already been evacuated.

"Where is everybody?" I ask.

"They're all down in the common room," he says, motioning ahead.

"What is this place? And why are there no people in it?"

"Oh," Dr. Haddox says, looking surprised again by how little I know. "Boston General Hospital, but this is a new wing. It's at minimal capacity. Come on, I think you and I will both feel better when you're in the common area."

As we're stepping past the nurses' station, I spot a phone on the desk. "Can I try to call my dad here?" I ask. I do want to call him, but it is also a test.

"Of course, absolutely," Dr. Haddox says without hesitating, and he seems genuinely relieved. Like he'd love nothing more than for me to have that conversation. He steps forward and hands me the receiver. "Dial nine to get an outside line."

I still expect for something to stop me, for Dr. Haddox to have some sudden excuse. But then the phone is ringing, the call going right to voice mail. I leave a message. "Dad, it's Wylie. I'm at Boston General Hospital in the—"

"Dwyer Wing."

"Dwyer Wing," I say. "These people brought me here. They're from the NIH. They're saying I and some other people have some PANDAS thing. Can you come here? Or call? As soon as you can?"

I hang up, look at Dr. Haddox. "He can call me, right?"

"Of course," he says. "We're hoping he does. As I said, we've already left several messages. Dr. Cornelia specifically said that—"

"Wait, who?" My heart has picked up even more speed.

"Dr. Cornelia. He's an immunologist who is affiliated with Metropolitan New York Hospital. He's my supervisor at Cornell."

Dr. Cornelia from Cornell, of course. I should have made the connection as soon as Dr. Haddox mentioned some "disorder" and the NIH. Obviously, it's all connected. I consider calling my dad right back, adding that Dr. Cornelia is involved. But I am now afraid of giving up to Dr. Haddox the connection between

Cornelia and my dad. Right now, at least, it still seems like Dr. Haddox has no idea who I am.

"Do you want to try to call someone else?" Dr. Haddox motions to the phone for emphasis. He wants to be sure I know he's not standing in my way.

I nod as I dial Jasper's number. When the call goes again straight to voice mail, it makes my stomach lurch. I wish I hadn't called.

I think about trying Gideon, too, but he was so very angry this morning. And then there is the fact that he pointed them in the right direction without even warning me. What if he is glad this happened? What if he doesn't try to hide it? And beyond Gideon there isn't anyone else to call except Rachel. But I want to talk to my dad first before I invite her to wade in and maybe make things worse. I don't trust Rachel's judgment, at all.

"Anyone else?" Dr. Haddox asks.

I shake my head. "No, that's okay. Maybe later."

WE CONTINUE THROUGH two swinging doors into a small lobby area. Creepily empty, too, like everywhere else, but for the furniture— two smooth, light-gray leather sofas across from each other and a steel-colored rug with a grid marked out in even, cream-colored lines. There's also a coffee table and a group of sleek armchairs lined up along one wall. But there aren't any magazines stacked up on the tables or discarded coffee cups on the sideboard. Like no one has ever really been here. Like no one is supposed to be. The signage on the other side points this way and that—*Francis*

J. Dwyer Memorial Wing to the right, *Staff Meeting Room* and *Augustus Burn Center* left.

I'm about to ask where Dr. Alvarez is. To demand that we find her so she can tell me what she knows about Jasper when we turn a corner and almost collide with her.

"There you are," Dr. Haddox says.

"I'm sorry, Wylie, that I took so long." She smiles. But she's uncomfortable.

"Did they find Jasper?" I ask.

"Not in the—no," she says. "Which is a good sign. The police said they are confident that if he did fall they would have spotted some sign by now." She hesitates, trying to choose her words carefully. "I guess they know where people usually turn up from the currents . . ." She glances in Dr. Haddox's direction. "I did ask them to confirm with Jasper's parents that he made it home safely. If I were you, that's the only thing that would put my mind fully at ease. The police promised to call me back personally on my cell when they'd confirmed. And I promise, I will call Dr. Haddox as soon as I hear from them."

She says this with a kind of grim determination—like staying on the case won't be easy, but she's up to the task. I want to find it comforting, but it is just the opposite. Still, overall I do feel less panicked about Jasper, but that's an instinct that would be easier to follow if Dr. Alvarez didn't still seem so upset.

"What's wrong then?" I ask her. "You seem more worried than before."

Dr. Alvarez smiles in a way that is not at all convincing, then puts a kind hand on my arm and squeezes. "Nothing—

nothing about Jasper. I just—don't feel well. Maybe something I ate." That's a lie for sure. No matter how good Dr. Alvarez's intentions, that does not make it any more comforting.

"You should go home, Dr. Alvarez. Take care of yourself," Dr. Haddox says, and he does not mean by drinking some ginger ale and going to bed early. This talk of sickness is a cover for something else. And they both know it.

"I'm sorry," Dr. Alvarez says to Dr. Haddox before walking on.

He nods. "It's not your fault."

Dr. Haddox and I watch as Dr. Alvarez heads back the way we came. We are quiet until she disappears around the corner.

"Come on, the common room is down this way," Dr. Haddox says.

AT THE END of the hall is a set of locked windowless doors. Dr. Haddox touches an ID to the keypad, and the doors buzz open. He waves me in ahead of him.

The common room is even more inviting than the fancy lobby. Sparkling white and spacious, the room has floor-to-ceiling windows running across its length and modern furniture—a low sectional with bright pillows and an earthy, burnt-orange shag carpet. The furniture is organized in three separate seating areas and the back has a half dozen café tables near a galley kitchenette, complete with refrigerator and sink. It's like the lobby area of a fashionable but inexpensive hotel. And—as promised—there are more than a dozen people clustered around the room in different groups. They are all girls, all wearing matching gray sweat suits. Just like mine. Though some of them have already adapted the sweats to suit their own taste—sleeves rolled, legs pulled up over the knees. They are still wearing their own shoes, too, which in the cases of high heels, look outright weird.

All girls. And Dr. Cornelia is involved. Dr. Cornelia of the Outliers-are-all-sick school of thought. These things are not unrelated. These girls aren't unrelated, even if I don't yet understand how they connected us.

They are leaning up against the windows, flopped across the fancy-ish couches. A couple laugh and point at something as they stand too close to the big-screen TV on the back wall next to the emergency exit. I think I might recognize some of them.

At least one goes to Stanton Prep, class president or something. I saw her speak at the annual awards ceremony last year when Gideon won the science prize. She had on the same bright-red lipstick that she's wearing now, seriously out of place with the sweats. She is pretty with a dark, blunt bob, setting off her chalk-white skin. There's another girl I definitely recognize from Newton Regional. She is tall and model-thin and strikingly beautiful with thick black hair and flawless skin—Becca, I think her name is. She's one of the girls in heels, platform sandals to be exact. Somehow, though, she manages to pull it off. Becca ran in the same circles with Maia, but I don't know whether they were actually friends. There was a rumor Becca was a heroin user. A pretty believable one if I recall.

I wonder if Jasper was friends with her. The thought of him makes my chest ache. But he is okay, he has to be. I know it, too. Don't I? I think so. I hope so.

There are two other girls on the far side of the room that I think I also might recognize from school. I am pretty sure the one with the red curls under a bandanna and freckles is named Elise. She started at school right before my mom's accident, in the middle of the year. Cassie told me later that Elise had gotten in trouble for stealing huge boxes of Trident gum from the Rite Aid and reselling them at school. Cassie also told me Elise was a transgender girl, pleased to be in the circle of people who were first trusted with that information.

Dr. Haddox's phone rings then, startling me. "Ah, I'm sorry," he says, digging in his pocket for it. "This is Dr. Cornelia. I called him earlier to tell him what happened to you. I should speak with him."

"But please, check again about my friend, too. Jasper Salt is his name."

Dr. Haddox nods. "I'll do everything I can."

And then he steps way out of earshot as if it's not at all suspicious that he doesn't want me to hear his conversation with Dr. Cornelia.

I don't doubt Dr. Haddox is well intentioned. But wanting to believe you are doing the right thing does not actually make it so. And I may not know exactly what is going on here—where it starts or where it ends—but I feel certain that Dr. Cornelia being involved is a very bad thing. For all of us.

It isn't until Dr. Haddox steps back out the doors he came in that I notice the two large, muscular men standing on either side of another set of doors across the room. These have a small window in each. Doors to the outside or the main section of the hospital. The men are wearing dark, fitted uniforms with lots of pockets, and they're staring straight ahead. They seem armed, though I don't actually see any weapons.

A couple of the girls have noticed me—the girl with the bright-red lipstick from Gideon's school looks especially intrigued. And I feel anxious—the regular old, Outlier-unrelated kind—with their eyes on me. Though, as was true when I raced after Cassie, trying to get my footing in this emergency, five-alarm situation is keeping the worst of my anxiety drowned out.

Apart from the two girls watching TV together, everyone else is keeping their distance from one another. Actually, the rest of the girls seem completely separate and alone. Unhappy, but also not terrified.

I watch Becca make her way over to one of the guards. Stalking more than walking, like some sinewy cat creature even in the unflattering sweat suit. The one guard looks delighted but not surprised that she has come over. Like he has beautiful girls seeking him out all the time, though he is short and balding and has a bit of a paunch. Becca props herself on the back of the couch nearby, one leg swinging back and forth like a metronome. I try to imagine her with a needle in her arm, and—oddly—I can, though I am not sure this makes the rumor any more true.

Even from all the way across the room, it's obvious that this flirting is an act. You don't need to be an Outlier to see that. Still, the guard is buying it completely. He leans in close to say something to her, his chin lifted in this absurd, cocky way.

"Hey, what's your name?" comes a voice from behind me.

When I turn, there's a petite girl swallowed by her big sweat suit and even bigger glasses. And she's standing *right* next to me. She's only a couple of inches too close, but those last inches are the most important ones. Maybe because of her nearness, the girl's emotions wash hard, and unavoidably, over me, and they are a scattered mess. She's a little scared and a bit worried. *And* a lot excited? Why is she excited? Am I even right about that? I feel dizzy trying to get a better fix on her. Her feelings are flashing at me like strobe lights, too bright and then gone. All I want to do is back up and close my eyes.

"Hello? What's your name?" she asks again. Louder this time.

"Wylie." I take a step back, hoping she doesn't follow.

She looks skeptical. "What kind of name is that?"

"My grandfather's," I say, trying to stay polite. I can't afford to offend people yet.

"I'm Teresa," she says, then rolls her eyes. "You know, like *Mother* Teresa. My grandmother is super religious." She stares at me for a minute longer, then smiles in a way that makes me queasy.

"Do you go to Newton Regional?" I ask, though I don't recognize her. Anything to create some noise that might distract me from her the piercing static of her jumbled feelings.

"Oh no," she says, like that is the most absurd suggestion ever. "I'm homeschooled. My grandmother used to be a high school science teacher, so she thought she could do a better job herself. She's all over it."

"How long have you been here?" I ask.

"Four long-ass hours." Another voice from behind. When I turn, it's the class president from Gideon's school. Up close she has elaborate, perfectly applied eye makeup. When she tucks her hair behind her ear, I catch sight of her bracelet—diamond encrusted. I am guessing they are real. Gideon always was the poorest kid at his school. "Hey, do I know you?"

"No, but my brother goes to Stanton Prep," I say, surprised that she recognizes me. Or maybe she recognizes Gideon in me. We are twins after all.

"What's his name?"

"Gideon."

She wrinkles her nose. "Nope, never heard of him." She snaps the woven, black bracelet on her other wrist. Nervous and sad— she's very easy to read—annoyed, too, but that seems secondary to being nervous. "I'm Ramona."

When I turn, I see that Becca has slunk her way over.

"And I'm Becca," she says.

"Yeah," I say, already dreading the awkwardness. "I think we went to Newton Regional together. I used to be friends with Maia, a long time ago."

"Oh yeah?" Becca asks but not like she's especially interested. "I don't remember anyone from there. I was so high all the time. And then I stopped going."

"Stopped?" I ask. And it comes out so weirdly judgmental. I will myself to stop talking. Because what I really want to do is ask her if she knows Jasper. And I have the nagging feeling she might say something that would make me even more worried about him.

Becca shrugs. "Getting clean is a full-time job. But I am now. I've been doing everything they said I had to do to graduate on time. I've been seeing my therapist, and I have a tutor and whatever." She shakes her head. "Which is why this is such bull-shit."

"Almost nobody in here has been in regular school for a while. We've figured out we have that much in common on our own," Ramona says. "They keep saying they're going to explain everything, including, like, why us. Why are we here? But they haven't told us shit. They just keep on saying that it's somebody else who has to tell us. First, it was Dr. Haddox, now he says it's the NIH. So we're guessing it has something to do with the not being in school, even if it is all for different reasons—Becca's got the drugs, Teresa's homeschooled, which—let's face it—seems best for everybody." I look over at Teresa to see if she's noticed the dig, but she doesn't seem to be listening. "That girl over there had some kind of eating thing. That girl has some klepto thing. I was 'bullying' somebody. Which, by the way, I totally was not."

"They didn't tell you about the PANDAS?" I ask, not thrilled that I might have to explain it.

"Oh, they told us *that*." Ramona waves a hand. "That's their *story*. But we *all* think that's bullshit. My parents were super psyched, though, that there might be some 'explanation' for what's 'wrong' with me." She shrugs. "They'd take hearing I have the plague as long as it was proof that it doesn't have anything to do with them. I told my parents this crap had holes in it and they were just like, whatever, fix her."

What Ramona hasn't mentioned, though, is being an Out-lier or Heightened Emotional Perception or anything like that. I should tell them, at least offer it as a possibility. But something stops me. It will sound slightly insane. And it will be hard to explain. But that's not what's holding me back. I'm also not ready to hand over the only thing I have: my secret. Keeping it doesn't make me feel like a good person. But that doesn't make it any less of a good idea. And, in my defense, "reasons for me to trust people" have been in short supply.

"This is so dumb," comes a voice from below me. It's only then that I notice the pair of feet propped up on the edge of the couch to my right, legs stretched out the length of it. There's a book blocking the girl's face. George Orwell's *1984*.

"What's dumb?" Becca asks whoever is behind the book.

"All of you, trying to figure out what these assholes are actually up to," the voice goes on. I look at her hands, the tattoo of an infinity symbol visible on the inside of one wrist. "Whatever you think, the truth is probably a thousand times worse. And they aren't going to come clean because you guess right."

"Who's 'they'?" Ramona asks, annoyed but a little wary, too. At least I think that's what she's feeling. With so many girls around it's impossible to get a clear read on anyone.

"Depends on the situation," the girl behind the book says. "*They* as in: not us."

She has a point. One thing I have definitely learned since what happened at the camp in Maine is that who is "in charge" can be way more complicated than it looks.

"I saw you talking to that guard, too," Ramona says to the girl with the book. "You sure he hasn't told you anything?"

"I haven't been talking to anybody," she says.

"I saw you," Ramona presses.

"Then I suggest you get your eyes checked."

"Hi," I say, hoping the girl will lower the book. The eye

contact might help me get a read on her. As it is, the buzz of the group is deafening. "I'm Wylie."

Finally, the girl puts her book down. She has gorgeous, amber eyes and long, dark brown curls. She is unnervingly pretty. She raises a thick, arched brow. But I still can't read her. Like, *at all.* Sometimes people's feelings are muddy, but this girl is like a brick wall.

"Yeah, I know what your name is because you told Teresa less than a minute ago," she says sharply. But while she sounds annoyed, I can't feel it. "And, you know, if that's your way of tricking people into telling you *their* names, you should come up with a new strategy. Because *that* one is dumb."

"Don't mind Kelsey," Ramona says. "She's kind of . . . a bitch. It seems like she can't help it."

Kelsey's eyebrows bunch. "Just because I don't feel like playing doomed Nancy Drew with you assholes doesn't mean I'm a bitch." She readjusts herself on the couch and lifts her book again. "They have two days to do their stupid tests and observe us or whatever. At least that's what my parents agreed to. And that's it. We're all just going to have to hope that they don't implant some shit in us or poison us while we're here."

"They said no one with Ebola was ever actually in here," Teresa says, sitting on the floor now and gripping her knees as she peers around. I am glad the collective static is at least keeping me from reading her. I'd be glad to never again feel what's going on inside of her. "Do we think that's true? Maybe they want to infect us on purpose or something. Like Kelsey said."

"I did not say infect," Kelsey mumbles. "I said poison."

"Stop it," Ramona says, rocking on her heels again. This time it's three tugs at the bracelet and then three more. A little OCD maybe, but what I feel coming from her is more complicated. It's mixed with rage, the kind that could make you bully somebody. "Why the fuck would you even bring up Ebola, Teresa?"

"Besides," Becca points to the security guards. "They'd at least be wearing masks or something."

"Right, good point," Ramona breathes. "See, Teresa. Now shut the hell up."

"What does Ebola have to do with anything?" I ask, and I don't like how it is ringing a bell with what Dr. Haddox said earlier.

"This part of the hospital." Becca motions to the room. "Remember when people in the US were getting Ebola a couple years ago? They built it to quarantine Ebola patients. Dr. Haddox told us they never ended up using it because people stopped getting sick."

"Oh," I say, and all of that would make sense.

"You feel worse knowing that, don't you?" Kelsey asks me. I look at her, but don't answer—she's right. I can't say why that Ebola detail is so unsettling, something too real about it maybe. I did hear they built a hospital to be some kind of quarantine center a couple of years ago when Ebola was all over the news. I do remember being shocked about how they could just lock people up that way. And now here we are. Locked inside, just like they were. "Well, that's why I don't want to play detective. Because most of the time, the truth is even worse than whatever you're afraid of."

10

SOMEONE RIGHT BEHIND ME CLAPS LOUDLY THEN. IT'S BECCA, WHO'S MOVED TO the center of the room. She claps again, two more times, like she is calling a classroom of little kids to attention.

"Okay, two truths and a lie," Becca says. "Let's go. Everybody's in, period. I need a goddamn distraction."

There's some unhappy grumbling. But mostly people seem glad for something to do. And my initial reaction is no. How can I play a game when I don't know yet whether Jasper's okay. But, at the moment, what I really need, too, is a distraction. It feels like my sanity might depend on it.

"What's two truths and a lie?" Teresa asks, like she's afraid playing it might involve getting in trouble.

No one answers her. Instead, everyone crowds around Becca, including me. Even Kelsey is standing now, though she doesn't look like she's making any promises about playing along.

"Jesus, back up and sit down," Becca says as we push closer like starving mouths to feed. "Give me a little room to breathe. I usually play this game with way more drugs and way fewer people."

Eventually, everyone sits in a large circle on the floor, legs crossed, shoulders hunched like much younger girls. Becca is the only one still standing in the center now, all of us waiting for her. And expecting much more than a simple game. Like we want her to lead us to real answers. Becca isn't ready for all that pressure, though. Soon her face gets stiff and loses color.

Looking at Becca, I wonder how things might be different if she knew that she was an Outlier—assuming that I'm right and she is. If she knew that part of what she is feeling in that moment could be what *we* are all feeling. It's been different for me since I found that out. Each one of us might still be broken in our own way, maybe even in ways that won't be easy to fix. But understanding this one part of ourselves could make us see our whole as something more complicated than just wrong.

Maybe having one another—not being alone—would make a difference, too. And, no, I don't know for sure yet that these other girls are Outliers, but even thinking that they might be, that I could be with people just like me, has made the ground feel steadier underfoot.

"I'll do it," Ramona says, stepping up and waving Becca away with warm, sisterly annoyance. Like freezing up is the kind of thing that happens to everyone all the time. "You sit."

Becca shuffles away and takes Ramona's spot at the edge of the circle, then hugs her long legs into her chest and presses her mouth against her knees. Becca is too far away for me to be able to read exactly what she's feeling. But whatever it is: she looks like she hates herself for it.

"Okay, two truths and a lie," Ramona says, like she's flipping through her mental Rolodex in search of the rules.

Teresa raises her hand. "This isn't going to have anything to do with, um, s-e-x or something, because—and I know this is going to sound weird and stupid . . ." She stares down into her lap. "I can't talk about that stuff. I know that my grandma isn't here to actually hear me, but it would take six minutes off her life."

And the way Teresa says it is like it's an established thing— this six-minute rule and her grandmother's life. Like she's already cost the old woman hours.

"It doesn't have to be about sex," Ramona says, but Teresa is still frowning. And, in fairness, we all know that everything with people our age eventually becomes sort of about sex.

"No sex then," Kelsey says, like we are dumb for not coming up with this obvious solution. "No truths or lies about sex. Period," she says. "No one should have to be any more uncomfortable than we already are."

And there, in Kelsey's unexpected compassion, is the potential. For all of us. If we stick together.

"Fine, whatever," Ramona says, annoyed. Like she was specifically looking forward to talking about sex. And, meanwhile, I am stupidly surprised that not mentioning sex will be so hard for everyone else. Because it will be so completely easy for me. "Now, can I explain how to play?"

"Yes, please," Teresa says, beaming.

Teresa isn't the kind of girl who would ever have been part of a group even if she had gone to school with other kids. So being in here with this group is probably her first chance. The truth is it's my first chance in a long time to be a part of a group again. Maia and those girls are like another life.

"All right, we'll start with . . ." Ramona looks around, points to red-haired Trident Gum Elise. "You. You say two things about yourself that are true and one thing that is a lie."

"And tell the person next to you which is the lie," Kelsey says, shrugging when Ramona looks at her. "Keep people honest."

"Yeah, okay, fine." Ramona looks back at Teresa, then rolls her eyes. "And not about sex or anything actually fun apparently. The girl directly opposite you then guesses which two things are true and which is a lie. We'll keep score; whoever wins the most can have—I don't know—there's a hundred bucks in my wallet if and when they ever give us our shit back."

Elise looks around the circle nervously, then seems to decide that she will not cave to the pressure of so many eyes. Instead, she pulls her spine tall. She leans over as told and whispers to Teresa, who is next to her, before turning back to the group.

"I once rode a bull. I am allergic to peppermint and I love Brussels sprouts." She rattles all three off in a single rush.

"Okay, you." Ramona points at another girl on the opposite side of the circle, one with disturbingly doll-like eyes who I haven't heard speak. "Which one is the lie?"

"The peppermint," the other girl answers, sounding much more confident than her stunned eyes would suggest. "She's not allergic to peppermint."

Elise lets out a surprisingly exasperated huff. Annoyed that she was found out so easily. "Whatever."

And so we go like that around the circle for maybe fifteen minutes. The game moves fast. We have people whose favorite color is not green, who hate pizza, and who were once an expert at the balance beam. Somebody else has a phobia of peanut butter, a love of spiders, and hates her dad. Somebody has a girlfriend named Sid. Each time the lie is detected quickly and easily. Eventually, without any discussion, the lies and the truths start to get more elaborate and specific: it was snowing when I was born; my house number is 714. I once had a teacher named Rose. But the results don't change—because each and every one of us can pick out the lie all the same.

Because we are all Outliers. Every last one of us. And I might have suspected as much before, but now I am sure.

But from where? After what happened with Quentin, my dad has guarded the names of any additional Outliers he found in his exploratory tests. Tests he financed himself with a small loan from his parents. Tests for which there was no public record. No data trail. The only place he recorded them was on an actual piece of paper in his office. Maybe these are the Outliers the military found through their own "secret" research that my dad brought up and then tried to blow off.

I stare over at Becca to see if she suggested this game on purpose, to root out everyone's HEP, but from the flat look on her face, I don't think so. And when I look around no one else seems to notice how weirdly good we are at sorting the truths from the lies, or what that might mean.

That is, until I meet eyes with Kelsey and I feel a sharp jolt of recognition. Like Kelsey knows exactly what is up. But almost as quickly she looks away and I feel nothing.

Did that even happen? Did I imagine it?

Everyone should know they are Outliers. Shouldn't they? Unless knowing it somehow puts them at greater risk? After what happened to Cassie, it's hard to know whether it's safer to know nothing. Or everything. It depends on what this is. I need to talk to my dad. I need to call him again.

Trying not to draw too much attention to myself, I scoot back out of the circle, push myself quietly to my feet, and head over to the guards. Even with my eyes down, I can feel them watching me approach and wishing that I would not.

"I need to make a phone call," I say. And still the guards do not look my way. "Dr. Haddox said I could try my dad again. Where is a phone?"

Finally, they look at each other, trying to decide how to respond. The one who was flirting with Becca glances in my direction. "There's one on the wall over there," he says, and not very pleasantly. Our eyes meet only for a minute, but I get an awful, icy feeling. Like he is dead inside. If necessary, he will later deny that he ever said it was okay for me to use the phone.

The whole time I'm walking over to where he pointed, I wait for something to stop me. For someone to keep me from making my call. Or for the line to be dead when I pick up the phone. But a second later, my dad's phone is ringing again. My heart leaps when he actually answers.

"Hi, Wylie," he says, matter-of-fact, but a little out of breath.

"Just making my way through the terminal. Going to try to find this driver they sent for me. I don't usually care about this kind of thing, but having my name on one of those little—"

"Dad! Did you get my message?"

"What message?" he asks, still with the breathing hard. "Wait, hold on." A pause. "There's no alert yet, sorry. The phone was in airplane mode. Is everything okay?"

I can feel the guards' eyes on me. I need to choose my words carefully. They are looking for any excuse to step in.

"I'm in a hospital."

"What happened?" he asks, panicked already. "Are you okay?"

"I'm not hurt," I say. "But you know Dr. Cornelia from Cornell—he's got a bunch of us here. They are saying we have something called PANDAS."

"What?" He's angry now. Frightened and angry. "Have you where?"

"Boston General Hospital?" The dead-eyed security guard is crossing the room toward me. The fact that I am giving out my location maybe, or how upset I sound—something has made him second-guess his decision.

"Okay," my dad says, still wound up, but trying hard to pull it together. "And you're sure you're not hurt?" I consider telling him about the ambulance, the bridge. But it can wait until he's here. He's already worried enough.

"No," I say. "But I don't know what's going on and we're not allowed to leave. It seems like that Ebola thing."

The guard is behind me now. His deadness is creeping up

my spine. "Wrap it up. You can ask the doctor to use the phone again when he's back."

"I'm so sorry that I'm not there, Wylie," my dad says. "If I had known, I never would have—and I should have known."

"Hang up the phone," the guard says. The hairs on my arms lift. It's like I can feel his hands on my neck. "Now."

"Dad, what should I do?"

And I mean so many things. Do I cooperate? Do I scream and yell? Do I tell the other girls they are Outliers? It's now a question I am afraid to ask with the guard standing right there. And if so, what do I tell them? I hear my dad take a breath as my heart pounds. He may not be an Outlier, but he must know that I am choosing my words carefully.

"I'll be on the next flight back. And I'm going to call Rachel, too. There's no way this can be legal. I'll send her right away. Until she gets there, I don't know what to tell you. Part of me wants to say—"

"Dad, I only have a second—"

"Hang up," the guard says again. More forcefully this time, and he is even closer now. Maybe close enough for my dad to hear him.

"Wylie," my dad says, more urgently. "Trust your instincts."

The line goes dead. The guard has put his finger down over the base of the phone, ending the call. "Like I said, you can call back when the doctor gets here."

When I meet eyes with the guard again I feel it so clearly: violence. He's hungry for it. Like some kind of animal. A bear, or maybe a wolf. And for the first time, I feel in actual, physical danger. But I need to try to reach Jasper, too. I can't wait any-more for Dr. Alvarez to do as she promised and send news. I need proof that Jasper is okay. And I need it now.

"I have to call someone else," I say, because I do. I can't wait anymore for word about Jasper. "He's a friend. I need to make sure he's all right."

"Like I said: no more calls," the Wolf says. "Besides, it's par-ents only. We can't have you all tying up the phone talking to boyfriends." The way he says "boyfriends" sounds so dirty it makes my skin crawl.

"Dr. Haddox let me call him before."

He glares at me. "Then I'm sure he will let you call again. When he gets back."

He's hoping I'll argue, so that he can shut me up once and for all.

"Fine," I say finally, handing the receiver back to him. "Here."

WHEN I TURN back from the phone, the girls have left their game. They are spread across the room in much the same way they were when I first walked in. I drift back to where we had formed our circle, looking around at them. Hoping to feel some kind of sign.

Tell them they are Outliers? Don't tell them? Tell them all about Quentin and Cassie and my dad. Or just some of it.

It sounds so easy: trust your instincts. But I've spent so much time disregarding my feelings, so long telling myself that all of what I'm feeling is suspect and wrong, that I'm not sure anymore how to read those messages that my gut is sending me that are right. And at least some of that cold burn in my stomach right now is still regular old anxiety. And maybe Dr. Shepard is right that someday I will know exactly where that line is between the terror that lies inside of me and that which I can feel in the world. But today is not that day.

I think back to that last night when my mom went out for milk. I did have a bad feeling about her leaving as she walked past me and out the door. I didn't want her to go. But I had pushed that instinct away. Decided to keep my mouth shut instead, so I didn't let my worry run the show. And with my anxiety, so many times that is the right call, even now it is. But not always. That time I had been right to worry. Wrong to ignore my instincts.

And I'd been right about Jasper being in trouble. I don't feel like he is anymore. I am so hoping I am right about that too. I'm just scared I'm confusing my hope with the truth.

The other girls have to be given the same chance to feel their way through this. The way I am trying to now. Little by little finding my footing in this unexpected place They should know about my dad and his research, about Dr. Cornelia and his bizarre ideas. They have the right to know that they might be Outliers.

11

"HAVE YOU READ THIS?"

When I look down, Kelsey is stretched out again on the couch. Was she there the whole time? "What?"

"I asked if you had read this book?" She thumbs through the last pages of *1984*.

"Oh, yeah, I guess," I say, trying to figure out why we are even talking about something so trivial when the world is exploding. "I don't remember it."

Kelsey frowns down at the copy of *1984* in her hands. Then she seems to come to some conclusion before holding it out to me. "Take it," she says, and her feelings are, as usual, a brick wall. I've only been knowingly reading people for six weeks, but I've never felt anything remotely like it. "You can have it."

And the way she says it, it's like she's giving me this great gift, which annoys me way more than it probably should. "Yeah, no thanks," I say. "I'm not in the mood to read."

"No, I mean it. Take it," she says, waving the book at me again. "You need it. You should read it again."

The heat rises to my face. Now I am actually getting pissed. "I don't want it."

"Except you do," she says. "But you have to promise me you'll read it, all the way to the end again. And then after, we should, you know, talk about it. Like a book club or whatever."

Reluctantly, I take the book from Kelsey and stare down at its worn pages. Pages read so many times that the spine has been repaired more than once. When I look back, Kelsey is reading a new book, *Fahrenheit 451*.

When we meet eyes again, her feelings suddenly crash over me—anger, outrage, righteous determination. Commitment. Then almost as fast: nothing. Like a light switch. And she has this expression on her face, too. *See?* That was a demonstration. Proof that she knows what she's doing—even more, she knows that I do, too.

"Wait, what was—"

But the windowless doors buzz and Dr. Haddox steps through before I can get my whole question out. "I'm sorry I've been gone so long. I know I promised you all more information," he calls to the group. His voice is rushed. "But I do have some good news."

"Did you find out if my friend is okay?" I ask.

Dr. Haddox looks confused, like he's forgotten all about Jasper, and I feel that he has. "Well, um, no——"

"We can go home?" Ramona asks, appearing next to me, arms crossed tight.

"Um, well, no, but the series of tests came in from your initial blood work—and I know some of you were never tested. But we already have enough preliminary data to confirm that there is no concern about any of you being contagious," he says, making a baseball umpire's safe-on-base motion with his hand.

"Contagious?" Becca snaps, working her neck to the side. She's pissed, but scared, too. "Who said anything about contagious?"

Dr. Haddox's eyes get wide, out of his depth again. "Well, um, we were pretty sure it wasn't communicable," he stammers. "But it is, um, good to get confirmation. It is strange that there would be so many instances of PANDAS in such a contained geographical area. That was part of why we—or they—wanted to have all of you here."

I can only imagine now how those living room conversations had gone with the other parents. How easy it would have been to scare them: Do you have other children at home, elderly neighbors? Because we can't be sure they are not at risk. We don't know what exactly this illness is. And we can't be sure that it won't take a turn for the worse. It would be best to have trained medical staff on hand as a precaution. Yes, only a precaution. Protect their children, that's what good parents would do. Just in case.

"This doesn't have anything to do with Ebola, does it?" Teresa asks as she comes to stand next to me. She sounds frightened, but I also feel like she's—weirdly—smiling on the inside, like some wicked little kid messing with someone.

"Ebola? No, no. Of course not," Dr. Haddox says, looking confused and a little exasperated by the question. "As I said before, no one with Ebola has ever even been in this building. But it is understandable that you would all like more information. And luckily"—he crosses the room to the far set of doors, peers back and forth through the small glass windows like he is looking for someone outside—"someone from the NIH is finally here. He can offer you a much better explanation of how you all might have contracted the initial strep infection." Dr. Haddox exhales. He is relieved, but not *for* us. He is glad to be relieved *of* us. We are about to become the NIH's problem. "Let me step out and see where this elusive Dr. Frederick Mitchell is."

Dr. Frederick Mitchell. The name trips an alarm in my brain. *Dr. Frederick Mitchell, Dr. Frederick Mitchell.* Then it comes to me: the huge, barrel-chested man who came to our house a few weeks after my mom died, months before Jasper and I ever went to Maine after Cassie. I remember his strange way of talking and his ill-fitting glasses. I remember how sure I was, even then, that he was not who he claimed to be. And now, here he is. It all but seems to prove the connection to my dad's research.

Dr. Haddox holds the door open behind him, moving to the side to let another man through.

And there he is. I want to be seeing things, but I am not. The same hair, same eyes. Still handsome, but this time he is in a suit and the way he carries himself is completely different. He has perfect posture and a confident stride. Nothing about him is like a wounded dog.

"Excellent, so this is Dr. Mitchell from the NIH," Dr. Haddox begins.

But *this* Dr. Frederick Mitchell isn't *the* Dr. Frederick Mitchell who came to our house. No, the man standing there with the handsome face and the steady posture is the one who convinced Jasper and me to trust him. The man we listened to and followed into that dark, abandoned camp. The man who we were grateful let us come along. The man who had such a real-sounding stutter until it vanished instantly.

Officer Kendall of the Seneca police.

In my head, I shout: Everyone run! That is a bad, bad man. But I can't. I shouldn't. There's a chance Kendall doesn't know that I am here. And so I hide, duck farther out of view. I squeeze my body tight so I don't tremble.

Jasper. He is the only other person who was there with Kendall. Who knows him like I do. I need Jasper there to tell me I'm not imagining things. That this man really is Kendall.

"Thank you, Dr. Haddox," Kendall says, stepping forward. "And thanks to all of you for your patience and understanding. This is quite an unusual situation, and it's taken us a moment to get our bearings."

He sounds like he has spoken to hundreds of patients, hundreds of times before. Comforted them and reassured them, dispensed complex medical information and delivered damning diagnoses. Who is this man? For all I know, he is an actual doctor. Maybe he was lying before up in Seneca.

"Please," Teresa says. Her voice is high and shrieky. But I am still close enough to feel that excitement underneath. Like she's waiting for the real show to begin. "What's going on?"

"First of all, I want you to know that you will all be fine," Kendall says.

"Yeah, not buying it," Ramona says, resting a hand on her hip and pursing her lips. "What are you going to say? That we're all going to die?"

"That is a totally reasonable question," Kendall says. The picture of calm. And then he looks from Ramona to the other girls as I tuck myself farther out of sight. I want so badly to be able to read him, to have some feel for whether he's telling the truth. But I am too far away and there are too many other people. "All I can do is give you the information we have and hope that we can earn your trust. You all are truly going to be completely fine. The NIH is merely concerned about how you would have contracted this particular strain of highly unusual strep, not the severity of your illness."

"'Highly unusual' how?" Ramona asks.

"Unusual in its high percentage of conversion to PANDAS and in its transmission. It seems the strep you contracted must have been either food or water borne. Strep can be contracted that way, but it is not typical."

Becca's face puckers, then she points at Dr. Haddox. "He told me that we probably got it because people are gross and don't wash their hands."

"That would certainly be one possibility," Kendall says.

"And what are the others?" Kelsey asks, shifting forward a bit so that I have to be careful to stay behind her.

"Our working theory is that the strep was introduced at one or perhaps several local food establishments you all frequented— a frozen yogurt shop in Barkwell Shopping Center is one possibility—in an intentional act of bioterrorism. After getting the initial heads-up from some online chatter, it was the credit card receipts from your parents, combined with the fact that you have all been out of school, that led us to you."

I know the yogurt place, and I *have* been there. But then, most teenagers in a thirty-mile radius have probably been there—it constantly has a line out the door. And from the way everyone is muttering and looking at one another, we were all on that line at one time or another

"Terrorism?" Teresa yelps, which is weird after the delay. She even clamps a hand dramatically over her mouth. Excited. I still feel it though. Why do I keep feeling that? It does not make sense.

"Bullshit," Ramona says skeptically. "If these are 'symptoms,' why have I always been this way? Also, why would a terrorist make a weapon that doesn't actually kill anybody? That would be so stupid."

"First of all, PANDAS can exacerbate preexisting conditions," Kendall goes on, so polished and smooth. Even Dr. Haddox seems unnerved by his ease. "Secondly, we have credible and specific intelligence that suggests this was merely a test run. Their intent could be to try again with a more effective agent or simply to unnerve the community by demonstrating their capacity to introduce an infection."

Kendall is so persuasive, even to me, and I know better. Is it possible that any of this is true? That we are sick because someone made us sick on purpose? I feel someone staring at me then. When I glance over, it's Kelsey. *This is bullshit*, that's what she's feeling. *Total bullshit*. And maybe I can't read those exact words. But I don't have to. Her emotions are completely clear.

Kelsey turns back to Kendall and raises her hand. "Excuse

me, but if we're not contagious and we're not going to die, then we can go home, right?"

"I want to *go home*!" Becca cries out suddenly. That same switch has flipped as before when she had to leave the game. "I have to go. I can't be in here. I feel claustrophobic."

"Listen, this is a lot of information to take in at once," Dr. Haddox says, stepping forward and raising his hands. He feels responsible for all our bad feelings. "You will all be fine. It's important to remain calm."

"But if this is an act of terrorism, we need to gather as much information as we possibly can from you," Kendall says. "So we can find the people responsible."

Now, that is definitely a lie. I had second-guessed myself, but this whole thing fits way too perfectly with Dr. Cornelia's career in need of a rebuild. And I am the only person in this room who knows Kendall is lying about who he says he is. I have to say something. My instincts are shouting that loud and clear.

"Did you tell everybody's parents about Dr. Cornelia and his book?" I ask. But I know too quietly. I am going to have to speak up. I am going to have to raise my voice.

"Sorry, did someone say something back there?" Dr. Haddox asks. "We couldn't hear you."

I take a deep breath and square my shoulders as I step forward.

"Did you tell the parents that the doctor in charge here has a book he is trying to sell about this exact scenario? Pretty big coincidence, right?" And my voice is loud and strong, vibrating in my chest. I keep my eyes on Dr. Haddox. I am not ready to face Kendall. "Also you can't keep people locked up against their will because that's better for your investigation."

I know that much thanks to Rachel, who made it clear that I never had to talk to anyone about what happened up at the camp in Maine if I didn't want to—not that Agent Klute and his friends had ever returned. Unless they have. Maybe *this* is them in one way or another.

"No, I suppose we can't," Kendall says, eyes locked on mine. I am still too far away to read him, but I can see from the look on his face that he knew I was here the entire time. That he is here *for* me. "This situation has many moving parts, however. Many things are not what they seem. It can be difficult to follow, but you should try."

It's a message directed right at me. *Difficult to follow, but you should try.* But it's not a threat. I feel like he is trying to help me.

"Wylie's right," Ramona says, stepping over to stand next to me. She flicks her bracelet once, but in a way now that's almost imperceptible. "It's a free country. You can't pretend you're helping us so that you can make us help you."

"Yeah, you can't keep us here," Becca says.

"Yeah," Kelsey says, next to me now, too. Committed to commotion, I get the sense, more than cause. "Let us go."

And I don't know who starts it, but soon everyone is chanting: "Let us go!" Everyone but me. I stand silently. My eyes are locked on Kendall in the swell of a revolt of my making. "Let us go! Let us go! Let us go!"

Kendall's face is calm and still, as if this is exactly what he planned. Like he is already focused on the next steps.

"Okay, everyone calm down," Dr. Haddox calls.

The security guards seem annoyed by the noise but not actually concerned. "Quiet!" the Wolf shouts.

Kendall glances away then, distracted by something. He digs around before pulling his phone out of his pocket.

"I apologize," he says, looking first at Dr. Haddox and then right at me. "I have to step out and take this."

It's a sign: *It can be difficult to follow, but you should try.* Officer Kendall has already turned elegantly for the windowed doors, toward the Wolf and his partner in front of them. The doors to the outside. In a moment he will be gone. I need to go after him. I need at least to try. *That* is my instinct right now. And I need trust it, just like my dad said.

I walk quickly but calmly—at least that's what I try for— toward the water fountain. It's in the general direction of where Kendall is headed, the water fountain, but a good enough excuse that no one will wonder where I'm going. I get there just as Kendall reaches the guards.

There will be the buzz and then the doors will open. Not for long. I'll have to bolt between the guards and hope they are too surprised to grab me.

It takes longer than I expect, though, for the guards to get the doors open for Kendall. Their key cards don't work until the third try. Waiting, my lips get icy in the flow from the fountain. Finally, I hear the buzz. And then the doors are open, and Kendall goes through.

It is my moment. *Go. Go. Go.*

I lunge after Kendall into the brightness of the hall. I brace for some kind of pain: a baton cracked against my knee, my face smashed against a wall. A hand on the back of my neck, pulling at my hair.

But there is this moment, this sudden gap in time. Then somehow I am through the doors. I am *in* that hall. And there is Kendall, already some distance ahead.

There's a loud shout behind me. One of the guards finally. "Wha—Hey!"

But the door clicks shut before they can grab it.

"What are you doing here?" I shout after Kendall as I start down the hall. "What is this?"

He does not speed up, but he doesn't slow down either. Instead, he just walks on in his nicely tailored suit and his hard leather shoes—pound, pound, pound. And, yet, somehow he is still so far away.

"Hey!" I shout again, and I sound so angry. Because I am. I am filled with rage. Kendall might not have killed Cassie, but he played a part in her death. "Who are you?"

But still Kendall ignores me. He will not do that. I will not let him, not this time.

The door finally opens behind me. I can hear fast footsteps behind me as I start to run.

I need to reach him before they reach me. I can feel my heartbeat in my ears as I sprint until I'm finally close enough to lunge for him. Fingers outstretched. And I want to do more than stop him. I want to scratch him, to tear into his skin. But instead I am suddenly too close. My face bangs against his shoulder and then we are somehow falling forward. *On purpose*, that's what I think. We are falling not because I knocked Kendall over, but because he wants it that way.

When my knee hits the floor, the pain is a jolt of electricity.

Kendall somehow lifts me effortlessly off him as he spins around then holds me hard by the forearms and jerks my head close.

"Get out now," he whispers in my ear as he shoves something into my hand.

A piece of paper, cardboard, something folded and sharp and square. And then I feel how Kendall feels: desperate and regretful. Sorry. *This* is his way of making amends.

I manage to tuck the paper into the band of my underwear just as the guards pull me away from Kendall. He gets to his feet calmly and smooths out his clothes.

"Let go!" I shout, kicking at them, which only makes them tighten their grip. There is no point in fighting, but I can't stop myself. "You're hurting me!"

When the Wolf appears over me he is all squinted eyes and gritted teeth.

"Wylie!" It's Dr. Haddox, his face suddenly there, too. He has a needle in his hand. "We need for you to calm down."

And I feel his regret then. Different from Kendall's, which is about the past. Haddox's is about now. About this. It's not what he signed up for. Not at all what he wanted to do.

12

I OPEN MY EYES TO DARKNESS. WHEN I TRY TO MOVE, MY FACE ACHES. KENDALL'S shoulder, the officers wrestling me to the ground—there are many possible explanations. The drugs have blotted them out.

Get out now. That's what Kendall said, and he'd meant it. He was worried for me, too. He's lied about so much. But in that one moment in the hall, he was telling the truth. I have no doubt about that.

When I lift my arms, I brace for them to be strapped down once more. But they are not.

I get out of bed slowly in the dark, a hand on the wall as I feel my way toward the light switch by the door. The fluorescent bulb overhead flickers before it finally catches. I'm in a small room with a bed like the one I first woke up in, but I don't think it's the same one. This one smells like fresh paint. It makes me woozy all over again.

When I turn back toward the bed, something sharp pokes into the skin above my hip bone. It isn't until I've dug it out of the waistband of my underwear that I remember Kendall's note. I can't believe it's still tucked in there.

My hands shake as I unfold it. I don't know what I expect. Some terrible explanation? Some new detail that makes everything worse. But there is only an address and some instructions: *323 Gullbright Lane, press buzzer in this order: 1.5.3.4.2. Ask for Joseph Conrad.*

I don't know what is more insane, the fact that Kendall thinks I might go where his note says, or the fact that I am actually considering it. But my gut is telling me I should. Trust my instincts. That's all I can do.

I'm feeling even more unsteady as I make my way back toward the bed and spot Kelsey's copy of *1984* on my bureau. I put it down in the common room before I went after Kendall. Kelsey came back and left it for me while I was sleeping? That's awfully insistent. I pick the book up as I make my way to the bed.

I need to call my dad again. Need to talk to Jasper. For either I'll need Dr. Haddox's permission, otherwise the Wolf will surely stop me again. But will Dr. Haddox be on my side anymore? I've tried to run for a second time. I've made him feel bad for having to drug me again. People can hold their guilt against you.

Still, I have no choice but to try. I'll just need to march out to the common room and demand to see Dr. Haddox. And I will right after I've worked myself up for another fight. I take a deep breath, exhaling as I flip absentmindedly through the pages of Kelsey's book.

And then my heart catches.

There's handwriting. Notes all over the pages of Kelsey's copy of *1984*. The word BLOCKING, and under that, a list in all caps and dark print, deep grooves left by a ballpoint pen. *BELIEVE THE LIE* is number one.

My hands tremble as I turn the pages—two parts scared, one part relieved. I've already glimpsed enough to know that what's written in the pages completes a loop. It explains why Kelsey was so hard to read and the way she was looking at me. Like we shared a secret.

I flip randomly through the pages, trying to figure out where to start. I settle on page 83. In the margin, there's a date: June 12, and a one-line entry as if from a diary:

> I knew you were going to start crying before you actually did.

It's signed K. Kelsey doing the writing, probably. I don't know for sure who the *you* is yet. The next entry is from June 21.

> I knew Mommy and Daddy were going to have a fight before Daddy got home. I knew that Daddy would tell a lie during the fight about his job. But that Mommy would believe him.

This one is signed G. Kelsey's sister maybe, I'm guessing from the way she refers to her parents—as if they share them. Another minute of flipping through the book and it's obvious that they used it as a journal traded between the two of them. And G is apparently Gabrielle. There is one place where it is fully spelled out. Looking at the dates, it seems like the entries start on the front inside cover, then jump to the back inside cover, then over the title and end pages before eventually starting again randomly at page fifty-six and running almost to the end of the book up and down the margins.

Why are we using a book? G asks at one point. *We could get a blank notebook. WITH MORE SPACE.*

The next day, the answer: *Because they'll come looking for it eventually. K*

Kelsey and Gabrielle keep pretty detailed notes: when they seem to know things before they happen; when they are right about somebody's feelings; when they suspect someone is lying; when they finally have proof. They treat it all like a game. Each time they are proven right, they record it in all caps and with a star. *DOUBLE POINTS!*

I wonder how Gabrielle has been lucky enough to avoid being locked in here. I flip back to the beginning to see how it started. How they first figured out reading people was an actual thing they could do. Because Quentin told me, and then my dad confirmed it, and even then it took weeks for it to feel real. And Gabrielle and Kelsey didn't have anyone telling them anything, much less their scientist dad.

I told you today. And the weirdest part was how you said "me too" right away like you'd been waiting. K

And so it had started small with trust and a secret confession from Kelsey, and from there they tried reading people together, seeing if they were right. They had practiced on each other, too. They learned most of the things that I had about crowds making it harder and eye contact making it easier. The only difference was that they'd had each other to share it with. It makes my chest ache imagining Gideon and me, or better yet Cassie and me, or some sister that doesn't exist, going through this whole thing together. Having each other.

It's the first that time I realize me not wanting to be an Outlier comes down to that one sad fact. I don't want to feel more alone. I don't want to claim this new part of me if it means putting more distance between me and the rest of the world. Not when we are already so far apart. But maybe if there were Kelseys and Gabrielles, maybe if being an Outlier meant becoming part of something, I'd feel differently. Maybe being an Outlier could mean finally finding a place where I belong.

Pretty soon, I start to skim. There is way too much to read, and I am too impatient. But I do pause on this list:

1. Get better with concentration and practice
2. Blocking; pretend it's the truth
3. Hard in crowds; eye contact helps
4. More than just reading feelings? Someday, the Future??? ☺

Blocking. That must have been what Kelsey was doing when I couldn't read what she was feeling, when she was like a brick wall. It takes a couple of minutes of looking to find the spot where Kelsey and Gabrielle go into more detail on the whole idea of "blocking"—controlling their own feelings so that others won't be able to read them. In theory it sounds simple, but without another Outlier to test me, how will I ever know that I'm doing it right?

I close the book and take a deep breath. I need to talk to Kelsey. I need to understand what she knows and figure out why she gave me the book. I mean, obviously she knows this is something we share, but what is it she wants me to do with this information?

Before I worry about that, though, I need to call Jasper and my dad. If I can't, or can't reach them, there can be no waiting—not for my dad to get back from DC or for Rachel to kick up a fuss. Or to find out whatever it is Kelsey really wants me to know. I need to go now. We all do.

THE HALL IS empty and quiet when I finally step out of my room and make my way down to the common room. I hope to find Dr. Haddox there. Hope that he is not too angry at me for running after Kendall, that he will be willing to overrule the Wolf and let me call my dad again and then Jasper. At this point even leaving another message for Jasper will be better than nothing. And I'll start with an apology to Dr. Haddox. It can't hurt to start there. Even if I don't really feel sorry at all.

I'm hoping to see Kelsey stretched out on the couch, too. I imagine what I'll say to her. Everything from: "So, hey, cool book," to "So you're an Outlier, too." It all feels so totally awkward and wrong, especially when there's a good chance she's never even heard the word "Outlier."

But when I finally enter the common room, I am startled by

the utter silence and the almost dark. There is no Dr. Haddox, no Kelsey stretched out on the couch. There is no one anywhere. The common room is empty. Not pitch-black, but the overhead lights are off. When I turn toward the windows, it is night outside.

It couldn't have been much past three or four in the afternoon when Kendall walked in. I was knocked out much longer than I realized, hours even. Who knows what could have happened since then?

"Hey, you okay?" A man's voice. When I turn, there are two new guards at the windowed doors. At least neither is the Wolf.

"Where is everyone?" I ask.

"Um, asleep?" the guard on the left with the full beard and the thicker waist says. He looks at his watch. "It's past two a.m. You need us to get a doctor or something?"

Mostly he's hoping I'll go. I can feel that much. I am making him nervous being here. And he doesn't even know that I am the one who tried to run. He's afraid of something happening, of things ending badly. He does not trust himself to be restrained. These men, whoever they are, are not regular hospital security. It is not until that moment that I am sure.

Maybe I've been seeing this entire situation wrong. Maybe there isn't one thing going on, one group of people. There could be—like Kendall said—many moving parts. There's Dr. Haddox—and his boss, the fame-chasing Dr. Cornelia. There's the NIH and the guards who seem more like Agent Klute and his friends. Who's to say they aren't each on their own team?

The thought of my problems multiplying in that way makes

me shudder hard. And that makes the other officer step forward. He is thinner and with a beard, too, but his is spotty and mangy. "Something wrong with you?"

Yes. No. Yes. Such a simple question has become unanswerable. I shake my head too hard and too many times as I back toward the door.

"No, I'm fine," I say, sounding far from it. "Is Dr. Haddox anywhere around? Because I was hoping to use the phone."

The guard with the full beard raises an eyebrow at his partner. This asking about the phone has shifted something. "It's two a.m. Like I said. He's home asleep. And you've got to get clearance from him for the phone."

"You sure you don't need help?" his partner asks, but like his "help" is not going to be a thing I actually want.

"No, I'm fine," I say again.

I spin around and head back the way I came.

BACK OUT IN the hallway, I look up and down the row of closed doors. I want to find Kelsey's, but I have no idea which room is hers. And following up my tackle of the "NIH doctor" with waking everyone up in the middle of the night probably isn't going to help my situation.

Instead, I head back to my room, crawl into bed, and turn on my side. Curled up into a C, I try not to think. But my mind spins anyway, and straight to Jasper. Is he really okay? Did Dr. Alvarez actually even speak with his mom? Deep down, I still do *feel* like he is okay. I believe it. But I'd feel a whole lot better if I had actual proof.

My mom is probably the only person who could really convince me that everything is going to be okay anyway. And she won't be convincing me of anything ever again, of course.

So instead of feeling any better, I toss and turn. For so long that eventually I pray not for sleep, but just for dawn.

※※※※※※※※※※※※※※

"I'M TELLING YOU that I have a bad feeling about him, that's all," I heard my mom say as I made my way up the stairs a few weeks before her accident. I braced myself thinking that I was overhearing my parents having yet another of their increasingly frequent fights.

But when I finally got to the top of the steps and peered in the door, they were the picture of domestic bliss. My dad was folding laundry, my mom cross-legged on the bed, surrounded by a ring of photographs. She was in between actual assignments, which meant she had to be working on one of her freelance projects, which always involved trying to expose one injustice or another that never seemed to fully materialize. Having spent so much time in war zones, she was especially obsessed with the military and proper oversight. So far, none of my mom's extracurricular activities ("conspiracy theories," my dad had teased) had gotten very far. But that had only made her more intent. Her thick black glasses were halfway down her nose as she selected shots, inspected them, and then discarded each, one by one.

I sat down on the landing, close to their bedroom door, curious now. It wasn't anger I had heard in their voices, but it had been something.

"He's *in* AA," my dad said. "Don't people always go a little overboard at first? It's like part of the program." My dad laughed a little. "The program. See the little pun I made there. And the kids say I'm not funny anymore."

"It's more than AA," my mom said, then shuddered hard. "I'm telling you. When Vince came here to get Cassie today, I didn't even want to let her go with him. He seemed, I don't know, deranged."

"Deranged?" My dad laughed again.

"Okay, fine, maybe deranged is a bit much," she said. "But seriously off. I even considered calling Karen about it."

"You didn't, though, right?" my dad asked nervously. Things between my mom and Karen had occasionally been rocky. My mom had thought "fitness camp," in particular, was a terrible idea, especially for Cassie. And she told Karen as much. Their relationship had never fully recovered.

"No, but only because she must already know what he's like, right? This isn't the first time he's been back from the Keys."

"I'm sure she knows," my dad said. "And everything is relative, you know? Karen is probably glad Vince isn't an angry drunk anymore."

"He got ordained, too, did you hear that?" she said.

"Some kind of online thing."

"There are worse things than becoming an internet minister."

"I know," my mom said quietly. "And I'm not trying to be judgmental. But I just—he gave me such an *awful* feeling. Like hair standing on end. He seemed so angry underneath all that Zen. And at *us*, Ben. Why would he be angry at us?"

"He wouldn't be. He's not," my dad said. "Listen, Vince has always had issues. Maybe he feels like we took Karen's side in the divorce. We kind of did."

"I don't know, I still—maybe we should warn Karen," she said. "We might regret it if we don't."

"And we could regret it if we do," my dad said. "I mean, things with Cassie and Wylie—I don't think we want to rock the boat any more than it already has been."

I winced. I had been hoping I was imagining that things between Cassie and me had been falling apart. It hadn't even occurred to me that it was so bad my parents had noticed.

"Obviously, Cassie and Wylie are what's important here," my mom said. "Anyway, it was only a feeling. And it's not like reality and my feelings always go together."

"I don't know," my dad said. "In my experience, sooner or later they usually do."

"WYLIE, IT'S ME." A whisper, only three words.

I'm awake now. But confused. I must have been dead asleep. And it's— there's something pressed over my mouth. So hard I almost can't breathe. I reach up in the dark, feel a hand clamped down. Kendall? I was wrong. He's come back to kill me after all?

Suddenly, there is a glistening set of eyes only inches away.

"Don't scream." It's a voice I recognize. One that makes my heart leap.

As the hand finally lifts, I squint. Try to make out more of the face in the dark. Afraid I am replacing some stranger's face with one I would so much rather see.

But no, it really is him. It has to be.

"Jasper?"

13

"SORRY," JASPER SAYS QUIETLY, SITTING NOW ON THE BED A LITTLE DISTANCE away. My eyes have adjusted so that I can see the faint outline of him in the darkness. "I didn't mean to scare you."

I reach forward and grab onto him, not convinced he's there.

"What happened to you?" I ask, finally releasing him. I have so many questions. "Are you okay?"

"Shh. I'm screwed if someone finds me in here. We both are."

He gets up. I can hear him shuffling around near the wall. When the light near my headboard finally goes on, I brace myself. For Jasper's flesh to be waterlogged, to be peeling off his bones. But even in the gray light of the hospital room, he looks better than he has in a while.

Jasper smiles and lifts the badge that's hanging around his neck, then sits back down on the bed next to me. It's a hospital

ID that says *Janitorial Staff.* "Not bad, huh?" He looks down, admiring it. "I took my mom's while she was asleep and doctored it. If I hadn't been so busy with hockey maybe I could have gone into the fake ID business or something." His smile fades, and all I can think about is how terrified I felt, looking for him in that water below. How relieved I am that he's okay.

"Jasper, what happened on the bridge?"

"I think we should start with what the hell this is."

And I think of pushing again, making Jasper explain first, but then I am not sure I'm ready for his reply.

"Some doctor other than my dad is claiming that the whole Outlier thing is caused by some illness," I say, much more matter-of-factly than I feel. "I mean, no one's said the word 'Outlier' in here. But that's the subtext. My dad says this guy's whole thing is bullshit."

"Well, looks like somebody believes it." Jasper motions to the room. "Your dad must be losing it on them."

"He will," I say, swallowing back my unease. "I talked to him on the phone, but he was in DC. He is coming back, but he hasn't gotten here yet." And it makes me feel even worse saying that out loud. More desperate. I consider going into more details— the strep, the PANDAS, the bioterrorism—but that's not going to help. And there's only one thing I absolutely need to tell Jasper. "Kendall was here."

"What? Where?" He jumps up, fists clenched. And the look on his face: like he will kill Kendall when he finds him. It reminds me of the boy I thought he was. The boy maybe he still is, but only partly. His fists relax like something has occurred to him. "Wait, are you sure it was him?"

He's got doubts. And not only about this. Like he wonders if the stress of this situation has me imagining things. And fair enough. Since the day Kendall left us in that cabin, he's been a ghost. The Seneca police department acknowledged that someone fitting his description had worked for them. And they admitted that they had sent said person up to the camp in search of our missing friend—though they'd made clear they had no idea we'd gone along (which was also true). As it turned out, Kendall was a recent hire—not the lifelong town resident Quentin had claimed or maybe even believed him to be. Who had lied to whom was still an open question, but whoever Kendall was, he had vanished after leaving us at that camp.

Until now.

"He was pretending to be some doctor from the NIH, but it was definitely him. I saw him up close. I ran after him and tackled him."

"You *tackled* him?" Jasper looks alarmed.

"You had to be there," I say, then hand him the folded note. "He gave me this and told me to get out of here. It's an address."

"*Obviously*, you should get out of here. Thank God Kendall came all the way here to point that out." Jasper takes the note but keeps his suspicious eyes on me. He shakes his head and hands it back to me without reading it. "Wait, why are you even giving this to me? How stupid does he think you are?"

"Yeah, except why would he—"

Jasper holds up a hand. "No, Wylie. And I mean *seriously* no. Who cares what he's doing or why? You need to get out of here. That's what we need to focus on. That's why I came. Throw that note away."

"He feels bad about what happened," I say. And I sound so naive. No, not naive—just stupid. Still, I can't stop with my explanations. "He came here to make up for what happened. That's why he gave me that note."

Jasper's nostrils flare. "He said that to you?"

"No." I hold his stare. "I felt it."

Jasper starts shaking his head. "Wylie, that's crazy."

Crazy. I don't want the word to hurt my feelings, but it does. "Awesome," I say quietly.

"I didn't mean—you know what I meant, Wylie. Crazy to listen to Kendall. Not that you're . . ."

He doesn't finish the thought and I stay quiet, staring down at the folded note. Jasper's doubt is fair. Completely. But that doesn't make him right. I have to trust my instincts. It's all I have. I want to let him off the hook, though, especially when he's already done so much for me. "It's not your problem. I mean, *I* am not your problem."

Now that he's okay, all that intensity I felt for Jasper in the past hours feels like a fever dream, exaggerated and outsized because of my fear. Jasper and I are friends. I care about him. But that's all. Anything else is just me being confused.

"You are not my problem, huh? Wow, thanks so much. That makes everything so much better," Jasper says, obviously hurt. But he shakes it off. "Listen, Kendall's right that you should get out of here. When I first went to the main part of the hospital looking for you, they totally denied that anyone was even in this part. Even *after* I told them I saw you brought in here. I think they actually believed it. Whatever this is, it's messed up enough for them to be hiding it really well."

"How did you even know I was here?"

"I followed the ambulance from the bridge."

"So you were on the bridge?" I ask, feeling this weird mix of dread and relief. It brings all those other feelings for Jasper right to the surface again, the wrong, confusing ones. I jam them back down harder this time.

"Yeah. I was on the bridge." Jasper frowns and nods, looking down.

"Why?" I ask.

"I was thinking about, you know, taking a time-out."

The fact that he can be so nonchalant seriously pisses me off.

"What the hell does that mean?" I snap. "Actually, no. Don't—don't even say it." I cover my face with my hands and try to swallow back the burn in my throat. This conversation is not making it easy to keep those wrong feelings in their rightful place. "Jasper, how could you even—"

"I don't want you to feel bad or anything. Trust me, it was—you are, like, the only good thing in my life." He pauses and it gets awkward fast.

"Was it the pages from Cassie's journal that . . . ?" I ask, but I don't even want to specifically say what I mean. It will just make it more real. "I saw them in your room. That must have been awful to read that after— Who do you think is sending them?"

"I don't know. Maia, maybe," he says. "She said something about cleaning up Cassie's room with Karen. And then she kept coming by and wanting to talk about how upset I was. Like maybe she was hoping I'd need her."

The thought of Maia doing that to Jasper makes me *way* angrier than it ought to. Like it's something she's doing to me.

"That's sick," I say. "She's sick."

"Yep. But it wasn't just the journal anyway. And it wasn't even just what happened to Cassie at the camp. It was way more complicated than that. It was a whole bunch of stuff: my mom, my dad, the future, the past, now. Suddenly it got all mashed together in my head and it felt like too much."

"But you changed your mind," I say. "And that's the important thing."

He nods and smiles with half his mouth. "Because of you."

"Don't say that." This time I snap at him so hard it surprises me. But I can't be responsible for saving Jasper. I am already such a mess. And I have such a shitty record of the people around me surviving. "Please, don't . . ."

Also, this whole conversation is making it harder to stay in the friends zone where we belong. I squeeze my eyes shut. Hope that I don't cry.

"I didn't mean it like that," he says, though he kind of did. I can feel it. "But you coming to the bridge helped short-circuit the whole thing. I was up there and I was thinking hard about it, but then I got worried it might not be a clean fall. Or that the bridge wasn't tall enough."

"Jasper," I whisper. It's terrifying to hear him sound so matter-of-fact.

He and I stare at each other for a minute more, and I feel a hard tug toward him.

No. Whatever that feeling is—it's one instinct I will not follow. Jasper and I are friends. We are better off that way.

"Anyway," Jasper goes on. "I walked down the far side of the bridge to check out the drop. And I was on my way back up already wondering what the hell I was doing when I saw them putting you in an ambulance with Boston General's name on it. And you were totally out cold. Like lifeless." He shudders, remembering. "I started to run up to stop them. But there were too many of them. So I decided instead to steal some poor kid's bike and come here." He is staring at the side of my face. And I can feel that he isn't going to stop staring until I look up at him. And so I do. "Two seconds on that bike and I realized that I wasn't thinking clearly. That I wasn't thinking at all. The scary thing is how it feels now like someone else was on that bridge. I can't even believe I thought about it. I don't think I ever would have actually done it. It was just this moment in time. And now it's gone."

I nod. "Make sure it stays that way," I say. "I can't—" My voice catches. "Just—no time-outs. For anybody."

"Okay," Jasper says, and I feel him about to reach out to touch me—a hug maybe, a hand on my arm. But he doesn't. Part of me wishes he had. The smarter part is glad that he did not.

"Do you think I can get back out with you?" I ask.

He shakes his head. "This is only an ID. They'll have to buzz me back out."

"There are fire stairs," I say. "I saw them in the common room. There's an alarm over there, too. What if we pull it and then take off down the fire stairs? Don't they always have to leave those doors unlocked?"

Jasper frowns. "The stairs and alarm are a good idea, but isn't that right in view of the guards? But there's got to be another alarm, over here maybe. If you head over to the stairs out in the main room, I can find it and you can take off out the fire exit. Even if I get hung up, I have the ID. You're the one who needs to get out without anyone seeing."

The other girls. I still haven't told them anything: not about being Outliers or my dad, or people like Quentin. I didn't warn them about the danger I am sure they are in. How can I leave them there so totally unprepared?

"I can't," I say.

"Weren't you the one just asking—"

"I know. I know," I say. "And I do need to get out, definitely. But the other girls—they don't even know that being an Outlier is a thing."

"Then we can get out and send your dad back to tell them all about it," Jasper says, and he's annoyed. I can tell. Maybe it's even fair. After all, he went through a lot to get in and now I am refusing to leave. Or, you know, also maybe because he cares about me. "It doesn't have to be you who stays, Wylie."

And maybe I feel overly responsible for these girls because of what happened to Cassie. That doesn't necessarily make the feeling any less real, or right.

"But it does have to be me," I say quietly.

"You and I both know what happens when you hang around to see this shit play out, Wylie. It doesn't end well. Ask Cassie." Jasper's voice catches on her name. He looks down. "Listen, I get that you care about the people here." He hesitates, looks away as he shoves his hands into his pockets. "But I only care about you."

He's confused now. Like I was when I thought he was gone. Once all this bullshit is past, and the world is quiet, Jasper is going to realize what I already know: that he is better off without me.

"It's not just that they are my friends or something," I say, steering this conversation hard back to the point, and away from us. Jasper will thank me later. "I had an actual chance to tell all of them about being Outliers. And I didn't. Partly because I was worried for them. But partly because I was worried for me. I have to stay and warn them, then I will go."

Jasper stares down. Finally, he nods. Before he can say anything else, there is a noise in the hall.

"You should go before somebody finds you in here."

"Okay," Jasper says. But not like he thinks it's okay at all. He just seems sad. And that feels like proof somehow that I'm right. That he will be better off if we keep things between us clear and simple. That I will be too.

"Can you do something for me, though?" I ask.

"Anything."

"Stop by my house and check for my dad? It seems like he should have been here by now."

"Sure, yeah, of course," Jasper says, glad to have something to do.

There's another noise in the hall, like a door opening and closing. Jasper stands.

"Can you take this, too?" I hand him Kelsey's copy of *1984*. "Hold on to it."

He looks down at it skeptically. "Really?"

"It has some notes in it that are important." Kelsey might be mad that I gave it away. But it is for safekeeping.

"Okay, but on one condition," he says.

"What?" I ask, reminded of that last phone call Jasper and I had before the bridge.

"That you promise me you'll be okay."

"Definitely." I smile. Whatever I say won't be any more true than what Jasper said to me. Right now, the truth is out of both of our hands.

"And get out soon," Jasper says. "Because I'll be waiting."

14

I WAKE TO LOUD VOICES IN THE HALLWAY. JASPER CAUGHT? MY HEART IS RACING as I lurch out of bed and throw open the door. But outside it's only Becca and Ramona laughing loudly right across the hall from my door.

"Wylie, you have got to hear this shit," Becca says, striding over to me and waving for Ramona to follow. I catch the time on the hallway clock: seven thirty. Morning. I feel relieved to have survived the night. Becca looks up and down the hall like she wants to be sure no one is listening, leans in close. "That asshole guard said he would let me go if I had sex with him."

"What kind of idiot says that outright?" Ramona chimes in. Once, then twice she plucks at her bracelet.

"Men are so stupid," Becca says.

"What an ass," Ramona adds before her eyes shoot over to me

like she's just remembered something. "Hey, wait, speaking of asses, what the hell was that, you running after that guy yesterday? That was whacko. And I mean for real. Like fucking nuts."

"Yep, full-on psycho," Becca says.

They are both looking at me like they want an actual explanation for my outburst.

"I didn't believe what he was saying." I shrug. "I wanted him to tell us the truth about why we're here."

"No offense," Ramona says, crossing her arms and seeming more suspicious now, "but isn't that the second time they had to drug you?"

"Yeah, didn't you do the same kind of thing when they were bringing you here?" Becca asks. And it's the opposite of the you-go-girl compliment it could be. "I heard you beat the crap out of the EMTs."

They aren't on my side anymore, at least not necessarily. There is still a line between crazy and *crazy*, and I might have thrown myself on the wrong side of it.

"Chanting 'let us go' is one thing," Ramona says. "Attacking people is kind of another."

This particular moment—when I have zero credibility—doesn't seem like the best time to tell them about being Outliers and my dad's research and all of it. But I have no choice. All I've done is wait.

But when I step forward out into the hallway, my foot knocks into something on the floor.

"What's that?" Becca asks, pointing to something white and balled-up in my doorway.

I crouch down to look. It's one of the scratchy, hospital-issue towels they've given us. When I put my hand on top, there's something hard inside. Something bigger than my spread-fingered hand. I press down, trying to figure out what it is without taking the towel off. Already I have the most awful feeling I know.

"Why don't you look?" Becca asks—a totally reasonable question. One that I can't possibly answer.

"I . . ."

Instead, I scoop the towel up, bolt back inside my room, and slam the door. I can hear Ramona and Becca whispering on the other side for a minute. It sounds like they are debating whether one of them should go after me—it's a "you do it," "no, you do it," kind of exchange. Finally, they decide against it altogether. Soon their voices are drifting away.

My ears are ringing as I step to the bed and rest down the towel and its mysterious cargo. I take one last deep breath before I tug hard on the towel like I'm performing a magic trick. I try to quickly close my eyes. But it's too late. I've already seen what's rolled out: a plastic baby, covered in red.

My heart surges as my stomach pushes up into my throat. A baby like the ones left on our porch? Here? Now?

Who left it? Absurdly, I think of Quentin torturing me from the grave. I think of Jasper doing it in some twisted act of betrayal. My mind spins frantically forward.

Wait. No. I will not do this. This must be exactly their point—whoever they are. This must be what they want: to make me suspicious and paranoid. But I will not line up the suspects.

I will not try to get to the root of this mystery. No more. Not after everything. The whole point is to make me afraid, or to make me lose my mind for real. And it will not work. Not this time. I will show them. I am not scared. I am not going to hide. Not anymore.

I jam my feet into my flip-flops, grab the baby by a leg, and yank open the door to my room. I stride hard down the long hallway, heading straight for the common room. My heels strike the ground harder with each and every step. *Boom, boom, boom.* Until it hurts. Until I am glad for the pain.

Go to hell. Go to hell. Go to hell. I chant in my head. *You will not make me feel worse. You will not make me more afraid. You will not make me hide or doubt myself. And I do not care who you are. I do not care why. Because I decide. I choose how I feel.*

My face is hot when I finally race out into the common room and the security guys startle to attention. The Wolf is there. If I were closer, I could probably feel him thinking his awful thoughts about me, imagining my neck in his hands. But I am glad he is here. I want him to see how little I care, too.

My eyes move from the guards to Ramona and Becca, standing next to each other toward the back of the room. And Kelsey is there, stretched out on the couch, a book in her hands. All of the girls are there. All watching me. It's hard to believe we have any connection anymore. Not with the way they are all looking at me.

Becca and Ramona are shaking their heads a little. Open mouths. Appalled. Almost as if they are saying: *Don't. Don't do it. Whatever you're thinking.* Dr. Haddox is at the back, talking to

Elise, and he looks concerned. Probably that he will have to act again to stop me.

Their eyes are all still on me when I finally stop in the center of the room and lift that baby high over my head. Despite their staring. Despite their disapproval. And just like that, a valve opens up inside me, and out pours only rage.

"Whoever left this for me can go to hell!" I scream so loud it burns my throat. I look around some more, wave the baby again over my head. "And when I find out who you are, I will make you sorry. I promise I will."

Cassie. That's who I feel like. When she climbed up on top of that stranger's car all those months ago on my behalf. At the time, I had wanted nothing more than to feel that kind of anger. Had believed it would devour my fear. And I'd been right: I am not scared anymore. But I hadn't considered the cost. Because when I look out around the room, at all those startled eyes, I don't feel strong. I feel trapped. Like whoever left the baby wanted exactly this to happen: for me to look like I was finally losing it. Now there is no way that anybody is going to listen to me about anything—Outliers or otherwise.

And so, I turn toward the tall garbage can nearby and crack the baby down into it. So hard that for a second I think I've broken the bin. But the top just sails round and round until finally it slows to a stop.

I'm still glaring down at the trash can's spinning lid when I hear a whimper close to me on the floor. When I look over to the side there's Teresa, knees clutched to her chest, trembling.

"Are you okay?" I ask, feeling a hot wave of guilt. "Did I hurt you? I didn't mean—I didn't see you there."

But when Teresa looks up, her face is so swollen and red and tear streaked. She looks like she's been crying for a while, way before me and the baby and the trash can.

"Can you help me get out of here?" she begs.

"Um, I don't think there's any way—"

"I mean out of this—back to my room? I don't want everyone to see me upset like this."

And the truth is, I don't want them staring at me anymore either. Slamming that baby into the trash was the end of my rage. But without it, I am no longer invincible. I'm not sure I am all that strong.

"Yeah, okay," I say. "Let's go."

TERESA'S ROOM IS at the end of the hall. With its two windows, it is much brighter than mine. Outside, the sky is a sharp blue, and sun streams through. It's so cheerful that I might even be able to forget there ever was a doll. That is if my hand weren't throbbing from where I was gripping it.

"Thank you for helping me," Teresa says. And she is weirdly peaceful now, which is almost as unsettling as her excitement. Or her sobbing. I realize now that none of Teresa's feelings ever seem to fit the situation. That's what makes them so uncomfortable.

"No problem," I say. "What happened? I mean, why were you so upset out there?"

"I spoke to my pastor on the phone."

She was allowed to call her pastor? I think, but try to stay focused.

"And he made you cry?"

She shakes her head. "He's not like that. That's why I started going to meetings instead of my grandmother's church. He's more progressive. I've made a lot of mistakes, though. Some sins you can't make up for."

This sadness is real and, for the first time, crystal clear. And it runs so deep that it makes my chest ache.

"What sins?" I ask. After her grandmother's six-minute rule. It's hard not to feel like she's exaggerating about what kinds of things she might have done wrong.

"Boys. Most of them I didn't even know." She glances over at me, and I try not to twitch. Sex? I didn't see that coming. But it could explain some of her jumpy, chaotic feelings. Maybe she's pushed some secrets so far down that when they pop back up, they spray out like fireworks. "One time, I even hitchhiked to a rest stop and let this one old guy pay me. I don't even know why." She takes a breath, and this time when she exhales her whole body sags. "I felt so bad all the time about myself even before that. Doing terrible things just gave me something specific to hate myself for."

"People make mistakes," I manage, grabbing out of thin air Jasper's words to me all those weeks ago. But I need to say something more. The thing they all need to know, but right now Teresa especially. "Also, I think there's a chance that all of us here—that we're extra sensitive to other people's feelings. My dad researches it. Anyway, that could be part of why you felt bad about yourself."

I wait for the onslaught of questions. *What do you mean, extra sensitive? What research?* Instead, I feel a new wave of peace when she smiles at me. And then sympathy—for me. Like I am even more deserving of pity than her. It makes me super uncomfortable. Teresa reaches up and takes off her necklace.

"Here, take this. As a thank-you for being so nice to me." She extends a small gold cross on a delicate chain. "My grandmother gave it to me. She said it would protect me from all bad things, even the ones in my own heart." I eye the chain, which I do not want to put on. Like *completely* don't want to, though I can't exactly explain why.

"You should keep it," I say. Force a smile. "If your grandmother gave it to you, it must be special."

"No, really." Teresa steps closer, already holding out the two ends of the necklace so that she can put it on me. "You need it right now more than I do." I resist the urge to stop her as she clasps the delicate chain around my throat, then leans back to see how it falls on me. "Perfect."

"Thanks," I say. "And I wouldn't worry about the things you did in the past, or how you've felt. I don't think any of us are sick, not like they're saying." Hearing myself say it out loud is a relief. It's not so insane after all. It's simple even. The other girls will believe me. They'll have to. "Anyway, I think sometimes not understanding yourself can make you feel worse."

"That's what my therapist says. Or I guess *she* didn't say that. She made it so that I would figure it out by myself."

"Ah, I'm familiar with that technique." I smile, for real. It is nice having this in common. "When my therapist does that, I fall for it every time. Usually, she's right."

Teresa actually smiles a little for the first time. "Is yours pretty, too?" she asks. "Sometimes I think that's why I fall for it. Because my therapist is like this perfect china doll in her big red chair."

15

OUT IN THE HALLWAY, I LEAN BACK AGAINST THE WALL. PRESS A HAND TO MY chest to try to slow down my pounding heart. Teresa is one of Dr. Shepard's patients? Does that mean everyone else is? Is that what actually connects us? But it doesn't explain so much else: like how we also just happened to all be Outliers. Whatever the truth, I don't believe for a second that Dr. Shepard intended me—or us—to be locked away. No possible way.

Still, I would feel much better if I had proof.

WHEN I COME back into the common room, I feel all eyes on me again—the guards, all of the girls except for Teresa. Luckily, I don't see Dr. Haddox anywhere. One less person to be self-conscious in front of. And everyone else has shifted around some, is preoccupied now. Kelsey is stretched out on the couch,

Fahrenheit 451 in her hands. I try to ignore the Wolf's eyes digging into me as I cross the room to her.

"Hey," I say to Kelsey, not sure where to begin.

She looks up and raises an eyebrow at me. "You seriously know how to lie low, don't you?" I try to read whether that's an insult or a joke. But there's the brick wall again. At least I know now what it is: she is blocking me.

"I guess." My episode with the baby is too much to explain at this moment. "Listen, something here is seriously messed up."

She keeps her eyes on her book. "What was your first clue? The guards or the doctors or the Ebola hospital?"

"I think we should go," I say. "Like get out right now. All of us."

"Sure. No problem." Kelsey's voice is deadpan. Then she hooks a thumb toward the guards without looking their way. "Running out the doors worked so well for you last time."

"My dad is a scientist and he's discovered this thing. The thing both you and I can do, feeling other people's feelings. Your book? *1984*?"

"I have zero idea what you're talking about," Kelsey says, and when she finally stares right at me, her wall is pulled high and tight. "I can't feel anything."

Okay, she obviously doesn't want to talk about any of it outright. There are other things I can say.

"Listen, I've been in a situation like this before. We shouldn't wait. It can turn really bad, all of a sudden. We should make some sort of plan. Get the other girls out, too. We need to convince them they're in danger. Because we are." I lean in closer to

Kelsey. It's not the most subtle thing with the guards still eye-balling me. But I don't have a choice. "I think we should create a distraction. Like the fire alarm. And then we should run."

"Assuming I did have any idea what you were talking about"—Kelsey makes a big point of looking over her shoulder toward the fire alarm, then glances once in the direction of the fire stairs—"your little plan sounds totally doomed to fail. Besides, I can tell you for sure that those girls"—she motions toward the back of the room, toward Becca and Ramona, who are still staring at us and whispering—"aren't going anywhere with you. They think you've lost it."

"Yeah, I realize that," I say. "But they'll listen to you."

"And why would I tell them anything?" She shakes her head. "You know what your problem is?" This time when she looks at me, she isn't blocking anymore. She wants me to know that she means this thing she is about to say. Her fingers trace her infinity tattoo, then point at me. "You worry too much about other people. You and I should leave together, on our own. We can send help back for them. That would be better for us. *And* better for them."

Back up goes Kelsey's wall. Just like that. Like she wants to show me how good she is at turning it off and on. Like she wants to remind me that there is still an *us*—her and me—and a *them*—the rest of the girls. We might all be Outliers, sure. But that does not mean we are all created equal.

"Listen," Kelsey goes on, more softly. "I just want to be careful. And I think you and I could—I think we could help each other and help everyone else." She pushes herself up from the couch.

"Where are you going?" I ask, sounding—and feeling—panicky.

"Um, to the bathroom," she says, rolling her eyes. "Listen, just relax. I'll be right back. And we can figure out a plan."

AFTER KELSEY IS gone, I look over at Becca and Ramona, but they immediately look away. It's kind of hard to blame them. We have only known one another for twenty-four hours. Loyalty born out of fucked-up necessity only goes so far.

I should have told them sooner about my dad and his research, the camp and Cassie, about being Outliers, all of us. Piled on top of all the other weird crap that I have done, the Outlier thing is going to sound like something I made up.

Still, I have no choice but to try. And while Kelsey is away. She wants me to keep it quiet and I don't want to piss her off, but there is no way I am leaving without telling the others. It's all fine and well to say we'll send people back for them. I won't make that choice for the other girls. I won't leave them here to wait. No matter what Kelsey thinks.

"HI," I SAY once I am standing in front of Becca and Ramona. I hold up an awkward hand in a half wave.

"Hey," Ramona says, glancing my way, then back down at the floor. Becca doesn't say a word. She's staring out over the room, like she's surveying the edge of a battlefield.

I am in a hole that I am going to have to climb out of. The truth is always a good place to start.

"We used to get those babies at our house," I begin. "The

dolls like the one in the towel. Somebody left them on our door-step. We thought it was somebody harassing my mom because she was this news photographer and people were always sending her hate mail." Ramona has looked up at me. But Becca has not. "I think that they were actually for my dad; he's a scientist and there were some people who didn't like his research."

"What kind of research?" Becca asks with a suspicious edge.

"Wait, I know." Ramona snaps her fingers like it's just come to her. "Stem cells!"

"No, he was looking into—"

A loud shriek blasts through the common room, making us all jump. Silence for a second, then it comes again. My heart races as I look around. People have their hands over their ears to block the shrieking sound. Even the guards look confused. It isn't until I see the flashing light in the corner that I realize it's the fire alarm.

Did Kelsey decide to go ahead and pull it? Maybe something happened, maybe she realized there wasn't time to wait after all? I have no choice but to tell Becca and Ramona about the plan now, and quickly.

"I think maybe—"

But when I turn, they've already hurried over—like every-body else—toward the guards and the emergency exit doors. This wasn't how our escape was supposed to go. We haven't even worked out the details. And this is the opposite of subtle. The Wolf is standing in front of the exit door already, stopping the girls from heading down. There will be no way to sneak past him in the confusion. No possibility of slipping away.

"We have to go out!" one of the girls near the door shouts. "We can't stay here."

Do I actually smell smoke? I could be imagining it, haunted as I am by fire.

"Calm down! It's just a drill!" the Wolf shouts right back at her, then calls to his partner. "No way I am letting any of them outside unless someone tells me I have to."

We are rats. Trapped in a cage. *Get out now.* Kendall was right. We need to go.

Dr. Haddox strides into the common room back from where our rooms are and with him a wave of actual smoke, unmistakable now. Not a false alarm. Not my imagination. Somewhere, something is definitely on fire. Was this what Kelsey went to do when she said she was going to use the bathroom? Did she send a trash can up in flames? But why didn't she warn me? Unless there wasn't time. Maybe something happened.

"We have a situation." Dr. Haddox waves at the guards. "Take them out until the fire department gets here."

"Outside?" the Wolf snaps. "They'll be much harder to contain. We can't be held responsible if—"

"Then don't go all the way outside!" Dr. Haddox shouts back, then rubs his forehead, trying to calm down. "They can't stay in here. It's not safe. Go down to the bottom of the stairs, but not all the way out then. That way at least they won't be stuck up here with the smoke. I'll be back."

Dr. Haddox disappears then, back the way he came. Back toward our rooms and the emergency.

"Come on!" the Wolf shouts at us like this is all our fault.

"Let's go, let's go. This way. We'll hold inside the stairwell, couple flights down. Should be fireproofed."

"I'll bring up the rear!" his partner shouts.

And still on and on goes that ear-piercing alarm. It has my nerves jangling. It's hard to think, much less to come up with a plan.

"Okay, come on! Follow me down!" the Wolf barks like a drill sergeant. But he is nervous now, too. Even with all the other people around, I can make out the hint of it. He'd be okay doing whatever it took to stop us from getting out of line, but he's not interested in consequences. "No one leaves the building. Stay behind me!"

We move in an orderly single-file line, Becca and Ramona way up near the front. Much too far away to tell them that this was part of a plan. And what does it matter anyway? It's not like we can get past the Wolf. I am pretty sure he would kill any one of us, just to prove that point. Not to mention: Where the hell is Kelsey? And Teresa? It's a risk to draw attention to Kelsey being missing if she's the one who started the fire, but what if she started it, only to get overwhelmed by the smoke? I need to make sure she's okay.

I turn back to the other guard, the one bringing up the rear. The less asshole-ish one.

"I think there could be people still back there," I tell him. I don't want to mention Kelsey—in case she's responsible. But it's not practical, not if she truly needs help. "Maybe two girls. Teresa and Kelsey. Somebody has to check."

"What?" he asks, still encouraging me ahead, waiting for me

to move through the door and on down the stairs.

"There are at least two girls missing!" I shout. "They could still be trapped back there."

"Okay, okay," the guard says, glancing back over his shoulder. "Follow everyone else down. I'll go back."

I STARE AFTER him, breathless, as he leaves me there alone. There is no one watching me as he disappears through the doors. All the other girls are on their way down. I keep following them, inching slowly until I am through the doors and into the cool, concrete stairwell. And then, suddenly, the answer is clear. Up.

The déjà vu makes me shudder. All those weeks ago when Agent Klute showed up at our door, I did exactly that: ran up. It didn't work then. Maybe because it was supposed to work now.

Fast though, too. And quiet. Before anyone turns. Before any of the girls notice me or think to ask—however innocently—"what?" Or "why?" Or "where are you going?" While the sound of stomping feet in the stairway is still deafening. While no one will be able to hear my feet headed the opposite way. My breath comes hard as I sprint up the steps, two at a time, not looking back. And then I hear the Wolf's voice echo up.

"You got them in the back there?" he calls to his partner.

I freeze, heart thumping.

"I think he had to go check for missing people," one of the girls mercifully shouts back. I brace for commotion, for the Wolf to investigate. For something that leads him right to me, one flight up, heaving. But it never comes.

"Okay, come on! Keep moving!" is all he says. "Keep together and in line."

And so I race on, farther up. As I duck around the wall to the floor above, I am still waiting for the guard below to call after me. For one of the other girls to notice me missing and to say something, even just offhand. But no one does. It's only me and the stairs and my breath—up and up and up.

But the doors on the floor above are locked. And I begin to doubt this plan of mine. If I can't get out of the stairway and into one of the upper floors, they will find me eventually. And I'm pretty sure there will be very bad consequences, especially if it's the Wolf that lays his hands on me first.

Which means that this has to work. This way up has to be a way out.

I run up three more floors, past three more locked doors. But at least there are no voices coming after me, no thick smoke gathered up there at the ceiling. Nothing to stop me from continuing until finally I reach the very last door. The top of the stairs, the door to the roof. I hold my breath as I push on the metal bar. Dread it being locked, too, like all the others.

But then, there is the door, giving way. And with a gasp I am there. I am outside in the sun and the fresh air. I am free.

Or I feel that way for a second. Because being trapped six floors up even outside on a roof isn't exactly the same thing as being in the clear.

Realizing that suddenly makes how pleasant it is on that roof—warm and sunny with big, puffy white clouds floating slowly above the tops of the bushy, bright-green trees—seem creepy. Makes the hum of the big air-conditioning units threatening. Still, I am so grateful to be away from the shrill scream of that fire alarm, from the heart-twisting smell of that smoke. At least up here there is space to breathe. Even if the freedom is mostly an illusion. And I still believe that there must be some way out. That I came up here for a reason. That I was right to trust my instincts.

I'm still standing with my back pressed against the door when I hear the fire trucks arrive. Even so, not necessarily a real fire, I remind myself. Could be something small that Kelsey started in a trash can. Just smoldering enough to trip the alarm as she bolted down another set of fire stairs.

I inch my way closer to watch them arrive. First one truck, then two more, followed by a red-and-white fire department SUV, and a fire department ambulance, which seems kind of like overkill given that we're *already* in a hospital. But the firefighters certainly do seem to be taking things seriously. They leap fast from their trucks, gear on, tools in hand at a full-on jog.

What if I really am trapped on the roof of a burning building, high above the flames? I am pretty sure that is the opposite of the place you are supposed to be in a fire. After Cassie, my mom, what if this is just my turn?

I shudder and push the thought away as I back away from the edge of the building. I try to focus instead on the much more likely thing: me getting caught. I need a good place to hide. Finally, I see a spot that looks promising and tuck myself out of sight between two ventilation units on the far side. Enough of a view to see someone coming, enough space to slip out and run if they do. I'm also a distance from the worst of the air conditioner roar. I'm not sure how much I could take of that sound gnawing away at the inside of my brain.

Waiting on the roof is my plan. Not because it is necessarily the best plan, but because it is the only one that I can think of. The firefighters will need to make sure that the fire is out first. At some point, all the girls will be brought back up the steps and into the common room and there will be a check to see if everyone is accounted for. Only then will they notice me missing. In there is a window, a narrow one. I will have a few minutes probably, five or maybe ten, to get from the roof, down and out the door.

I have to hope that Kelsey got out some other way. And if she did not, I will be coming back anyway for all the girls I did not warn. When I do, I will get her out, too.

I will know it is time to go down once the firefighters start to leave—between now and then all I can do is wait. And that would be fine if the black tar rooftop wasn't a giant sucking magnet for the sun's rays. Within minutes, it goes from a little warm to burning hot in my hiding spot. I am so thirsty, too. I can no longer remember the last time I had something to drink.

Time grinds down. Minutes ooze into what could be awful, uncomfortable hours. Or maybe only more minutes. Everything feels muddled and confused. I try to think cooling thoughts. Cool, happy thoughts.

And, so, I think of the first cold, happy place that jumps to mind: Crater Lake.

THE LAST BIG trip my mom and I took before she died was our farthest ever, to Crater Lake in Oregon.

It was the third week of August—a week before the start of junior year. By then, Cassie had been back from her fitness camp for two weeks with her brand-new body, more stylish clothes, and notable disinterest in everything I had to say. I didn't realize the change in Cassie's feelings right away, but my mom wasn't nearly as slow on the uptake. She could see the writing on the wall, which is why she suggested the long trip for just the two of us.

"I think we should do a full-on blowout this time," my mom had said. "Northwest coast. We can hike up near Mount Rainier, then drive down to the Oregon coast. I have a whole extra week now that my trip was canceled." Though she was also somewhat disappointed about this, I knew. The trip had been for one of her personal freelance projects. An anonymous source had said they were willing to give her a tour of some off-limits research facility (which sounded super sketchy to me) so she could take pictures that would reveal who knows what. And I guess she did take some. But then her source had disappeared—couldn't be reached, wouldn't return calls. Leaving her with time on her hands. "Come on, just you and me. It'll be fun."

Crater Lake was our last stop before heading home.

And it was as beautiful as my mom had promised: fir trees lush and tall, and with a sharp blue sky endless off the water. It was hard to tell what was real and what was a reflection.

It wasn't until we'd hiked most of the slippery distance down to the water's edge that my mom even mentioned the whole idea of swimming.

"Swim?" I asked, because I was sure she had to be joking. It was the deepest lake in the United States, with something like six species of fish that had been "introduced" over time. By whom? That's what I wanted to know. Plus, the lake could be as cold as thirty-eight degrees. I'd read all about that in the guidebook. "You can't swim in it."

And by can't, I mostly meant no sane person ever would. Besides, I wasn't a strong swimmer even under the best of circumstances. Like a warm pool.

"Of course *swim*," my mom said as she marched on toward a short dock that extended out some distance into the lake. A dock she had clearly been aiming for all along. "You can't come all the way to a place like this and not at least swim a little."

And from the way she said it, I already knew that "a little" actually meant a lot. She looked so excited, too. And there actually were a handful of totally insane people already in there. Remarking loudly: "phew, it's chilly!" or "refreshing!" Nothing unbearable or dangerous. But also nothing that sounded the least bit appealing.

"I'm not swimming," I said, quiet but firm as I

marched on behind her. And I meant it, too. I had been following my mom on these adventures for years now. And for years I had done everything that she wanted. I had climbed the mountains. I had camped—cold and terrified. I had rappelled. And yeah, all of that had given me something to hold on to at times when I badly needed a lifeline. I was grateful, but it also hadn't changed anything about me. I wasn't all better. I also wasn't a little kid anymore. I was entitled to make my own choices.

"If we go from here to that corner over there, it's a little over a half mile. Then we could rest on the other side and come back." All of this was based on advance research, obviously. Like she had committed a map of the lake to memory. She then produced from her pocket a small orange bag that was currently pressed flat. It took her less than a minute to inflate. "And we have this buoy for emergencies, in case you're"—she winked at me—"worried. It is totally safe."

She sounded so triumphant and looked so elated. I could tell that this was it, *the* moment that was to be the culmination of all our years of trips. The moment when her broken-winged little baby bird would, at long last, truly fly.

I probably should have been touched. Maybe even appreciative. But all of a sudden, all I felt was seriously pissed off.

"I'm not swimming in there," I said again.

"Oh, come on, yes you are." She waved me off like she

had about so many things, so many times before. Already she was taking off the clothes she'd worn on top of her bathing suit and folding them on the dock. "You swam a mile to qualify as a CIT this summer. We'll take a break in between. You can definitely get there and back, no problem."

I felt the tug of my own bathing suit beneath my clothes, which I'd put on that morning at my mom's suggestion without a second thought. "Just in case," she had said, as if one could never be sure when a swimming-related emergency might crop up.

"No," I said, crossing my arms. "I don't want to."

"Wylie, come on, you know that—"

"No!" I shouted, my heart beating hard. "I don't actually have to do everything just to prove that I can. Other people get to choose the things they do. Why can't I?"

Her lips parted then, like she was about to reply. But she took a breath. And her head tilted in that way it did when she was considering something intently. Finally, she nodded. "Okay," she said quietly.

And that was what I wanted, right? For her to back down. So why did it feel so terrible now that she had?

"Okay?"

"You're right," she said. "There are lots of different ways to be brave. Including knowing who you are. I just want to be sure that it's always you choosing what you want. And not your fear choosing for you." She took a breath. "Okay?"

I felt a wave of unease. I didn't want to swim in that

water. I resented her trying to make me. But me *not* swimming wasn't some casual, I-don't-feel-like-it decision. It wasn't really a choice at all.

"Are you disappointed?" I asked.

She walked forward and hugged me. "I couldn't be more proud, Wylie. Always."

I stood there on that dock as she dove into that icy water and watched as she kicked away from shore. And I believed she felt proud of me. The problem was I didn't feel proud of myself.

She'd gone only about a dozen strokes when I stripped off my clothes, took a deep breath, and dove in after her.

———————————

THINKING OF THE cold water of Crater Lake works to cool me off, but only until the memory is gone. Within moments I am baking again. When I think I can't stand the heat one more minute, I finally hear raised voices below.

I jump to my feet and head again to the edge of the roof. Sure enough, when I peer down the firefighters are climbing back into their trucks, tired but triumphant.

I have to go. Now. The fire is out, the emergency contained. And I don't see anyone evacuating. Which means they have gone back inside. Any second the head count will begin. Soon they will realize that someone is gone. And they will come looking.

16

I FLY DOWN THE FIRST THREE FLIGHTS OF STAIRS, SLOWING ONLY WHEN I HEAR the voices from our floor begin to rise. One of the guards is shouting directions to the girls. I catch bits and pieces. "Find an available room." "Transfer belongings." The girls' mumbling, grumbling. "Teresa?" someone asks. And then someone else replies. I can't hear what they say. I don't think I hear Kelsey's voice either. I hope that means that she has somehow already managed to get herself out the door.

I slide quietly past our floor and race the rest of the way down, so fast that I trip on my stupid flip-flops a few times. But I am too scared to slow down.

And no one stops me, no voice calls out. Soon I am at the bottom of the steps. Right in front of the exit door. My hands tremble on the bar as I look at the sign—*Emergency Exit Only*.

Alarm Will Sound. When the alarm goes off, they will know exactly where I am. They will come after me. And it will be broad daylight when I emerge. Not the best for a clean escape. Still, I have no choice. I take one last deep breath then push open the door.

There's no sound, though. No alarm, at least not one I can hear. And that's the last thing I think—*no alarm*—before I run.

The driveway is much longer than it looked from the roof. Longer and longer it seems, the faster I try to go. Soon my lungs are burning, my legs rubbery. But I keep my eyes locked on the city skyline ahead. There is only me and my breathing and the tall buildings in front of me. And I need to get there, to the crowds of Boston, where I can disappear.

Finally, the end of the hospital driveway is in sight. A stop sign and then the road, a main one—three lanes in each direction— that make the top of a T. Across the wide street is an office building next to some brick historic site, to the right a sandwich shop with people inside. That's my best shot. I have no cash or ID. No phone. I am just going to have to hope that somebody buying lunch in there takes pity on me. But I'll need a good story. A believable one that does not involve government quarantine or anyone chasing after me.

As soon as I step foot into the road there's a screech, tires skidding on asphalt. I brace for impact that never comes. Instead the sound stops and when I open my eyes, red metal is all I can see.

The car door swings open. "Come on!" Jasper shouts, waving for me to get in his brother's Jeep.

I rush forward and jump in. I barely have the door closed when he speeds away.

"Get down, get down. Stay out of sight."

I scrunch low, head below the window, knees on the floor as the car lurches forward.

"Was there somebody else, maybe behind me?" I ask, panting and grateful.

Jasper looks up nervously in the rearview. "I don't think so. I didn't see anybody."

His eyes lock on the road ahead. Like his plan is to drive as fast and as far as we can. And I am suddenly overwhelmed by panic.

"We have to go back," I say.

"Go back? No way, not right now." Jasper shakes his head. "You want to help the other girls, I know. But to 'go back' you got to leave first."

"One of the other girls, Kelsey, she helped me get out," I say, not mentioning the fire she might have started. "I think she was coming out right behind me."

"You *think*?" Jasper asks. He sucks in a sharp breath. "It's a huge risk to go back."

I push myself up into the seat.

"Just a quick flyby. To make sure. I don't want her to get grabbed because she's waiting for me."

"Seriously?" Jasper whispers. He already knows he's going to do what I want—he just can't believe it.

"Seriously." I watch the side of his face. "And thank you for going back, for coming in the first place."

Jasper takes a deep breath, shaking his head as he switches on his turn signal. "One quick pass and then we're gone."

WE ARE ABLE to pull into the lot on the opposite side of the hospital and park some distance away. We have a decent view of the Ebola wing, but are pretty well hidden. Jasper leaves the car running.

"What does she look like?" he asks.

"She's shorter than me with long, dark, curly hair. And she'll be in a gray sweat suit." I pull at mine. "Like this one."

"Okay," Jasper says, eyeing the side of the hospital. "And you think she'd just be hanging out in the open?"

"I hope not, but I want to be sure," I say, then try to change the subject. To buy myself some time. "Did you go to my house? Any sign of my dad?"

My stomach twists when Jasper looks down. He's been dreading this conversation. Now, so am I.

"Jasper, what is it?"

"He wasn't there." He brightens a little as he digs out his cell phone and hands it to me. "But there were thunderstorms last night. Maybe his plane couldn't land. He's probably still stuck in the airport in DC."

"He would have called," I say.

"How?"

"They let other people get calls," I say, thinking of Teresa's conversation with her pastor. "People that weren't even parents."

"Were they people who are scientists studying this whole thing?" Jasper asks. "Try him again."

He's right, of course. Because Dr. Haddox may not know who I am, but somebody surely does.

I dial my dad's number again. I am so relieved when it doesn't go straight to voice mail. But when someone finally answers, it's a young woman. I pull it away from my face, hoping that I've dialed the wrong number. I haven't.

"Hello?" I say.

"Hello?" she snaps back, much louder this time.

"Who is this?" My heart is drumming inside my rib cage. "Why do you have my dad's phone?"

"Well, that was *awful* accusatory," she says, and with an edge that makes me think I am exactly right to be accusing her. "I'm trying to be a Good Samaritan. And you're coming at me like I've done something. How about a thank you? You know what? Maybe I'll hang up now."

"Wait!" I shout. "Please don't hang up. I'm sorry. I didn't mean to—but this is my dad's phone, and I can't find him. Um, why do you have it?"

"I found it," she says, like that's obvious. "Probably he was doing his shopping, and it fell out of his pocket. It happens all the time to my boyfriend. I'm always telling him he needs a man purse, and he's like screw you, I am not carrying a purse. But I told him: You want to lose your damn phone?" She takes a breath like she's forgotten who she's talking to or what about. "Anyway, you can't carry your phone in your hand while you're shopping in a big marketplace like this. Too many distractions. You're *always* going to end up setting it down."

"What marketplace?"

"*Eastern* Market," she says, like that also ought to be obvious.

"Where's that?" My hand is trembling. And I want to scream at her. Demand that she explain everything to me, immediately. But she's already almost hung up on me once. I need to stay calm. Be patient. "I'm calling from Boston. I don't know an Eastern Market."

"Boston?" She laughs. "Well, we're in D.C., right near Capitol Hill. I'll tell you what. Because you're so far away, why don't you PayPal me some money for shipping, and, you know, to cover my inconvenience, and I'll send it right back to you today."

I hang up once she's texted me her contact information. A name and a P.O. box that could belong to anybody. Part of me doesn't even want the phone back, like having it in my possession guarantees my dad isn't going to reappear with an explanation for all of this.

"What is it?" Jasper asks when I hang up.

"Somebody found my dad's phone in DC in some random market in the center of the city. Last time I talked to him, he was in the airport. He said he was going to turn around and be on the next flight home. Why is his phone not in the airport?"

"Okay." Jasper is trying not to seem freaked out. It would be more convincing if I couldn't read him so easily. "Maybe he got delayed and didn't feel like waiting in the airport. Or somebody could have stolen his phone and brought it to that random place. Just because the phone is there doesn't mean that he ever was."

"Yeah," I say, swallowing hard in a mostly useless attempt not to cry. I turn toward the window when my eyes start to burn. "What did Gideon say when you went to the house?"

Jasper closes his eyes. Again, I feel his dread rise. This is what he doesn't want to talk about. The house.

"Gideon wasn't there. No one was," he says. Jasper looks down at his hands. "But the door to your house was kind of open a little. I could see that before I got out of the car. And so I went in. Your house is kind of messed up."

"What does that mean?"

When Jasper turns to look at me, there's no mistaking just how bad he feels for me. "Actually, your place was totally trashed, Wylie. Drawers pulled out, papers all over the place. A front window was smashed."

"What?" Panic floods my stomach, making me nauseous. "Why?"

"From the mess, I'd say they were looking for something."

I wrap my arms around my waist and squeeze, but I shudder hard anyway. "And there was no sign of Gideon at all?"

"For what it's worth, there wasn't any sign that anything *bad* had happened to Gideon either," Jasper says, and this thought honestly reassures him. "I checked and there wasn't like blood or a shoe left behind or anything."

My eyes are wide. Jasper squeezes his eyes shut. He knows he has said the exact wrong thing.

"Oh, my God." I dial Gideon's number, pressing a hand to my mouth.

Gideon answers on the first ring. "Yep?"

"Gideon, it's Wylie. Are you okay?"

"Um, *yeah*," he says, all attitude. "Why wouldn't I be?"

"Have you talked to Dad?"

"Shhh. Why are you screaming?" he shouts back. "Stop yelling or I am going to hang up on you."

"I'm not yelling," I say, though I can hear myself—I am totally yelling. "When did you last talk to Dad?"

"I don't know," Gideon say, distracted. I probably caught him in the middle of playing a video game. I can almost hear the clicking of the controller. "Like yesterday, I think."

"What time?"

"I don't know. He was on the way to the airport."

My heart sinks. I spoke to him after that. Gideon probably won't know anything I don't. But I try not to lose hope.

"What did he say?"

"The same stupid shit that he's been saying—oh, I'm so sorry. I love you both the same." His tone is nasty. Mocking. "Blah, blah. It's all bullshit. And I told him he could go to hell. I'm going to stay away for a while, too. Once I'm gone, we can see how much he cares," Gideon says. He sounds so pleased with himself.

"Where are you, Gideon?" I ask.

"Staying with a friend," he says.

"What friend?" My voice is rising. "This is serious. I don't know where Dad is, Gideon."

"Well, why don't you see if you can *feel* your way to him?" he says viciously.

"Gideon, tell me where you are." Though it's not as if there are that many options. He only has a couple of friends. "Stephen's?"

"Well, if you need to ask, maybe you're not so gifted after all."

"Gideon, this isn't a joke. I'm—" But he's already hung up. "Asshole," I whisper.

"At least he's okay," Jasper offers as I start Googling. "What are you doing?"

"Trying to find the office number for my mom's friend Rachel." It takes a few tries before I find her—Rachel O'Calla-han. A second later, I am dialing. "My dad said he was calling her. Maybe she knows something."

I get her voice mail. "Rachel, it's Wylie. I need to talk to you right away. I can't find my dad. Call me back," and at the last second I remember to leave Jasper's number.

I squeeze Jasper's phone tight after I hang up. The police. I know I need to call them, too. As a possible semi-fugitive, I don't love this idea. If it was legal that they were holding us—like Dr. Haddox said—that would probably make it illegal for me to leave.

The call with the police doesn't last long. They aren't inter-ested in my dad as a supposed missing person. It's like with Cassie, only worse: they are all about why they can't do much to find a person who's vanished. They take down his name and a description and the few details about his travel I know. The only part they perk up about is his phone. That's when they start asking about me. Demanding to know who I am and where I am calling from. I hang up when they ask for my number and loca-tion. I never even get to telling them that someone also broke into our house.

After that, Jasper and I sit in silence. We have a good view of the building and even some of the exits. We've been there going on ten minutes. There's still no sign of Kelsey.

"You're sure you didn't see anybody running after me?" I

could have sworn there was. And maybe they grabbed Kelsey—that's what I'm thinking. "When I came out?"

"I don't think so," Jasper says.

That should be good news—except it doesn't feel like it.

"Kind of weird, isn't it?" I ask.

"Every part of this is weird, Wylie."

"But I mean, the fire door said it had an alarm. I didn't hear it, so it must be one of those silent ones. For sure, they'd know someone had opened it. After all the secrecy, I run out and no one even bothers to come after me?"

"Maybe they were too busy dealing with the actual fire alarm, which was seriously loud, by the way. I could hear it from the road. Maybe they didn't even hear the door alarm," he says. "Or maybe they couldn't chase you once you got outside. It would draw too much attention."

Even with Jasper's eyes still locked on the side of the building, I can feel something awful has occurred to him.

"What?" I ask. "What's wrong?"

"Nothing, it's just . . ." He looks down at the steering wheel, traces a right half circle with his finger. "There's nothing on the news about this. And I mean like nothing *at all*. I checked online, and there's not a word anywhere. Wouldn't somebody have said something to someone?"

It doesn't make me feel better, but it's also not a surprise. Uncomfortable silence is a thing I have become accustomed to. "I don't know. What happened at that camp was a nonevent and *thirteen* people died. I'm not sure I understand anything anymore."

"Yeah, except all these girls are going to come out eventually," Jasper says. "Even if the parents are being quiet now, they probably won't be once their kids get home and tell them about all this bioterrorist whatever. Everyone's eventually going to know about this."

"Unless," I say, and already I know I'm on to something. "The girls *don't* come out."

Jasper makes a face. "And how would they explain that?" he asks. "'Sorry, I know we said we were bringing your daughter back, but . . .'"

"How about something like a tragic fire that burns the hospital to the ground, accidentally killing them all?"

That's it. *That* is what I've been worried about: the girls—all of us—being erased. The fire might not be it, but something terrible is about to happen to those girls. Something permanent. And I need to get them out before it does. Me. Because I'm the only one who knows.

I feel so sure of it, too. It's the same way I felt about Jasper and the bridge. The way I felt about my mom that last night when she walked out the door for milk. Like something awful had already happened. I was right then, all those times. I'm not always right to worry—not by a long shot—but I'm sure that I am right now.

WE SIT IN silence for a minute more—or maybe five or ten. It feels like a long time as I scan right and then left across the edge of the building, still looking for Kelsey. But I don't feel anymore like we are going to find her. In fact, I feel like Kelsey is gone.

The only people we see are two women speed walking down the driveway, a groundskeeper, and two nurses headed toward the main entrance for their shift, bags over their shoulders, coffee in hand. I push up so I can get a look farther down toward the emergency room entrance. If I were Kelsey, I might head over there—more people, more places to hide. But the only person hanging out in front is a heavyset guy smoking.

"Oh wait, I have something for you," Jasper says, digging around in the piles of trash in the backseat—food wrappers, newspapers and magazines, empty soda cans. He seems happy to be able to focus on something that won't be upsetting. "Sorry it's such a mess in here. I've been kind of camping out since I saw you."

"This whole time?"

"Yeah, I mean I went to your house. But then I came back here to the parking lot. I wasn't sure when you'd make it out, so . . ." he says. But trying to make it seem like no big deal.

Something more than gratitude swells in me so fast I blush. Despite myself.

"Thank you, Jasper." It feels totally inadequate. And also incomplete. "For everything."

"I said I would be here when you got out." He sounds offended I'd doubt him. He's still digging around his trash-covered back-seat. "Ah, here it is."

When he turns back, he is holding out Kelsey's copy of *1984*.

"Oh, thanks."

But the book feels so much less important now compared to getting the girls out, finding my dad. I will read what's inside, and I will figure out what it all means at some point. If and when I find Kelsey again, maybe she and I can even help each other somehow—or maybe she can just help me. Maybe that's the truth. When I take the book from Jasper's hands, something falls out. It isn't until I pick it up from the floor that I realize it's Kendall's note.

I take a deep breath as I stare down at it. Just when I was wondering what we should do next: an answer.

"Can you take me somewhere?" I ask Jasper.

"Sure," Jasper says without hesitating. He's so glad to leave the hospital. "Where?"

"Someplace you are not going to want to go."

17

WE DRIVE INTO CAMBRIDGE, PAST THE IMPOSING IVY-COVERED BUILDINGS OF Harvard and the packs of jostling students so filled with all that promise and possibility. I fixate on one girl walking alone. She is tall and slim with short jaggedy hair, but cut intentionally that way unlike mine. She even has a backpack like the one I used to carry. It's amazing how she and I could look so similar and yet the gulf between us is infinite. Permanent maybe, too, I beginning to realize.

By the time we park in an alley a few blocks off Harvard Square, a full-blown summer storm is overhead. There is a distant rumble of thunder, and the air feels heavy and wet, even inside the car.

Without pressing for details, Jasper drove all the way to the address I gave him following the GPS on his phone, pulling into one of the only open parking spots a couple blocks away. He was so happy that I'd agreed to leave the hospital that he probably would have gone anywhere. But I could feel him getting more anxious the farther we went into the Cambridge side streets.

"Okay, now you have to tell me where we're going," Jasper says as he turns off the engine.

"To the address I gave you," I say. And I know it's stupid to delay the inevitable, but I do anyway. "That's where we're going."

He rolls his eyes. "Yeah, I got that part. I mean what's at this address?"

Really, I shouldn't drag Jasper into—well, that's just it. I don't even know what I'm dragging him into. I can't do that without telling him what's going on.

"It's the address that was on the note Kendall gave me." Even without looking at him, I can already feel Jasper's anger in my toes.

"The same Kendall who locked us in a cabin in the middle of the woods so some maniac could try to saw open your brain? I get it, you want to help the other girls, Wylie, but this is—"

"I believe him," I say. "The way Kendall looked at me and handed me that note. Listen, I can try to explain what it's like to have this Outlier thing. How sharp and clear it can be. Maybe someday when my dad gets all his research done there will even be some way to measure it. To hold it up for everyone to see. But right now, it's only a feeling. *My* feeling. And I can't promise you that it's right." I turn to look at Jasper. "Also, technically, I don't think Quentin was going to saw open my brain." I smile, trying to lighten the mood. It's not working.

"Do you think this is some kind of joke?" he snaps.

"Listen, you don't even have to come—"

"Don't give me that bullshit," he says. And he is angry. Angry because he is worried. "Obviously, I'm going to come. And you know it."

Do I know that? Did I realize that when I made Jasper drive me here? Maybe.

I will do this on my own, there's no question about that. But I would prefer to have somebody with me when I knock on this door. And I would prefer for that person to be Jasper. I feel how much he wants to hear that. He needs me to say it: that I want him with me.

"To be clear, I would like you to come with me. *You* specifically because I trust you and you make me feel . . . better." I wince. Wow, for someone who can feel everyone else's feelings, I am still shit at talking about my own. Even the ones that I am willing to admit, which—I am beginning to realize—may be far less than their true sum. "But I won't be mad if you don't come. And you won't be abandoning me. I can and I will do this on my own."

Jasper looks up at me out of the corner of his eye, then ahead again through the windshield. Finally, he nods. His anger has vanished, replaced by a faint twinge of satisfaction. And warmth. That was exactly what he needed me to say. And there it is: the first time that I've used what I know from being an Outlier to make someone feel good, to make things better. For a moment it lifts the heaviness off everything. For a second, it gives me hope.

IT STARTS TO rain as we climb out of the car. Huge, scattered drops plunk to the ground as Jasper and I lift our hoods and follow the little blue dot on his shielded phone through several more rights and lefts, deeper still into the maze of narrow Cambridge streets. The stormy blue-black sky makes it seem much later than four p.m.

When we finally turn onto Gullbright Lane, the sky opens and it begins to pour. Jasper tucks his phone into his jeans, trying to protect it from the rain as we dash down the street looking for number 323. People have newspapers over their heads, jackets pulled up as they sprint for cover. I'm glad for the rain, though. Now everyone is running from something.

Finally we spot 323, about halfway down the block. A narrow, run-down, pale-blue Victorian divided—judging from the buzzers—into five apartments, the lower windows covered from inside in some kind of brown paper. We hover under the short awning as I dig out Kendall's note with the code.

I'm shaky as I step forward to the panel of buzzers stacked up in a row, each with a small number taped alongside. I try not to think about what will happen. Maybe I will ring all those buzzers in the order Kendall said, and everyone in the building will burst angrily to the door. And who could they be? My fingers are trembling as I punch the first button and then the next.

I hold my breath until I am done. Then I wait for the door to spring open, for some terrible possibility I haven't even considered. But nothing happens. The door doesn't open. No one jumps out. There is only silence.

"Try it again," Jasper says, which surprises me. I'd have thought he'd be happy for any excuse to turn around.

And so I press the buttons again in the order Kendall's note instructed. This time I hold each number for longer. My finger is still on the last button when the door finally opens. But only a crack. Whoever is inside has left the chain across.

"What?" A male voice, deep and aggravated. On the upside, at least he didn't come charging out the door.

"Um, we're here to see Joseph Conrad," I say.

It feels reckless, like I'm taping a target to our backs. And yet—a bigger part of me is pushing onward.

"What?" the voice barks.

"Joseph Conrad?" I offer again.

The door snaps shut without a reply. There are voices inside, followed by other sounds: cabinets opening and closing, footsteps. A beat later the door opens again, this time a little wider and without the chain. But more like someone forgot to be sure that it was all the way closed than an actual invitation.

I look over my shoulder at Jasper. If he tries to stop us again I might listen. But he nods a little—*go ahead*—and so I push open the door with one spread-fingered hand all the way until it bumps back against the wall to be sure there is no one hiding back there.

I take a deep breath as I step into the darkness inside. The smell hits me first. Mildew and dust and something else, thick and rotten. My throat clamps shut and I try not to gag.

"Hurry up," comes a voice to our right in front of the blotted-out windows. "And close the goddamn door."

In the dim light, I can make out only a short, slight outline. He sounds super pissed, but at least he isn't huge.

"You sure?" Jasper asks.

I nod, though I am not sure that I am sure, and motion for Jasper to close the door.

"Come on, come on," the small guy says, stepping from directly in front of the window so we can see something of his face now. He has messy, shoulder-length hair and a bony face. He's wearing oversized clothes—a green denim army jacket and super-low, baggy jeans. Massive black gauges stretch out his earlobes. Both the clothes and his angry voice seem meant to make up for his size. He's waving us toward the back of the room. "Let's go. Hurry up."

He was expecting us—or somebody like us—but he's also annoyed that we're there. He heads past us toward the back of the room and jerks open a door. Dim light from a stairway down brightens the room. I can see now he is even younger than I thought. And smaller.

"Hello?" he snaps, waving us toward the steps. "Come on, let's go. They're down there."

Jasper peers in the direction of the stairs without taking another step. "They who?"

"Fuck off," the kid spits back, like he's sure Jasper is messing with him. He pulls himself tall, too, for emphasis. Or taller. "Get down there now or get the fuck out."

Jasper makes a noise then: something between a huff and a laugh. Then he closes the space between them and I think: *don't Jasper*. This will not end well. But he is already looming over the jittery kid with the stretched-out ears.

"What did you just say?" Jasper asks.

The kid leans in. Stupidly unintimidated. "I said: get down there or—"

Jasper has grabbed him by the throat. In one hand. And so fast and sudden that I have to blink to believe what I am seeing. But there is Jasper, this small kid's neck locked under the fingers of one hand. He has him lifted, too. On his toes. It is not the first time that Jasper has done this either. He is too good at it. A complete and terrifying natural.

"Jasper," I whisper.

Finally, he loosens his grip a little and the kid starts to cough.

"Who is down there?" Jasper barks.

But instead of answering there's a flash of movement as the kid's arm jerks back and then forward.

Then: stillness.

The kid has his arm outstretched, a short knife only inches from Jasper's neck.

"Stop!" I shout, staring at that knife so close to Jasper's skin. This is all my fault.

Jasper raises his hands in surrender. He is afraid now, I can feel it. But not nearly as afraid as he should be. "Okay, man, I don't—"

"Shut the fuck up!" the kid screams, his voice shrieky and wild. "Asshole, do you *not* fucking see that I am the one with the goddamn knife?"

It's when the kid readjusts his grip on the knife that I notice the tattoo on his hand. A grid of nine black circles arranged in a perfect square. I have seen something like that before. Where?

When? Who? Then it comes to me. On the neck of one of the two men we passed coming out of the main cabin up at the camp. Level99. Hacktivists, that's what Quentin called them.

I have to think. I have use what I can feel to help Jasper. What is it that this kid is worried about? What is it that he actually wants? What can I do to get Jasper away from him in one piece? I try to see past his fear to what lies beneath. *Concentrate. Concentrate.* Not to fuck it up. That's what this kid wants, to prove to Level99 that he should get promoted off the door. But he is scared. And fear can make a person do anything.

"Level99 is expecting us," I say. "You can ask them. My name is Wylie." It's a risk. Despite Kendall's note, I seriously doubt they're expecting us. But this kid won't check. He's too worried about bothering them. "We're supposed to be here. We knew the code. They'll be pissed if we don't show up."

The kid keeps his eyes locked on Jasper, knife still right at his throat. "Then go," he says. "Get the hell downstairs."

I tug gently on Jasper's arm, trying to get him to move. "Come on, Jasper. Let's go. They're waiting."

THE STAIRS ARE narrow and uneven and creak hard underfoot. I brace myself against the walls as I make my way down, feeling both better and worse with every step. Better that the knife is farther away, worse that we are getting more and more trapped inside this house. And I realize then that it doesn't even matter if Kendall was telling us to come here because he truly believed we should. Doesn't matter if he was telling the truth. Kendall had no way of knowing exactly what would happen once we got here. What that kid would do. How I would respond. How Jasper would.

Outlier Rule #4: Someone telling the truth—isn't the same thing as them being right about what will happen.

Behind me, Jasper is breathing hard.

"I'm so sorry," I manage. "This is my fault."

Though the choking is on Jasper, that's for sure.

"Yeah," he says, more angry than I had expected. "It is."

Eventually, the stairwell opens up on one side, and when my head clears the ceiling, I lock eyes with the person seated at the desk below. It's the blond guy from the camp with the beaked nose and the dark circles under his eyes. The one with the game board on his pale, ashen arm. It's obvious he recognizes me, too. And not in a good way.

"Shit," he says, annoyed, exhausted. Like I am yet another human spill he will now be forced to clean up.

Beyond him there are a dozen young women and men sitting at a long table in the center of the room, headphones and hooded sweatshirts on, hunched over laptops. And beyond them is a partial wall, a light in the corner as though there might be another desk there out of view. If the people at the laptops notice us, they pretend not to. They don't even look up. It is stuffy and dim down there, and there's a distinctly sour smell—too many pairs of jeans worn too many times.

"I don't know why the hell you're here," the blond guy says, sizing Jasper up as he comes into view, "but we're done with you. Period. That comes straight from her."

I am close enough now to read the newspaper clippings taped

above his desk—*Emails Surface Proving FDA Fast-tracked Profitable Painkillers over Lifesaving Cancer Meds* and *Servers Down at Oil Giant Following Spill.* There's a big white bedsheet tacked to the opposite wall with the game board spray-painted below the words: *Courage is the price that life exacts for granting peace. Amelia Earhart.*

"What 'comes straight from her'?" a girl shouts from behind the partial wall.

"I'm handling it!" the blond guy shouts back with an edge. Like he and the girl are already in a fight about something else. "You don't want to come out here. Trust me."

"Oh, please," comes the snorted response.

When the girl finally emerges, she is petite but muscular, wearing boyfriend jeans and a snug white tank top that sets off her crimson lace bra and her olive skin. Her black hair is held up in a high, thick ponytail, and she has piercings that run the length of one ear. Near her collarbone, she has the same game board tattoo.

"Riel, you didn't have to come out here," the blond guy growls at her. "I'm handling it."

"Handling it," she snorts again, like that's the most absurd thing she's ever heard. "And thanks for telling her my name, asshole. Well done."

The blond guy frowns and looks down.

When Riel turns in my direction, her eyes search my face so intensely that it feels like she's climbed inside me and is busy inspecting my internal organs. Contempt, that's what I read when she's done. But it is so complete that it seems weirdly suspect. Most people usually feel more than one thing at any given time.

"Who are you?" she asks finally. Her eyebrows bunch sharply when I stay silent. That's when she glances up and notices my hair—which I can only imagine now looks full-on insane. "What's wrong with you? Why aren't you talking?" She's still pointing at me when she turns back to the blond guy. "Does she not talk?"

"She's the one from the camp," he says, like this alone explains everything. And in a way I suppose it does. "Her dad's the scientist. You know, she's the 'Outlier.'" He hooks quotes in the air as he shakes his head. "I told you not to come out here."

Of course they've got opinions about me. Level99 were the ones combing through all our personal data, heading off my dad's texts. They might know more about me than I know about myself.

"Nothing Quentin told you was true," I begin. But when Riel spins around, her wide-eyed fury knocks the wind out of me. "I just mean whatever he told you about what he was doing up at that camp. It wasn't what he said."

Riel starts to laugh, then bats her eyelashes viciously. "No. Fucking. Way." Like I'm the idiot. But however angry she is at me, she is even angrier at Quentin. I can feel that much. "What was the giveaway for you? Your dead friend or the eleven people somebody shot?"

"Twelve," I say, trying not to flinch. It's a small thing, but I don't like the idea that she's getting the number of people they found wrong. "Twelve people were shot."

"Sure, if you count your friend as one of them," she says, rolling her eyes. "I said shot, not dead. And, personally, I wouldn't want to group her with the rest of those psychos."

I want this not to matter, this inconsistency. But it was something that I had my dad follow up on specifically. I kept holding out hope that Lexi or Miriam had made it out alive. I wanted hard numbers. Real facts. But then sometimes the police count the "shooter" among the dead and sometimes not—there could be a totally logical reason for this inconsistency.

"Whatever." Riel shakes her head when I stay silent. And for a split second she feels sorry for me. A little guilty, too, about what happened to Cassie. But it's just a flash and then it's gone.

"Kendall told me to come here," I say. "I don't know if you met him at the camp, but he—"

"Kendall?" She steps forward and points a furious finger right in my face. "Did that lunatic follow you here? Because if he did, I swear to God, I will have your ass kicked." She nods her head in the direction of the blond guy, who seems to accept this as his role: head ass-kicker.

I feel Jasper shift behind me like a guard dog ready to lunge. *Not again*, I think, *not yet*.

"Kendall wouldn't have to follow us," I say carefully. "He's the one who gave me this address."

"Goddamn it!" Riel shouts, putting her hands to her head. "Well, we can't stay here then." She's not talking to me anymore.

"Seriously?" the blond guy asks. Disappointed, not concerned. He looks around. "I like this place."

Riel takes a deep, exasperated breath, then turns back to me.

"You come clean right now, and I mean right this goddamn

second, about why and how you're helping Kendall, and maybe I won't drain your dad's bank account."

"I'm not helping Kendall." I raise my hands like she has a knife pointed in my face. And she might as well have. I can only imagine how Level99 could wreak havoc on someone's life. "Kendall found me in the hospital and told me to come here." I hand her his note. Her eyes narrow as she looks at it. "They have this group of girls, all of them are Outliers like me, at least I'm pretty sure. I don't know how they found them or what they're planning to do to them but—"

"Wait." She holds up a hand and cocks her head to the side skeptically. "They who?"

"The NIH, I think—that's who they said was in charge. But it didn't feel like the truth, to be honest. They said we all had some kind of bioterrorist strep. There's some immunologist guy who's trying to say that it explains the Outliers."

She crosses her arms. "And you believe that?"

"No, I don't believe that," I bite back, and from the look on her face, too hard. "That's why I got out. But the other girls are still in there and I think they are seriously in danger. Like maybe they are going to get rid of them."

"And why would they want to do that?" she asks. As before, all I can feel is her deep contempt. The question is a test. Like she already knows the answer, but wants to see if I do.

"To stop this whole thing from coming out maybe. My dad was getting funding for a study that everybody would have known about. And at some point, people are going to be pissed if they can't be Outliers, right? Especially the guys." Riel rolls her eyes—I can't tell if it's directed at those "guys" or my suggestion that they exist. "Anyway, I guess Kendall thought you could help me at least get the girls out."

"Don't you think it's a little suspicious that Kendall, of all people, would try to save anybody?" she asks.

"I think maybe he regrets dropping us off at the camp."

"Oh, you don't know, do you?" Riel smiles. "Who do you think killed all those people up at that camp?"

My ears ring, and my cheeks feel hot. "That's not . . ." But I can't even muster up the stomach to defend him.

"Oh yeah, it's true. We *saw* that asshole," she goes on, pointing two fingers toward her own eyes, then at me. She can tell that she's shocked me, and she is glad. Maybe she fell for Quentin, but at least she is not as stupid as me. "We left a couple cameras up there. Because I didn't *trust* Quentin. I don't *trust* anyone." Except I can feel for a second that maybe she did trust Quentin more than she wants to admit. "I knew there was a chance some seriously bad shit was about to go down. And I mean, there are trees and whatever, so we couldn't record everything. But we saw enough. We saw Kendall stroll right into that camp with this huge freaking gun."

"Jesus," Jasper says quietly, lowering himself down into a chair.

"Oh look," Riel says, turning to Jasper like she's forgotten he was even there. "It speaks."

"But why?" I ask. And I know that's a stupid question—especially under these circumstances. But I can't help it. I need to know.

"Power. Control. Secrets. Who knows?" She waves her toned arms around. "*Kendall* probably doesn't even know exactly. Whatever shady bullshit acronym he pretends not to work for probably just told him to go forth and kill. Isn't that how all of the worst things happen? People 'just doing their jobs'? Everyone getting a little taste of evil without having to swallow down the whole monster sandwich."

"But why would he come to the hospital to warn me then?"

"How the hell do I know?" Riel snaps. And I can feel Jasper silently shouting: *exactly!* But he doesn't say a word. Then something else occurs to her. "Or maybe you were *actually* better off in there. Did you ever consider that?"

No. I won't. I can't. I still need to believe that Kendall sent us to Gullbright Lane for what he believed was a good reason. And that reason has to be saving the other girls.

"You don't have to help us," I say.

"Um, yeah, *correct*. I do not," Riel says.

"But we do *need* help. Those girls do. Because I just—"

"Let me guess, you have a bad feeling," Riel says, and she's aiming for snide. But she doesn't get all the way there. "You have fully drunk your dad's Kool-Aid, haven't you?"

And now, I'm pissed. "You know what? Fuck you," I say. "My best friend *died* at that camp. She died helping us try to get away from Quentin. And *you* helped him do that. You are responsible."

"Bullshit." Riel glares at me, but her guilt blooms like a rash. I feel her try to knock it away. "What that asshole did to you and your friend has nothing to do with me. Your dad was the one who was hiding shit. If he hadn't—"

"How can you possibly try to blame Wylie's dad?" Jasper asks. And not even angrily. Like he legitimately can't believe *Riel* believes that. "Quentin did all of that. And whatever, I get it, you thought you were doing the right thing, but you did *help* him."

And I can feel that Jasper finally believes this—maybe for the first time: that Quentin killed Cassie; that he is not to blame. If we get out of this basement in one piece, at least he will take that with him.

"No, no, no." Riel waves a finger. "That asshole Quentin lied to us, same as he lied to you." She is bothered that he was able to, though, more ashamed than she is letting on. "It happens. Nobody's perfect."

"Nobody's perfect?" I ask. And I hope I sound as disgusted as I feel. "Cassie is dead. And all those other people—"

"You're going to try to blame that shit on us, too?!" the blond guy shouts. He recoils when Riel shoots him a look.

I stare at Riel until she finally looks back at me. Contempt once again—flawless and complete. And hard like molded plastic. I am not going to be able to force her to do anything she does not want to do. I'll have to hope she changes her mind.

"Listen, there is a doctor at the hospital named Alvarez and another one named Haddox," I say. "And the professor guy is named Cornelia, and he works at Metropolitan New York Hospital. You can check it all out yourself. If there's anybody who deserves your help, it's those girls. They're all at Boston General Hospital."

18

WE WALK QUICKLY, AND IN SILENCE, AWAY FROM LEVEL99'S HOUSE. IT ISN'T until we're a block away that Jasper finally slows down. He had been even more worried in there than I realized. The fear is buzzing off him.

"You okay?" he asks when we are almost at the car. Like he is totally fine.

I nod. Then shrug. Then shake my head. "I had my hopes up higher than I realized. I thought following Kendall's note was going to explain everything."

"On the upside is the whole not being stabbed thing," he says, feeling bad, *really* bad that he escalated things. "I shouldn't have—I don't know why I grabbed him like that. I haven't done something like that in a long time."

"Yeah, that was, kind of—"

"Messed up," he says. "Sorry."

"Well, it was my fault we were in there in the first place."

Jasper smiles. "That's true."

His phone rings as he's unlocking the Jeep. He looks down, confused by the number. "Hello?" His face tightens as he answers. "No. Who's this?" A pause. "Um, because *you* called *my* phone?"

"Is it the woman who has my dad's phone?" I ask. I can imagine her jumping in without much explanation.

He shakes his head. "Yeah, Wylie's right here." He sounds offended. Rachel. I can hear her still talking as he hands me the phone. "Wow, she's a delight."

I take the phone and brace myself.

"Rachel?"

"Wylie!" she shouts. "What is going on? I just got your message. What do you mean your dad is missing?" She is way more worried than I want her to be. Also, it's obvious she knows nothing. "I tried his phone and some *lunatic* answered. She tried to extort cash out of me. What is going on? Are you okay?"

"Yes." But this isn't the time to be putting on a brave face. "I mean, I'm not hurt or anything. But I do need your help. Can we come see you?"

"Of course, of course." And I feel so grateful now that Rachel stuck around despite all the times I tried to kick her out of our lives. "You want me to meet you?"

"No, we'll come to you."

"Okay. I'm at the office. I'll be here waiting. And don't worry, Wylie. We'll work it out. Whatever it is."

WE PARK IN a run-down strip mall on the far edge of Boston. The lot is dotted with potholes, and two of the eight storefronts are empty. Four of the others have signs that look like they're from the 1970s—a dollar store, a hardware store, and a nail salon. There's a huge Michaels, too, shiny and brand-new; it looks like it was mistakenly dropped from a great height.

"Are you sure this is the place?" Jasper asks, looking around.

"This is the address Rachel gave me." I study the row of stores. "Maybe it's that one over there."

"Sorry, let me ask that question another way," Jasper says. "Didn't you say she was like super successful and went to Harvard Law School? How did she end up working here?"

I realize now that I don't know Rachel's whole story, only bits and pieces.

"Rachel used to be some kind of corporate attorney. My mom called her a 'fixer.' And she didn't mean that in a good way," I say. "But she defends people pro bono now. Trying to make amends for all the bad people she helped, and all the money she made. That's what my dad says. Oh, there it is, over there," I say, finally spotting a simple black-and-yellow sign that is identical to the nail salon's next door: *Rachel O'Callahan, Attorney-at-Law.*

THE DOOR IS locked when we reach it. There's a small handwritten sign taped inside that says *RING BELL.* It's a Sunday, after all. When I do, a crackly voice comes out garbled through the lopsided intercom.

"It's Wylie Lang to see Rachel!" I shout back, hoping they will understand me.

But there's just more loud crackling. I try again.

"It's Wylie Lang!" I shout a second time.

More crackling, even louder. Like whoever is on the other side is shouting now. The voice cuts off when the door buzzes open.

The waiting room is not much nicer than the outside of the office. Actually, it might be worse. There are a half-dozen cheap-looking folding chairs and an empty reception desk. Wood paneling and a linoleum floor. It smells of mildew.

"Um." Jasper starts looking around like he's got a lot to say but can't figure out where to start.

"Coming! Coming!" Rachel calls from down the dark hall, her voice an unmistakable mix of Boston and Brooklyn.

"Are you returning, Ms. O'Callahan?" a man calls after her. He steps out of Rachel's office and drifts in our direction. "Or should I just . . ."

"Sorry!" Rachel calls, though her eyes stay locked on me. "But I'll have to reschedule our prep session for later this evening, Doctor."

"Well, I'm sorry, but that won't be convenient for me." He sounds insulted. When he finally emerges from the dark hall, he is short and gray haired with a bulbous nose and huge ears. He has a thick unsightly scar on his throat, near his Adam's apple.

"I have you on a twenty-thousand-dollar retainer, Doctor. Paid out of my own pocket," Rachel shoots back, not even turning his way. "I decide what's convenient. I'll be in touch."

Once the doctor huffs out, Rachel locks the door behind him.

"Come on," she says. "Let's go back to my office. It's more comfortable in there."

RACHEL'S OFFICE IS indeed nicer than the rest of the place, if only a little. It's brighter and cleaner with new, cheap carpeting and the wood paneling is painted white.

"Okay, now, what the hell is going on?" She motions for us to sit in the worn wooden guest chairs facing her desk.

I'm so relieved to be there, but as soon as I open my mouth, my throat squeezes tight. I will myself to keep it together. "My dad was supposed to call you—"

It's too late. Already, I'm crying.

"Oh, sweetheart." Rachel jumps up and comes around the desk. She puts a hand on each of my arms, then shoots an accusatory look Jasper's way. Like he is somehow to blame. "Why was he supposed to call me? I never talked to him. Tell me what's going on."

And so I begin again, breaking down everything that has happened. I talk for at least five minutes without taking a breath. When I finally get to the part about calling my dad, Rachel stops me.

"So he was in the airport when you spoke to him?" she asks. "And then his phone ended up somewhere else in DC?"

I nod. "Yeah," I say. "There's no sign of him at home either, and he never came to the hospital. And he would have come if he could have."

"Of course he would have." Rachel goes to stand behind her desk. Then crosses her arms as she sits back down. She is *very* worried, though she is doing her best to seem not the least bit concerned. "Okay, well, at least his phone didn't turn up in Florida."

"Florida?"

"Oh, that blogger," she says, waving off her own suggestion. But now all I can think about is EndOfDays.com. "Sorry, I shouldn't have brought that up. Your dad wasn't worried about that. You shouldn't be. And this is going to be okay, Wylie. We'll find him. Do you know who he was meeting with in DC or what flight he was on?"

"The NIH and some senator, I don't remember his name. Something with an *R.* Russell or something like that. My dad was going to leave all his information at the house," I say. "But I don't even know if it's still there."

For the first time it occurs to me that my dad's itinerary and my house being trashed could be related.

"What do you mean?" Rachel asks.

"I went by earlier," Jasper says, then hesitates. "The house is kind of . . . It's trashed. Someone tore the place apart."

"What about Gideon?" Rachel asks.

"He doesn't know anything," I say. "He and my dad had a fight yesterday and he hasn't been back home. I called the police and told them that my dad is missing, but I don't think they are going to do anything about it. He hasn't been gone long enough."

"Okay." Rachel puts her two hands flat on the desk like she is about to push herself up to standing. Instead she looks me square in the eye. "We're going to find your dad and he is going to be fine."

"We need to get the other girls out, too."

"Of course," she says. "We'll sort out whatever this business is with the hospital. We will nail the people responsible."

But it's far down on her list, I can tell.

"No. I mean now," I say. "They're in danger."

"Danger?" Rachel asks, skeptical. "Like physical danger?"

"Something like that, I think." I hope she doesn't press me for proof. "And I didn't even warn them. I didn't tell them anything.

If you won't help me, I can go back there myself."

"Whoa, Wylie." She holds up her hands. "I'll do whatever I can to get the other girls out. But first I'm going to call the police about your dad. I'll see if I can find the itinerary at your house and we'll get him tracked down." She is all calm matter-of-factness now. "Then we'll deal with this situation at the hospital. I have a friend at the Justice Department. He probably has a contact at the NIH. Always helps to have an inside line. But I am on it, I promise." And for the first time since we left the hospital, I feel my body loosen the tiniest bit. "And listen, if worse comes to worst, we'll use your mom's journalist contacts to apply some pressure. The threat of a headline can be extremely motivating."

"Thank you," I say, and in that I hope she also hears: *especially because I was always such a bitch to you.*

"Of course," she says. Then her brow wrinkles. "Wait, so how did you get out of the hospital?"

"There was a girl I was with—she and I decided to pull the fire alarm," I say, making a point of not looking at Jasper. He knows I am deliberately leaving Kendall out as a contributing factor. Rachel would disapprove of Kendall's role in all this even more than Jasper does. "But then it seems like there was an actual fire. Everyone was kind of unprepared and freaking out. Even the guards. I was able to sneak out, but I'm not sure Kelsey did."

"Wait, there was a fire at the hospital?" Rachel asks.

"Yeah," I say. "I mean, I don't know for sure because I took off. But the alarm went off and I smelled smoke, and firefighters came."

"That's an odd coincidence," Rachel says. And she is suspicious, but I'm not sure of what or whom.

"What do you mean, a coincidence?" Jasper asks.

Rachel doesn't look at him. Instead, she keeps her eyes on me. "I mean, after the fire at the camp."

19

JASPER AND I RIDE THE T TOWARD BEACON HILL AND RACHEL'S BROWNSTONE. The few people on the early-evening Sunday train look so ordinary, reading their newspapers, fixated on their phones. Going about their day as if nothing is amiss. I envy them.

Rachel had insisted we go to her house. That she would handle looking into everything. I tried to argue with her, but she did have a point. If there are people from the NIH—or whoever—looking for me, I should stay out of sight.

As soon as I'd agreed, Rachel moved fast getting into details. Extra keys to her house, a card with all her numbers written down, a spare burner phone. She called it that too: "a burner." Apparently, this was not the first time she'd helped someone disappear. Rachel convinced us to ditch Jasper's car on a side street and take the train to her house. We were supposed to stay there until she came for us.

"Out of an abundance of caution, I'd keep that off as much as possible." She had pointed to Jasper's phone. "They'd first have to connect you with Jasper and then realize you're together to use it to find you. It's a long shot, but not impossible. Never ceases to amaze me what the government can accomplish when it wants to. And yet how little it gets done most of the time." The last thing she did was hand us a thick stack of twenties that she'd pulled out of a drawer. They were stiff and brand-new when she pressed them into my hand. "Definitely don't use a credit card, Wylie. They'll find you that way in a heartbeat."

And just like that, we were officially on the run. Again.

I'm startled back when Jasper puts his hand on my shoulder. "This is our stop," he says as the train rocks to a halt.

IT TAKES US a while to find Rachel's house in picturesque Beacon Hill with its fashionable storefronts and pristine brownstones. Her street is only a couple off Newbury, but without GPS, we walk in the wrong direction for a while trying to find it. We're about to give up and power up Jasper's phone for its map when I finally spot a bright-white house with a gas lantern out front—exactly as Rachel described. It's only a few houses down.

"Wait, I think that's it," I say, picking up the pace. "Down here."

I walk quickly ahead until I am in front of number 729—a massive, immaculately restored brownstone nestled behind two huge trees. It's the closest thing to a mansion that the city of Boston has to offer.

"Wow," Jasper says when he comes to stand next to me. He

sounds afraid to go inside as his eyes roll up and down the facade. "That's a super-nice house."

"Yeah, it is," I say, and there's no denying it, especially compared to her office. I don't want to be bothered by the disconnect, but it makes me uneasy. "Crazy nice."

INSIDE, RACHEL'S PLACE is even fancier than outside, restored historical details mixed with chic industrial furniture. The front of the living room has two huge floor-to-ceiling windows, one wall of exposed brick, and dark wood floors, which probably cost more to make look so knotty and worn.

"She lives here by herself?" Jasper asks, looking around at the vast emptiness. He's still trying to figure out Rachel. So am I.

"Yeah," I say. "As far as I know."

"As far as you know? I thought she was your mom's best friend?"

"She used to be. That's what I said." I don't want to explain Rachel's weird split with my mom, or her reappearing out of nowhere. If Jasper makes me examine it again up close, I will get suspicious. Too suspicious to let her help. And we need Rachel right now. My dad definitely does.

Jasper is still looking around the inside of her beautiful house. "Did that freak you out at all, the way she was all ready for us with a go bag?"

"She's a defense attorney."

"Um, yeah," Jasper says. "But I don't think they're supposed to help their clients get away."

"I'm going to take a shower," I say, because Rachel said we

could and I feel gross. Also, I desperately want to end this conversation. Jasper's points are too valid. "Don't break anything."

I STAND FOREVER in Rachel's fancy spa shower, trying to wash away the hospital. Soon my time locked up there starts to feel like some kind of weird, invented memory. Something I might even forget if it weren't for how responsible I feel for the girls I left behind.

After the shower, I head to Rachel's bedroom to change into the clothes she insisted I borrow. She said I could take whatever I wanted. Her massive walk-in closet is like its own perfectly arranged boutique, the expensive clothes all well spaced and nicely lit. There are dozens of built-in cubbies, too, each with only one pair of shoes. I've never seen anything like it, and it is completely overwhelming. I close the closet and turn to Rachel's large bureau, hoping there might be something less intimidating in there.

Sure enough there are jeans, but buttery and soft in a way I was not aware denim could be. Still, they are my best option. I pull out a pair and move on, hoping to find a nonthreatening T-shirt of some kind. It isn't until I dig way to the bottom of the second stack of shirts that I feel something like plain old cotton. As I'm pulling it out my fingers hit on something hard at the bottom of the drawer. I pull the T-shirts back and look. It's a small square box like the kind an expensive bracelet might come in.

Why would someone who lives alone be hiding a box at the bottom of her drawer? Who would she be hiding it from? I am about to pull it out and investigate, but something stops me. It's none of my business. Rachel is helping us. I don't want to jeopardize that by snooping through her things.

WHEN I GET back downstairs, Jasper is sound asleep on the couch. He's propped up stiff—feet square on the floor, arms tightly crossed. Only his head is tilted a little off to the side, mouth open slightly. I take a pillow off the bright-white couch opposite him. When I tuck it under his head, he shifts and leans into it in his sleep.

I watch him for a minute. It's easier to look right at him with his eyes closed. I am glad he is there, more than I am ready to admit. And not because I need him. I don't need him, not like that. I just want him here, which—it turns out—is actually way more unnerving.

I sit down on the couch across from him and dig out Kelsey's copy of *1984* stowed in the getaway tote Rachel gave us. There isn't anything else but to wait for Rachel to call with news. This time I start reading at the beginning.

Gabrielle and Kelsey had the benefit of each other for their haphazard trial and error, but I had the benefit of knowing that what I was doing—what I was feeling—was real, an actual scientifically verifiable thing. Because there are a bunch of places in the book where Kelsey and Gabrielle wonder whether they are making the whole thing up, imagining it. Whether they both might even be losing their minds.

I skip ahead until I get to the word *BLOCKING*, in all caps and boxed with several deep, dark lines. Followed by four numbered points:

1) BELIEVE THE LIE 2) Imagine a box 3) put your feelings in that box 4) stare at the flat black top, think of the box (only the box). G

But how are you supposed to do that while you're having a conversation with someone? K

IDK. Practice? G

From how good Kelsey seemed in the hospital at blocking, they must have figured it out eventually.

I try to do it myself now: I close my eyes and imagine pushing all my feelings into a box. I stare at the top of the black box. Try to think of only that. After a minute, I do feel emptied out, though I have no way of knowing if I've done it right, not without Kelsey here to try to read me. As much as I want to pretend that I have a leg up because of what I know from my dad, it feels more important that I am alone.

On a diagonal below the bit about the blocking I find the following: *Knowledge or cognition without evident rational thought. Intuition—as defined by Merriam-Webster's Dictionary.*

They figured out what I have: HEP is more than just reading people's emotions. Already practice has made me better. The real question is how much better we can get. What's the limit of what we can do.

I flip through the rest of the book to the end pages, which are filled with notes. Not all of it is about reading either. There are some exchanges about friends; some girl named Sarah on the volleyball team was causing Kelsey all sorts of problems—she made up a rumor that Kelsey had had sex with somebody who was married and old and, most importantly, totally disgusting.

There's something about Gabrielle's new-at-the-time boy-friend—a point of testiness between the two girls. His name is Leo Berkowitz, and he's a rower on the Harvard crew team, which Kelsey somehow makes seem like an insult the way she hurls it at her sister. A stupid cliché to date a "college guy," and, "ew, Harvard, gross."

But I know neediness when I see it. Kelsey is covering up for feeling abandoned. She's obviously hardened in the time since, because I can't imagine the Kelsey I met clinging to anybody. Later there is a mention of Kelsey getting high and Gabrielle not approving. *Drugs* I can imagine. There's a note from G: *I'm worried about you.*

The boyfriend is my first tangible lead back to Kelsey: Har-vard University, crew team, Leo Berkowitz. If I can find Leo, maybe I can find Gabrielle. I have a fantasy that Kelsey is already with her. If not, surely her sister will want to help me get Kelsey out.

I want to jump off the couch right now and run to Harvard to find Leo. But I should at least wait until I hear from Rachel about my dad, which is where Rachel's energy should really be focused.

Having reached the end of the book, I flip to the inside of the back cover, where my eyes land on another exchange enclosed by a dark, black box.

Snuck into the test!!! It was way too easy. That researcher guy may be super good at science, but he sucks ass at security. The creepy Dr. Caton guy totally bought my lost Univ. ID story!! K

My heart is pounding as my eyes search the rest of the page. Until finally I find it: AN OUTLIER. And then it says: WHAT THE HELL DOES THAT EVEN MEAN?

I'm still staring at the words, which are written in big block semi-hysterical letters, unlike the others, when the book slips from my hands and smacks against the floor.

Jasper, startles awake, bolting upright. "What's wrong?"

"Sorry, I dropped something," I say. "It's okay."

He sinks back against the couch and rubs at his eyes with the heels of his palms. "What's that?"

"It's that copy of *1984*. It belongs to the girl we went back to look for. I think she was one of the other three original Outliers."

"Oh?" Jasper narrows his eyes at me. He is confused and so am I. "And this is a good thing or a bad thing?"

"I'm not sure." That's the honest truth. "I guess it depends."

"On what?"

I think then of how wary my dad was about me meeting the other two original Outliers. I had assumed he'd been worried about us drawing attention to ourselves. And the truth was, I hadn't really had any interest in meeting them. But it could have been something else. Being an Outlier definitely doesn't mean that someone is automatically worth trusting. I've met Kelsey and she wasn't exactly sunshine and light.

"It depends on whether or not she's a good person."

My burner phone rings then with what I can only hope is Rachel's number. "Hello?"

"You guys okay at the house?" she asks. She sounds nervous. Whatever she's learned in the time since we left her office, it's not good news.

"Yeah, we're fine," I say. And suddenly I am swamped by dread. I've been worried about my dad, but I've controlled it by not letting myself go there all the way. Now, my grip is slipping. "Did you find my dad?"

"Not yet." She's measuring her words. "I just left your house, though. For sure there was someone there. Jasper's right. It's a mess. The police are investigating, and for now they seem to be buying the idea that you and Gideon are out of town—at your grandmother's house, I told them. They haven't asked to talk to you yet and they didn't mention your call. Between the state of your house and some random woman having your dad's phone, they at least seem to be taking finding your dad seriously. And I did find his itinerary, buried under a bunch of other stuff."

"Oh, good." But I don't really feel relieved. "Then we can call them and—"

"I already did," she cuts me off. "Apparently, Senator Russo wasn't even in Washington yesterday and had no plans to be. They have no record of anyone from their office ever being in touch with your father either," she says, then hurries to add, "He was on that flight, though, and he did land in DC. And, like you said, fifteen minutes after he was on the ground, he booked a flight back home. But—"

"He never got on that flight back," I say, finishing her sentence.

"No, he didn't."

"So now what?" I ask, and I am gripping the phone so hard my hand is aching.

"Surveillance video and cell phone data are the next places to check. It can take a little while to get all of that, but the wheels are in motion. There's a chance I'll have to go to DC to make sure it happens. But then I could also talk to that woman who has your dad's phone. She may know more than she realizes." Rachel takes a breath and sounds exhausted when she exhales. "Now, about the girls in the hospital, I—"

"No," I say, feeling a stab of guilt. I feel bad pulling Rachel off helping the girls, but I can't have her distracted from my dad. His situation suddenly feels so much more urgent. I just hope that isn't because I know something—something terrible—I don't even realize I know. "You need to find my dad."

And the girls will be my responsibility, I think but do not say. It's only fitting, though. I am the one who left them behind.

"But you and Jasper need to stay put in the house, Wylie." Rachel is already onto me. "I mean it. I don't want you deciding to try to get the girls out on your own or something. Besides, I've already talked to my friend at the Justice Department and his contact at the NIH should be getting back to him by tomorrow morning. It is a Sunday, so we have to be a little patient. We can talk more about it when I get home. I will help the girls *and* find your dad. I'm on it. I promise. You need to sit tight."

"Okay, yeah. Yes," I say quickly. Hesitation will be fatal. "Sure."

But I stop short of actually promising we will stay put. Because that would be an outright lie.

"I'll call you if I hear anything else," Rachel says. "And you can call me here, on my cell, whenever you need."

"Okay," I say, wanting to get off the phone before I say anything incriminating.

"This is going to be okay, Wylie. I'm here and I'm going to help you. Everything will be fine."

WHEN I HANG up, I go in search of a computer to track down Leo Berkowitz. He is a place to start. He is the path to Kelsey's sister, and she is my way back to Kelsey, one of the other original three Outliers. I feel a weird flutter—part nerves, part excitement—thinking of talking to her again. I wonder if Kelsey knows?

There is Jasper's phone, which we could use to find Leo. But turning it on is unwise unless we absolutely need to. Those are instructions from Rachel that I will listen to. Luckily, it doesn't take long anyway to find a slim laptop—elegant and expensive-looking in a leather case—in the corner of Rachel's kitchen.

"What are you looking up?" Jasper asks as he makes his way over behind me. I should come clean. Leave it up to him to make his own choices. The farther we get into this the higher the stakes are rising. I'm in this until we get the girls out. Jasper doesn't have to be.

"Kelsey's sister has or had a boyfriend named Leo Berkowitz," I say. "He's on the crew team at Harvard. I want to see if I can find him. Where he lives or a phone number or something." I look up at Jasper. "To be clear, Rachel told me that she wanted us to stay here, that she would look into what's happening with my dad and the girls at the hospital. But she can't do both, and I need her looking for my dad."

"Which leaves you to go back for the girls."

I nod. "There's a chance Kelsey is already out. That's what I'm hoping, I guess. Or if she isn't, that Leo will get us to Kelsey's sister and maybe she'll have some better ideas about how to get everyone out." And I do hope that—no matter how unlikely.

Jasper looks down like he's considering. "Okay," he says finally. Like he's come to a conclusion. "If that's how you feel, that's good enough for me." He motions to the computer. "Let's go."

But when I try to turn on the computer, nothing happens.

"Shit, the battery is dead," I say. "There's got to be a cord around here somewhere."

I push off the stool and open a narrow drawer to my right. Nothing. The huge kitchen is filled with drawers and more drawers. But I need to find that cord even if it means I have to go through every inch of the house.

"I'll help," Jasper offers and the two of us start opening one mostly empty drawer after the next. "She barely has anything in here. How does she even live?"

I shrug. "Takeout."

There are only two drawers left to look in on my side, one— thin and wide—probably holds silverware. And a smaller one that is our last reasonable shot. When I jerk it open a manila envelope slides hard forward and bumps against the front of the drawer. I freeze, staring down at it. At the words written on the front: *David Rosenfeld, January 12.* Unmistakably in my mother's handwriting. Dated this year, too, right before she died. I blink once, then again. I even shake my head.

All I can think to do is close my eyes again. Hope that when I open them it will be gone. "Do you see that? In the drawer?" I manage finally.

"Um." Jasper seems more confused than anything. "You mean this?"

When I look, he has the envelope in his hand like it is nothing. No. Big. Deal. And it wouldn't be maybe if my mom and Rachel had been in touch anytime in the past five years.

"Will you check what's in it?" I ask.

"Sure," Jasper says, but more hesitantly now. He pulls something out of the envelope and squints down at it. "They're photographs: a building, a few people. Do you want to see them?"

"Those are my mom's," I say, my voice trembling. "Rachel shouldn't have them."

Breathe, I tell myself as I stare down. But my lungs feel encased in cement. I grip the counter hard to steady myself.

"Is it possible your dad gave them to her?" Jasper offers.

"No," I say.

Because I do not believe for one second that's actually what happened. Finally, I get myself to take the envelope from Jasper, but still I do not look inside.

Instead, I move quickly out of the kitchen, opening every drawer I pass—the ones in the living room bookcase and then the foyer. Furniture, built-ins. Anything with a knob I can tug on.

"What are you looking for?" Jasper asks, following behind me. I can tell that he wants to know only so that he can help.

"For something else she shouldn't have," I say.

Like maybe something in a box shoved at the way bottom of her T-shirt drawer. I turn for the stairs.

"Where are you going?" Jasper shouts as I race up.

"She has this weird box in her drawer," I call back when Jasper finally catches up to me in Rachel's bedroom. I yank open her bureau and feel around underneath her clothes.

My hands tremble as I pull the box out. Even more so when I lift the lid.

Inside is a ring. A plain silver band like so many others. But when I peer closer, I can see words etched inside, part of a longer Yeats poem about love that I recognize. Because the whole poem is a piece of history. My history. My parents' history. The first half—*I would ride with you upon the wind*—is engraved in my father's wedding ring. The second half—*And dance upon the mountains like a flame*—is in my mother's ring.

And that's the ring sitting here now in Rachel's drawer.

20

IT TAKES US A WHILE TO GET TO HARVARD'S SPRAWLING CAMPUS, AND EVEN longer to find the information center. It is a little past eight p.m. when we finally get inside. We luck out on the woman behind the desk, a friendly grandmotherly type who seems not the least bit concerned that two random people want to know where any crew team members might hang out on campus during summer. Instead, she points us in the direction of the MAC, the Malkin Athletic Center, where some of the crew team apparently sometimes works out, even during the off-season. (The woman behind the desk does not approve of such a strenuous, year-round schedule—that much is clear.) We just have to hope that Leo is one of those summer holdovers.

We walk in silence across the dark, quiet campus, headed—at least we hope—in the direction of the MAC. Twice I stop to ask where it is, and both times we discover that we have gotten off course. Not terribly, but enough that it feels like a bad sign. Like maybe we will walk on and on in circles and never actually get anywhere.

Jasper doesn't point out how unlikely it is that this little excursion to the Harvard student gym will result in us finding Leo. Never mind the even slimmer chance that Leo will lead to Kelsey's sister. Or that Kelsey's sister will lead us to Kelsey. Or that all of us together will get the girls out of the hospital.

Jasper hasn't said one negative or discouraging word since we left Rachel's house. But I can feel how much he is thinking them. There is a part of me that wonders if he might even be right. The bigger part of me—the part of me that *feels*—knows, though, that we are headed in the exact right direction. That we have to be.

The endless walking does give me an unfortunate amount of time to think about my dead mother's ring somehow ending up in her ex–best friend's drawer, though. I'm glad I took it with me, that I am wearing it now on the chain Teresa gave me. And the photographs, too, stuffed into the tote bag on my shoulder. There is some comfort, at least, in having them close to me. Like I've just rescued some small part of my mom.

But rescued her from what? What could the ring and the photographs have been doing there in Rachel's house? When my mind drifts toward explanations, they are all too awful to let myself linger. The only thing I know for sure is that Rachel is hiding something.

The MAC is finally in sight when the burner phone rings

again. It's Rachel, of course. She's the only one who knows that phone number. Without a voice mail, the phone rings forever. A moment after it finally stops, a text comes instead.

Where are you? it reads. **I just got home.**

I take a breath and think about tossing the phone. But what if she's found out something about my dad? Whether or not she'll answer me truthfully, I have no idea. I don't know what Rachel's motives are for anything anymore. But I have to at least try.

Did you find my dad?

Not yet. You should be here Wylie. Where r u?

I think about sending her a nasty note back, telling her that I found the ring and the pictures. That I know she's lying about something. A lot probably. Telling her off would just feel good in the moment, though. I'm better off not revealing what I know.

Had to do something, I type, and it's slow going on that phone. **Be back soon. Sorry.**

No. Not safe. Come back.

"Rachel?" Jasper asks when I turn off the phone and jam it awkwardly into my pocket. "Do you honestly think she's involved in all this somehow?"

Is that what I think? No, not exactly. Something bad and deceitful, but not exactly that.

"I don't know," I say. "But something is not right."

THE HUGE, GLEAMING Malkin Athletic Center is buzzing with life when we finally get there. At the main desk inside is a heavyset, round-faced kid with hair hanging in his face, eyes fixed on his lap at what I'm guessing is his phone hidden from view. There's a big, unfortunate sign on the counter next to him that reads *No Admittance Without Proper University ID.*

"Hi," I say when the kid still does not look up.

"Yeah?" he asks and not at all in a friendly way.

Shame, that's what I feel when his eyes finally flick in my direction. There is no mistaking it. Like maybe we caught him surfing porn. But his shame feels less specific than that. For sure, he wants us to disappear. No, wait. That's not it. He wants for *him* to disappear.

"We're looking for my brother, Leo Berkowitz. He's on the crew team." I worked out the lie right after we left Rachel's house. And I feel pretty good about it. "There's been a family emergency. Leo's phone is off, and I can't find him. I know he comes here a lot."

Family emergency sounds like death or serious injury and is also vague enough to discourage follow-up questions.

"You got ID?" The kid points toward the sign. He is totally and completely unmoved.

"Um, I don't go to school here, so how would I have ID?" I ask slowly, trying to read my way through to this kid. Trying to figure out what might make me more sympathetic, make him more likely to help. But I am coming up empty. Like maybe nothing will. "I only want to run into the weight room and see if Leo is there or if anyone's seen him. It'll only take a second. Like I said, it's a *family* emergency."

But the kid is already shaking his head again. He points to the sign again. "No ID, no inside," he says, pleased with himself and the certainty of his job.

"Then could *you* go in the weight room and see if he's there?

Or if anyone knows where he is?" I ask. This is not my first choice, but I'll take it. I need to find Leo.

The kid makes a kind of snorting noise. "No way."

Ah, *that's* what his shame is about. The students who use the center. The athletes. At some point, he was harassed, made a fool of, casually abused by some big, muscular guys in that weight room. And ever since, he's kept his head so far down his forehead is attached to the floor. Or something like that. I'll have to use it, too. It's all I have.

"You know they'll do something *way* worse to you when they find out that you didn't let me see Leo," I say. "I mean, it *is* a family emergency. And they are his friends, right?"

The kid looks up wide-eyed, then pissed off. He is in a lose-lose situation now and he knows it. Finally, he shrugs like he doesn't even care anymore. Even though I can feel that he actually cares more than ever.

"Fine, but you only." He points to Jasper, then to the wall some distance away. "He waits over there."

I nod to Jasper before heading quickly back toward the glass-walled weight room, afraid the kid might change his mind. I practice what I plan to say to Leo again in my head. *I need to find your girlfriend. Something has happened to her sister.* And then he'll have questions, no doubt. I'll have to tell him the truth, no matter how unbelievable.

THROUGH THE GLASS window of the insanely huge weight room, I can see more than a dozen people—mostly bulky men, but a few women—making their way through reps on machines and with free weights.

When I finally step inside, the whole room does not screech to a halt like I'm afraid it will. No one even seems to notice me. I look around for someone who could be Leo, now wishing I'd stuck around Rachel's long enough to find that computer cord and search up a picture or two of him. It had seemed so much more important to get out. And more important than ever not to use Jasper's phone.

"Um, do any of you know where I can find Leo Berkowitz?" I call out.

No one even glances my way. I wonder if maybe I didn't actually speak. Until I meet eyes with one guy in the far corner, who shakes his head at his lifting partner. When the partner turns, I see he has on a Harvard crew T-shirt. He is sinewy and tall, his dark hair buzzed so tight that it looks gray. And he just looks like an ass. Not Leo. At least I hope not. He is way too far away to get a read on.

"Come on." A girl has appeared next to me. She is broad shouldered and tall, nearly six feet of pure muscle in her yellow shorts and neon-green sports bra. "Let's go. Out."

When I don't move, she puts a hand on my back and shoves.

"Hey!" I snap back at her even as I try to keep my voice down. Starting a commotion could get the kid at the desk to come after me. "Don't touch me."

But when our eyes meet, I feel it. Clear as day. She is afraid: *for* me.

"You're not supposed to come here," she whispers angrily as we step out of the weight room. Or that's how she sounds. Because what I feel when she finally stops to look at me is fear, not anger. "Didn't they tell you that?"

They who? There are infinite possibilities. None of them especially good.

"I don't know who you're—"

"Stop," she says, a hand raised in my face. And just like that all of her feelings vanish, and up goes that brick wall. Like Kelsey's.

"You're blocking me," I say, even though I would have said a second earlier that I would be better off not saying anything.

"You can't shut up, can you?" She's irritated. Or I'm assuming irritated. All I can read now is that brick wall. "Just go to Delaney's." She rolls her eyes when I stare blankly at her. "The *bar* where *Leo* works. And don't go around asking everyone where he is when you get there. He's the only barback with a ponytail." She pulls back and looks me up and down, then shakes her head. "Seriously, you have got to start keeping your mouth shut. It's bad for everyone."

And with that she turns and heads back toward the weight room. I watch through the glass as the guy in the crew T-shirt shouts something at her from across the room. But she just holds up her middle finger in response, which makes his lifting partner laugh.

WE ASK FIVE people on campus where Delaney's is and none of them have a clue. Jasper even quickly checks the map on his phone. It only takes a second to realize that Delaney's isn't listed.

"Now what?" Jasper asks, swiping his phone off and slipping it in his back pocket. "Maybe it's not even a real place?"

"It's real," I say, though I wonder again if my hope is getting in the way of my actual instincts.

We continue on through campus, asking student after student

if they've heard of Delaney's. Even though that is probably the opposite of keeping my mouth shut. Each time they say no. But then the students we're asking—the ones alone, carrying books even during the summer—are the exact wrong ones.

It isn't until we are almost at the gates on the other side of campus that I finally spot a much better alternative: a pack of totally wasted people.

"Them," I say to Jasper, pointing. "Come on."

And sure enough, when we finally stop them, Delaney's is exactly where they are coming from.

"It's down these teeny-tiny little street," one girl slurs, pointing toward the sky like the street is above her. Her thick white-blond hair is in two long pigtails that tick back and forth as she sways unsteadily. "And it's got a ½ on the door. 81½, 52½, 96½, I don't fucking remember. Do you guys?" Her friends mumble in the negative. "Anyway, that's it—the number, but no sign. And it's awesome." She nods knowingly, then places a finger squarely on the tip of my nose. "But it's a speak*easy*. So you have to look for the half."

FINALLY, WE FIND the nondescript door halfway down Concord Alley in a very old, dark building. It's wider than a single brownstone, but not quite as big as an apartment building. And the girl was right: a tarnished brass 89½ in the center of the door is the only sign. There are windows, but they are dark, maybe covered with curtains. When I go to open the door, I expect it to be locked. For someone inside to ask for a code, for a chain to keep us out. But the door opens easily. There's a second one inside, also unlocked, and beyond that a curtained vestibule. Pausing there, I can hear a single voice, speaking eerily into silence.

When I finally push my way through the curtain, there are in fact lots of people there, just all facing the stage at the far end, all quiet. The floor is covered with sawdust, and there are black-and-white photos of musicians hanging on the walls, painted a fading red. When I stand on my toes, I can make out a man at the microphone. Short and rumpled in a baseball cap and a baggy sweater, he sounds much more confident than you'd expect him to be. And no wonder, with the crowd hanging on his every word. Not that I can make any of them out. Back on my flat feet, my only view is a wall of backs, and his words are all muffled.

I meet eyes with a husky bald guy with hoop earrings and a black leather vest perched on a stool near the door. Definitely the bouncer. He squints at us, like he is trying to decide if we are worth the bother of pushing to his feet.

"Let's go," Jasper says, noticing him too.

We weave our way through the bodies, more tightly packed as we get farther back toward the stage, until finally there is a small corner of space near the bar—though kind of unfortunately right in the bouncer's sight line. Already the next person is onstage, a very tall girl wearing a beatnik paisley skirt and cowboy boots.

When I glance over my shoulder toward the bar, I can see a bartender hard at work, opening beer bottles and taking crumpled dollar bills. I don't think he's Leo. He looks older than college age, maybe even in his thirties. Also, he does not have a ponytail.

It occurs to me now how risky this is. My search for Leo has become a search for a guy at Delaney's with a ponytail. The girl in the green jog bra renegotiated my terms. She could be sending me to find anyone, theoretically. But one thing that was for sure not theoretical? Her blocking me exactly the way Kelsey did. That was not something she made up. And right now, that's enough for me. No, maybe not enough. But it's all I have.

Finally, I spot somebody farther down the bar, on the other side of the bartender. He is bent over and pulling glasses out of a rack like a barback and not a bartender might. When he finally stands, sure enough, I can see light brown hair pulled back in a short ponytail. Lit up behind the bar, his face is a series of elegant angles. Leo, definitely.

"Do these people actually think this is good?" Jasper whispers to me. He's listening to the girl up onstage, her face more and more flushed with each and every angry word. "All she's doing is yelling."

"Come on," I say, turning my attention back to Leo. He's ducked under the bar with his rack of glasses and is headed past us toward the back, the kitchen maybe. I watch him disappear behind a door that swings back and forth on its tight hinges. "I think I see him."

IT ISN'T EASY for us to make it the rest of the way through the crowd, but eventually we end up at the same door. I hold my breath as I push through, startle when I let go and the door makes a super-loud snapping sound. But Leo—if he is Leo—does not twitch. He does not look up. He just keeps on with what he's doing. Pulling out a clean rack of glasses, loading another dirty one into the dishwasher. But he has tensed. I can feel it.

"You shouldn't be in here," he says finally as he starts up the machine. He still hasn't looked in our direction. And he is wound tight. But I don't feel any actual anger coming off him. At least, not yet. Then again, we still have not made eye contact, which I get the sense is not an accident. "You're supposed to wait around back, in the alley. I take the empties out at midnight."

Like he knows exactly why we are there. Maybe the girl in the green jog bra told him to expect us.

I look down at my watch. "It's not even ten p.m.," I say, like that's the important point—that we'll have to wait two hours. "I need to find your girlfriend," I say carefully, bracing myself for sudden blowback.

"Oh yeah?" he asks, plucking a chipped glass out of the clean rack and tossing it into the garbage. Except it's not really a question. "I don't know anyone by that name."

"I have something for her." I dig Kelsey's copy of *1984* from my bag and hold it out to him.

Finally, he turns. As soon as he sees what it is, his eyes shoot back up to mine. And, wow, is he pissed. He steps forward and snatches the book from me so aggressively that I feel Jasper flinch. Leo flips through the pages, then glares at me some more. Yep. Definitely furious.

"Where the hell did you get this?" he asks. Or accuses.

"Kelsey gave it to me," I say, getting ready to bolt out the door. Whatever I *felt* was going to happen—it wasn't this. I have no idea what this is. I feel more lost than ever. "That's why I'm here. She and I—"

"Wait, who?" he asks. Confusion and disbelief have overtaken his anger.

"Kelsey," I say. "This is going to, well, sound crazy, but she and I were in this hospital together." My voice rises at the end like it's a question as my stomach twists. There's no way to explain a crazy situation that doesn't sound crazy. "And anyway, Kelsey gave me the book because, I think, we shared this connection." Vague, I am going to stay vague—not mention the Outliers, not yet. "And then she helped me get out and—"

"Wait, when?"

"When what?" Now he's more worried than angry—freaked out, actually.

"When were you in the hospital together?" He steps toward me with the book raised. Jasper moves forward, too.

"Um, this morning," I say. "Kelsey helped me get out, and I'm hoping that maybe Gabrielle has heard from her. Because Kelsey was supposed to leave with me, but I haven't seen her. I'm worried that she's still in the hospital. In which case, I think we should go back to get her."

"Well, that would be hard," Leo says. His voice is cold and flat. Dread—it's the only thing he feels. Overwhelming dread.

"Well, I know, it will be hard, but—"

"Kelsey is dead," he says with utter and undeniable truthfulness. "She's been dead for months. I don't know who you were with, but it wasn't Kelsey."

21

MY HEAD IS VIBRATING AS JASPER AND I STAND IN THE ALLEYWAY THAT'S alongside Delaney's, between Concord Alley in front of the bar and the back where Leo has told us to meet him. Kelsey dead? I feel sick. Sick that girl who claimed to be Kelsey was lying to me. Sick that this Leo person might be lying to me now. Both feel possible. Or maybe I want them to be.

Leo did agree to meet us in back at least. Not that he was happy about it. He also hadn't been forthcoming with any additional information. Not even when I tried to press—and I did try to press.

"I mean, maybe Kelsey isn't dead. Maybe she's missing or something?" I had offered when we were still inside Delaney's kitchen, still waiting for Leo to agree to meet us. "I was in the hospital with her. That's the truth."

"No," Leo had said again, simply. "She is definitely *dead.*"

And it did feel like he was telling the truth as he believed it to be. Though I have already learned that does not necessarily mean he's right.

Leo slid Kelsey's book onto a high shelf above the dishwasher before dismissing us. I wanted the book back, but didn't feel like I could argue under the circumstances, especially because he had agreed to meet us.

I pull Rachel's burner phone out of my pocket while we wait and turn it on. I don't want to talk to her, but I can't help checking in occasionally to see if she has learned anything new about my dad. As much as I don't trust her, I have to believe she would at least be straight with me about that.

I sit down on the curb as text after text comes through. Eight unread messages, all from Rachel, all some increasingly pissed-off version of: *where the hell are you?* No news at all about my dad.

"Oh, okay, we're sitting?" Jasper asks as he comes and lowers himself down on the curb next to me, then leans over to read the text. "Maybe she can explain," Jasper offers. When I shoot him a nasty look, he holds up his hands. "I'm only playing devil's advocate."

"Why?" I ask quietly. "She hates you."

"Gee, thanks," he says. "I don't know, but maybe that's why. Why risk being mean to me?"

"I don't know." I stare down at the disposable phone in my hands. "I have no idea what she would do, or why."

And that is definitely the truth. Do I actually think Rachel had something to do with my mom's death? No, not exactly. But Rachel has done terrible things for money, or so my mom once

said. And I already know now that anything is possible, that people are capable of much worse than I ever could have imagined.

"You know, before I ended up in the hospital, I finally went
to the police station to look at the case file from my mom's accident," I say.

"Really?" Jasper asks. "I thought they kept saying no."

"They changed their mind. I wish they hadn't. It wasn't at all
what I thought it was going to be."

"What do you mean?" Jasper asks.

"There was—they found a vodka bottle. Like my mom had
been drinking in the car before the accident," I begin. And suddenly I am flooded with the horrible sense that I am missing the
point. Like I felt on that bridge with those officers inching closer
as I looked for Jasper. "And, I guess, I—"

My voice cuts out. I am grateful that Jasper doesn't say any of
the annoying, empty things he might. Instead, he leans his body
closer to mine and wraps an arm around my shoulders. And
before I know it, I am curling myself against him.

"It makes me feel like I never knew her."

"You can be wrong about some things," he says, holding me
tighter, "without being wrong about everything."

And for a second I almost believe him. Or I want to. And that
is something.

There's a sharp whistle then from the far end of the alley.
When we look, Leo waves us down, then disappears around the
corner.

I AM WALKING fast by the time we get to the edge of the building,
not quite a jog but close. When I finally turn the corner, the

alley is almost pitch-black and narrower than I expect, filled with trash cans and Dumpsters. I see Leo, someone else, too. But they are tucked back in the shadows. Kelsey's sister, I am hoping.

"Explain where you got the book," Leo says. "The whole story, now. Or we're gone."

Finally, the person he's with steps forward from the wall and into the pale light. Even in the mostly dark, I recognize her right away: Riel. Level99, Riel. My heart drops. What the hell.

"What are you doing here?" I ask, feeling betrayed yet again.

"I ask the questions," Riel snaps back. "*You're* the one who has *my* book."

"Your book?"

"Yeah, *my* book. Where the hell did you get it?"

"From Kelsey," I say, though already I have a very bad feeling that I am wrong. About so much. And then, far too slow, finally it comes to me. "Riel is short for Gabrielle?"

"Very good," Riel says flatly, then punctuates it with a slow clap. "Leo already told you that Kelsey is dead. So where did you get the book? Tell the truth, too, or I will ruin you in ways you cannot even imagine."

"There was a girl in the hospital who *said* she was Kelsey, and I had no reason not to believe her," I say. "She gave me the book. She said she was going to sneak out with me, too, but then I lost her. She was amazing at blocking, too, just like it describes in the book. I honestly thought she was Kelsey, I swear." And I know I should probably leave it at that, but I can't. "I mean, is there any chance that—"

"Kelsey is dead!" Riel shouts, and I can read her easily now—suspicion and rage and pain. So much that it takes my breath away. "And I know she's dead because *I* was the lucky one who found her." She points a finger hard at her own chest. "I saw her skin tinged blue. A needle sticking out of her arm."

The horror that passes through Riel when she says the word "blue" makes me feel hot and nauseous. And in that moment, I am reminded of how only weeks ago I might have mistaken that feeling for my own. Now, I can see the difference. But still, it is awful all the same.

"I'm sorry," I say, and I am. For making her even think about that.

"You should be," Riel says, and when I try to read her again, that weirdly flat shield of contempt is back. It must be her way of blocking.

"Yeah, it's different from in the book," she says. Because she knows that I'm reading her. Has a decent idea even of what I'm thinking, maybe. She is good at this Outlier thing, too. Maybe as good as Kelsey was. Better than me, I am pretty sure. "If you make yourself a wall, it's pretty obvious you're blocking, right? At least to another Outlier. Using another feeling as cover? Much smarter. But that's not in our book because I only figured it out recently, *after* your dad killed Kelsey."

"What? My dad did not *kill* Kelsey. He didn't kill anybody."

"Well, he's the reason she's dead, and that's close enough for me."

"What are you talking about?"

"If he had *told* Kelsey more about his research earlier, what he'd found out about her, then maybe I could have helped her. Maybe I could have made it so she didn't have to numb herself with oxy and a whole bunch of other shit, so much that she'd end up OD'ing." But Riel does not believe my dad is to blame, not deep down. I'm not sure if it's deliberate that she stops blocking me. But I can read her clearly for a moment. And in her center is only grief, and guilt. "And so, yeah, when Quentin came looking for Kelsey and told me what your dad was hiding, I jumped at the chance to help shred your dad's data. Which, by the way, is all I thought I was doing: making it so he couldn't cash in."

But Riel did lie; that isn't lost on me. Quentin didn't trick her by lying. She offered to help to get back at him.

"And meanwhile you helped get Cassie killed," Jasper says.

"That sucks what happened to your friend," Riel says. "But if your dad had come clean from the start, none of this would have happened."

"He was trying to protect us," I say, though it may be more true that he was trying to protect me.

"Well, he did an awesome job," she says, her voice thick with something worse than contempt. Something that she wants me to feel.

"Somebody has him now anyway," I say. And then realize that's the best-case scenario. "Or something happened to him. Maybe they even killed him. So that should make you happy."

Riel doesn't even flinch. Instead, she shrugs.

"It's amazing what they think they can keep secret." She sounds insulted. "Or how far they'll go to try."

"So who was the girl I met?" I ask. "And how did she have your book?"

"I have no idea," Riel says, but then something occurs to her. "Wait, what did she look like?"

"Long, curly dark hair," I say. "Oh, and she has an infinity symbol tattooed on the inside of her wrist."

Riel looks in Leo's direction, then shakes her head again. "I should have known it was her."

"Who?" I ask.

"There were three of you, right?" Riel goes on. "Three original Outliers from your dad's test. Or that's what he told me when he called to warn Kelsey about Quentin, when it was way too late anyway." I am glad that my dad at least called. "That girl with the tattoo is the third Outlier. And I can promise you if she was in that hospital it's because she wanted to be."

The guard. *You were talking to him, too,* that's what Ramona had said to Kelsey. It had only been in passing. Not a comment that had really stuck with me. But maybe that was the link. That the Wolf had been Kelsey's way in, when the rest of us wanted out.

"How did you meet her?" I ask.

"She showed up at the house a couple weeks ago trying to get Kelsey to do something with her," Riel says. "I was her second choice when she found out Kelsey was dead. Like I was going to run off and do whatever she wanted. It sounded like Quentin had tried to use her, too. But she wasn't looking to help anyone but herself. She was damn good at reading people, though. I'll give her that. She must have grabbed the book when she was here.

And by the way, she added shit to the book. We never wrote about being an Outlier in there. Back then, we didn't know yet."

"What did she want you to do?" I ask. Do you think you're an Outlier too? is what I really want to know. But it seems pointless to risk annoying her when I already know the answer is yes.

"Who knows? I never let her get into specifics," Riel says. "Some way to 'cash in' on being an Outlier. She kept going on and on about how she and I could 'help each other.' She must have thought I was pretty fucking stupid—actually, no, I think *she* was pretty fucking stupid. Running around assuming everyone wants money? I don't want money."

"What do you want?" I ask.

She considers the question for a minute. Then turns to stare at me hard.

"Justice," she says finally. And I feel a flash of disappointment, like she already knows she's failed.

"Riel, we should go," Leo says, looking around nervously. "It's getting late. And with everything going on, I don't think we should hang around here."

"But . . ." I start. *Please don't go* is all I can think to say. I already know, though, that pleading won't persuade Riel to do anything. "The other girls. They're still in that hospital."

"Riel," Leo says, impatient. "We should go. Seriously."

"I know," she says, walking toward him. Leo and Riel start down the alley, but Riel stops and turns back to me when she's gotten a few strides away. "Well, don't just stand there like an asshole. Come on."

22

NO ONE SPEAKS AS LEO DRIVES US AWAY FROM DELANEY'S AND OUT OF Cambridge. Soon we are on I-93, leaving the city of Boston behind. As the lights shrink in the distance, my chest loosens a little. Even though I know that bigger problems lie ahead and not behind.

Jasper glances back at me from the front seat, where Leo insisted he ride. Riel is in the back next to me. These are their precautions. What purpose they serve, I'm not sure. But I knew better than to argue.

Jasper is worried about me. He is worried about himself. I can feel that so clearly it's almost like he is shouting it at me. He is hoping that I'm right that we should go with these excellent liars. I am, too.

"Where are we going?" Jasper asks when we have driven in silence for more than fifteen minutes.

"My grandparents have a house on Cape Cod," Riel says, like this explains everything. "We can't stay in Cambridge. Thanks to you bringing Kendall—"

"I didn't bring Kendall," I say. "*He* sent me."

"Whatever," she says, but more mildly. Like she knows the difference and maybe even believes me, but is also determined not to change her negative opinion of me in general. "Somebody else came by, too. Somebody we didn't know. Could have been a coincidence, but I don't think so. We were on borrowed time in Cambridge."

Riel rests her head against the window, eyes toward the darkness.

"Why are you helping us now?" I ask. Her change of heart is nagging at me.

She closes her eyes. Shrugs. "Because I can," she says. And for a second she lets me feel her guilt. "Because you need me to."

I WAKE UP disoriented and cloudy. I don't know how long I was out, but we are now in the middle of the tall Bourne Bridge, arced high above the water. When I was little, crossing that bridge was always the dividing line between the Cape and civilization, between life and summer bliss. I wonder now what waits for me on the other side.

Soon we are snaking along Route 6, which runs the length of the Cape. I recognize it, too. I try to hold tighter to my old sense of this special place—of sand and dried pines and hermit crabs and biking on the rail trail—but it's already slipping away.

A few minutes later we turn off onto a much narrower paved

road, which turns quickly into a dirt one, we bump slowly along. Another minute or two more, and I see water through a break in the trees up ahead. We hit a wooden bridge too fast, our tires rumbling hard over wooden planks. My teeth rattling.

"It's one of the little private islands," Riel says, like we all spend a fair amount of time in such glamorous places.

On the other side of the bridge the vibrating ends. When we come around a bend along the water, a large, dark house is finally in the distance. The moon illuminates the bay and I can see that the house is perched high at the tip of the little island, stately and beautiful with a pillared porch. Leo cuts the headlights while we are still a ways off and pulls into a shadowy spot on the far side of the garage, where the car is out of sight.

"We have to go in the back," Riel says. "And don't turn on any lights. The neighbors will call the police if they think someone's here. Especially if they think it's me."

"I thought you said this was your grandparents' house."

"My grand*father's* technically, and he hates me. My grandmother loves me," she says. "But no one cares what she thinks anymore because she left him years ago. She lives in Scottsdale now. My grandfather lives in Arizona, too, during the winter, but they've spent summers at this house since my mom was a kid. The neighbors are obsessed with my grandfather. They love to report back anything he might want to know. Honestly, he's an ass to them so I don't get it. But then he's a politician. They specialize in making people love them."

///////////////////////////////

INSIDE, THE HOUSE is even more beautiful. At least what I can see of it with the lights off. But it is surprisingly bright with the almost-full moon shining through the many windows. It's everyone's faces that stay mostly cast in shadow.

The kitchen is open and vast with white, polished cabinets, shiny stainless-steel appliances, and lots and lots of granite. There is a massive vase of white flowers in the center of an island, the bouquet carefully designed to appear gathered haphazardly. The flowers give the room a sweet, summery smell. Honeysuckle. I remember it from the little cottage we rented for years on the Cape back when my mom was alive.

"Why are there flowers if no one's home?" I ask, glancing over at Jasper. I can feel how not sure he is about us being stuck out here in the middle of nowhere. And the truth is, I feel more nervous now that we're in the house. Confined. "Are you sure somebody's not here?"

"I'm going to run to the bathroom," Leo says, excusing himself toward an even darker back hallway.

He has definitely been here before. He knows where to go even without lights, and as he brushes past me I feel a wave of disgust. He wishes we weren't here, too. That *I* wasn't, actually. He hasn't made eye contact with me once since we left the bar, but even so, I have been able to feel how much he doesn't like me. He doesn't approve of Riel bringing us along.

He loves her. I can feel that, too. All he cares about is protecting her.

"Trust me, no one's here," Riel says. "My grandfather doesn't come until summer break, which starts July fifteenth this year—I checked. Also, my grandfather's secretary said he's in all week. As for the flowers? Who knows? My grandfather's third wife—the second one left him, too—is some twenty-five-year-old who he may have lobotomized. That's the only explanation for how she can stay with him. She probably doesn't even know why she keeps the flowers coming." Riel tugs on the two tall refrigerator doors and stands in the glow of the stocked shelves. "I mean, look at all this food." She picks up a decorative little jar of some kind of jam. "Fancy even when no one's looking. Otherwise rich people dissolve into a puff of smoke."

This "I hate rich people" thing is an act. Or no. Not an act. An effort. Riel believes it, but it takes work to distance herself from what must be partly her own history.

"So he doesn't like what you do with Level99?" I ask, and I am not sure why—but this thing with her grandfather feels important to understand. No, *he* feels important to understand.

"That's what he says. But really he hates that I have a vagina and, you know, opinions." She shakes her head and I can feel how much she hates him. "My grandfather is all about 'family values' as long as you're not talking about his family because how can he claim to be so moral when his wives are not much older than me. And he uses his money to control them, until they break free and run away. It's gross. Really, he just hates all women because they keep dumping him. You remember that whole 'genuine assault' thing a few years ago?"

"Yeah, I think so." I do have vague memories of some politician saying something horrible along those lines. "Didn't that guy get impeached or whatever?"

"Nope. Alive and well and with a summerhouse on the Cape."

"Your grandfather?"

"Yep, and *wait* until he gets wind that this whole Outlier thing is something only girls can do." She whistles and shakes her head like she can't wait for it. "He'll make Quentin look totally reasonable. The idea that any woman could have something that makes her more powerful than him? It'll make him totally crazy. I mean, even more crazy than he already is. And my grandfather has actual power, not to mention lots of people who agree with him. I think he might even try to run for president someday or something. And then, seriously, God help us all." When Riel emerges from behind the refrigerator doors, she's holding bread and peanut butter in her arms. She pushes the doors closed with a foot. "You guys want something to eat?"

My stomach is tight after all this talk of her maniacal grandfather. But I should probably eat something. Maybe it's a good sign that Riel hasn't lost her appetite. She hates her grandfather, there's no doubt about that. But I don't think she's actually afraid of him.

"Yeah, thanks," I say. And a second later she is handing me a sandwich. She hands one to Jasper, too, and when our eyes meet, his brow wrinkles: *What are we doing here?* That's what he's wondering. *Are you sure we should stay?* These are valid questions. Except I can't possibly leave until Riel tells me everything. And watching her assemble her sandwich in the mostly dark, then push herself up onto the counter—her fuck-you to the rules of the house—I feel this twinge. There is something she has left out. Something important. Why did she have a change of heart?

Why did she let us come along?

"Did you look into any of the stuff I told you about?" I ask, taking a stab in the dark. "The hospital and everything?"

Riel nods, then takes another bite of her sandwich. Finally, she pushes herself off the counter and pulls out her laptop. The screen glows brightly in the darkness when she open it on the counter.

"You wouldn't be here if your story hadn't checked out. It wasn't easy to find, though, I'll tell you that much. There was nothing on the Boston General Hospital servers. Like the whole thing doesn't even exist." She waves me over as she clicks through some screens. "I had to get to the Dr. Cornelia guy first through Metropolitan Hospital and then find my way to a totally sketchy Gmail he's been using for this entire thing. By the way, no mention of the NIH anywhere. And then I searched for Alvarez like you said. And that's when I found this."

I step forward to the computer and begin to read an email open on the screen. It's from Dr. Cornelia to Dr. Alvarez.

"Read it out loud," Jasper calls from where he's still leaning against the wall near the door, arms crossed, like he's afraid of being blindsided by something if he commits to the center of the room.

"Thank you for your concern and your thoroughness, Dr. Alvarez," I begin to read from her screen. *"It is precisely this kind of dedication that makes me so glad that you are a part of our team. However, the issues you have presented have been assessed and determined to be without substantial merit or warranting further review. Do not raise them again or we will be forced to evaluate our future collaboration. Sincerely, Dr. Cornelia."*

"Well, actually, that was his reply," Riel says, reaching over to scroll down to the original message.

I read on. *"There is no medical justification for the hospitalization of these young women. Holding them at Boston General Hospital so that you can conduct some kind of investigation for personal gain is both immoral and unethical. There is insufficient scientific evidence of PANDAS infection or even underlying strep. If you do not inform their parents immediately of your limited basis in fact and give them the option to leave, I will go directly to the press."*

"And then this last," Riel says, scrolling some more.

"Dr. Alvarez, your contract as a research associate has been terminated effective immediately. You must report to hospital security upon receipt of this messasge. If we find you have breached your confidentiality agreement we will pursue legal action."

So that was where Dr. Alvarez had gone, and why she'd been so upset—she'd been fired.

"So I kept looking and eventually I found this in Dr. Cornelia's email contacts."

With a few more keystrokes, an email address pops up. It ends in @dia.mil.

"What is that?" I ask.

"Someone at the Defense Intelligence Agency," she says, tapping her keyboard once more. She stops and points at her screen. "Here's their website." And then she begins to read: "We provide military intelligence for warfighters, defense policymakers, and blah, blah. Warfighters? I mean, how is that even a word?"

"My dad thought the military had their own research project about the Outliers that was similar to his."

"Looks like maybe they're kind of territorial," Riel says. "Oh, and speaking of your dad . . ."

She heads back to her bag and pulls out a sheet of paper, handing it to me.

"What is it?"

"It was attached to one of the first emails from Cornelia to Dr. Haddox," she says. "Seems like that's how they found all of you. Or, at least, all of them. Your dad has a serious knack for losing important shit."

At the top there is a handwritten note: *Phase II Outlier Exploratory, Not for Publication or Distribution.* A note that is definitely in my dad's handwriting. But it's a photograph of the actual note, not a document.

"Somebody broke into our house," I say. Though already I know the timing doesn't make sense. We were all in the hospital by then. Whoever had the list had it much earlier than that.

But I know for sure my dad wouldn't give them our names. And I am not going to get roped into being suspicious of him like I was back with Quentin and the camp. My dad is a victim here, like us.

"I thought maybe we were all Dr. Shepard's patients?" I go on then, consider explaining who Dr. Shepard is before realizing that, of course, I don't need to explain because Riel must already know. Also, I never even got proof that was true. Teresa was the only person who ever said anything about Dr. Shepard.

"Dr. Shepard?" Riel asks. "I don't know about her. But I know for sure your dad was also advertising on campus for volunteers for his follow-up studies."

She looks away then, but if she actually feels ashamed of all the time she spent trolling around our private electronic lives, she hides it well.

"And none of this says what they are planning to do to the girls," I press. "Or why they have them in the first place. Did you find anything else?"

"Hey, it wasn't easy to figure out this much in a few hours," Riel says, defensive. "These people don't exactly hang out a sign. And then I got a call from Leo saying some random girl had Kelsey's book, which was kind of distracting, you know."

"Also, she doesn't work for you," Leo snaps as he comes back in. "If your dad hadn't tried to cover everything up to begin with—"

"I know, he messed up!" I shout. "No one is saying he didn't! But that doesn't have anything to do with this."

"*And* she doesn't owe you anything," Leo goes on. She's not obligated."

But all I can think is: yes. *Yes, she is obligated. Being an Outlier makes her obligated to help other Outliers.* I don't say that, though. Maybe I'm wrong. And I'm afraid suggesting that will make Riel angry.

"Listen, my dad definitely made mistakes, and Quentin exploited them, and if you ever talk to my dad"—my voice catches on the *if*—"he will be the first to take full responsibility for all of it. But he was trying to protect me—and he thought he was protecting Kelsey and whoever the girl is who gave me your book. He was afraid of this, something like what's happening right now, happening to the three of us. But he isn't hiding anything anymore. He's trying to get all of this out into the open. He went to DC to meet with the NIH to get public funding for his research and—"

The NIH. Dr. Frederick Mitchell. That was one lead I didn't give Riel. One place she couldn't have searched.

"What?" Riel asks when I stop talking midsentence.

"Dr. Frederick Mitchell from the NIH," I say. "Can you try to find something between him and Dr. Cornelia? That's who Kendall said he was. I think there might be a connection."

It's a feeling. An instinct. And luckily, that's not something I have to explain to Riel.

She nods as her fingers move fast over the keys. "Getting into the NIH system is even harder than the Department of Defense," she says. "And not because of security. Their system is so old it's barely an actual computer. This might take a minute."

I stand behind her as her fingers fly over the keys.

"How many are there? Outliers, I mean," I ask after a few minutes. She pauses and looks up. She is not blocking me anymore. And what I feel from her is a mix of nerves and a tiny flicker of hope—hope that she might find something in me that she's been looking for since she lost Kelsey. "I met someone at the gym and she made it sound like people came around looking for Leo all the time, which I'm guessing means they were looking for you. You've found other Outliers, right?"

Riel turns back to the computer.

"After I realized that Quentin was full of shit, but before we bailed from the camp, I grabbed as much of your dad's stuff as I could—background research, copies of sample tests, that kind of thing. Enough so that with the help of a few psych geniuses on campus here that Leo knows, we were able to assemble a basic Outlier self-test. Not like official scientific or whatever—there's a disclaimer. But so far it seems decently accurate."

"And what did you do with it?"

"Posted it online." She is proud of this fact, but also a little uneasy. "Now you can Google 'Feel Test' and find it."

"What's the point?"

"People have a right to know who they are," she says, seeming appalled that I don't realize that. But also I can feel her hesitation (despite her attempts to block me). Like she isn't entirely sure about these things she's already done. "Besides, if there's going to be a war, I'm sure as hell going to be ready with an army."

"A war," I say. Not a question. More an idea I am trying on for size. And it fits in a way that I wish it did not. "Can I ask you something else?"

"I guess," Riel says.

"Do you think being an Outlier is more than being able to read how people feel?"

"Definitely," she says without hesitating. "A lot more."

"Do you sometimes know that things are going to happen before they do?"

Riel turns and looks dead at me. "All the time." And I feel it then: that thing I had so envied when I read the notes in *1984*. What Riel and the real Kelsey had shared. An actual connection. "That's the worst part of what happened to Kelsey. I think I kind of *knew* it was going to happen. And I should have stopped her."

Outlier Rule #5: With enough practice we won't just be able to know people's feelings. We will know what's going to happen.

"But knowing that something bad is going to happen isn't the same thing as being able to stop it," I say.

"But it should be," Riel says. "It could be."

I stand by her side for another few minutes, then a few minutes more as she winds her way through a maze of computer screens.

"Wait, hold up, I think I might have something," she says finally, peering more closely at her screen.

"What is it?" Jasper asks, coming closer.

"I've found a Frederick Mitchell," she says. "But not in the NIH system. It popped up in Cornelia's Gmail. In an order for a shitload of morphine being sent to Boston General Hospital, Dwyer Wing," she says. "For the Frederick Mitchell project."

"The Dwyer Wing is where the girls are."

"If none of them are sick," Jasper asks, "why the hell do they need so much morphine?"

"Maybe so that the next time the hospital burns," I say, "there won't be anyone getting away."

23

"CAN YOU GET ME BACK IN?" I ASK, MY EYES STILL ON THE COMPUTER.

"Back in?" Riel asks.

"To the hospital," I say. "I'd need to go back in through the locked fire door. That Dwyer Wing is new and super high-tech, so the security probably is, too."

"Hmm," Riel says, narrowing her eyes at the screen as she begins to type. "Brand-new is actually better. The security might be online." Her fingers pick up speed. Soon she's found an article talking about all the building's bells and whistles, including naming the "cutting-edge" company that handles the security. "It'll take a while, but, yeah, I think I can probably hijack the system. Everyone thinks high-tech is better." She shakes her head. "You know what's better? A fucking combination lock."

"So you can unlock the fire door to the outside? You'll also have to get the door to the specific floor open. Those are locked, too."

Riel nods. "It'll take me a couple hours to get in, and I won't be able to keep any of the doors unlocked for long. You'll have to move fast." She looks up at me, and I can feel her certainty. I can feel also how much she wants to help now. "But, yeah. I can do it. We should agree on a time now. Texting back and forth while we're doing it is the easiest way to get busted."

I look at the clock. It's almost two. "How about four a.m.?" I ask. "That'll give me time to get back to Boston. And it'll be easier in the middle of the night."

"And let's go with four thirty a.m. exactly," she says. "But that'll be it. That will be your only chance."

"And then what? What's the endgame here?" Jasper asks. He has retreated to the wall, arms crossed again. "Think about how hard it was for you to get out before, Wylie, and that was alone. Now you think you're going to be able to walk out with a bunch of other girls? Why don't you send those emails to a newspaper or TV station or something? Get them on the case."

"Just an FYI," Riel says. "It's not like the press is always some avenging angel. Sometimes they care about the shit you want them to care about. And sometimes they don't."

"They're running out of time, Jasper." I look away from him and back at the computer. "I have to try. Even if I can't get them out, I can at least warn them about what's going on. I have to do that much."

Riel waves Jasper and me away. "In the meantime, both of you back off and argue over there so I can get to work. I'll tell you when I have something."

Leo comes to take our place, putting a protective hand on the back of Riel's neck. I am surprised when she seems to soften instead of knocking it away.

"I'M NOT TRYING to be negative," Jasper says once we've drifted back over to the kitchen table and sat down. He won't look me in the eye and he is clenching his jaw. "But there's no point in doing something that puts you at risk and doesn't help them."

I reach over, put my hand over Jasper's and squeeze his fingers. It feels so much less awkward than I expect it to. Because what else is there? There is nothing I can say that is going to make him understand why I am going to do this. "I need to do it."

Jasper is about to argue with me anyway when there's a loud knock at the front door, on the far side of the living room. We all freeze. Stare in the direction of the door. Even Riel's hands hover above the keys. Her face is tight in the light from the computer screen.

"Shit," she whispers, looking toward the door.

"I didn't see any lights," Leo whispers.

"My grandfather's office." Riel motions for us to go. "I'll get rid of them."

Even from the other side of the kitchen I can feel that she's not so sure.

"Coming! Hold on!" Riel shouts without moving, buying us time. "I'll be right there!"

WE FOLLOW LEO through a set of doors and into the back hallway. It is so totally pitch-black that we have to feel our way along the wall until we reach the first open doorway. It is brighter in the office, the moon reflecting off the water back there and in through the three windows. It gives everything in the room an eerie blue-gray glow—the dark wood bookshelves, the big mahogany desks, the walls of Riel's grandfather's framed awards and photographs, our faces. Leo waves Jasper off when he goes to close the door, then points to his ear. *Leave it open so we can hear.*

I lean against a bare spot on the wall and try to get myself to take a breath. I do not have a good feeling. I have a very terrible one actually. I try to tell myself that it's only my anxiety again—and it could be. Except, now that I can feel the difference that's easier said than done.

I try to focus instead on the framed certificate nearest me, with the curly cursive script and fancy shield in the middle. Hard to decipher in the dark. Finally, I see that it's an honorary doctorate in political science from the University of Arizona, awarded to one Senator David Russo.

Senator Russo. The senator my dad was meeting with? Has the monster that Riel described—the one who she is so sure won't sit idly by and accept the gender disparity in my dad's research—decided to stop the Outliers at the source: my dad?

I have begun to tremble against the wall. In the distance, there is the sound of the front door opening.

"Yeah?" Riel's voice is trying to sound blasé, even a little annoyed. But whoever is at that door is not who she expected. "What do you want?"

"Hi, ma'am." A man's voice, one that I have heard before. "I'm Agent Klute, and this is Agent Stevens. We're with the Department of Homeland Security."

Jasper nudges me. He's holding his phone out. And it is on, signal flush with all the bars.

"I thought it was off," he whispers in my ear. "I'm so sorry."

And what is there to say? One tap in the wrong place, or one too many. It's easy enough to think you turned something off when you didn't. I reach forward and put a hand on his arm to comfort him. To steady myself.

"Did something happen to my grandfather?" Riel is talking loud. Playing dumb. Making sure we can hear. Buying us more time.

"Not that I'm aware of," Agent Klute says, all smooth calm. I can imagine him smiling, too, with his big white teeth. "We're here for Wylie Lang."

And all I can think of is my bag—or Rachel's bag—out there in the kitchen with my mom's photographs.

"Wylie Lang?" Riel asks, her confusion reasonably convincing. Though it's hard to know how Klute is taking it. "It's just me and my boyfriend here."

"Well, we have reason to believe that she is here," Agent Klute says.

"And I have reason to believe you are wrong," Riel shoots back, standing her ground. It can't be easy. Agent Klute is intimidating.

"How about we come in and take a quick look around to be sure?"

"You have a warrant?" Riel asks.

"A warrant?" Klute asks, like she has inquired instead whether he has a unicorn in his pocket. There is silence. I imagine Riel glaring at him. I imagine Agent Klute glaring back. "Wylie is in serious trouble. Criminal trouble. I don't think your grandfather would be happy to hear that you're mixed up in something like that. If I were you, I wouldn't get in the way."

"So I'm going to take *that* as a no on the warrant," Riel says. "And so I'm going to close this door now. You feel free to knock again when you've got that warrant. I'll be right here, waiting. Bye-bye."

Agent Klute is still saying something when the door closes. The sound of the dead bolt thuds across the entire house. Then I hear Riel walking, calm and cool toward the back, surely for the benefit of Agent Klute, who might be watching through the front windows.

She sprints, though, when she finally hits the dark hall out of sight.

"Come on, let's go," she says when she turns into the office. She freezes when she eyes Jasper's phone on the table. She points at it. "Fucking seriously?"

"I thought it was off," Jasper says, pained. And I am so grateful to be able to read him—otherwise I might be suspicious. But there is no doubt, leaving the phone on, allowing us to be tracked, really was an accident. "I don't know what happened."

Riel takes a breath. She can also read him, of course. However dumb, she knows, too, that it was an honest mistake.

"Come on, you can't go out the front," she says. "And leave the phone, might make them think you're still in here. The way you're going, you won't be able to use it anyway."

WE RACE AFTER Riel down the hall to a set of French doors. My heart pounds as I get ready to run. I think about where the bridge is, how we will manage to keep out of sight on the expanse. What we will do when we get to Route 6. Hide in the woods? Try to hitchhike?

When Riel opens the doors, a strong, salty breeze blows through. I am about to step out when I see the water down below. The back of the house is propped high on stilts. There is a narrow widow's walk with a ladder at one end. Below is a thin stretch of black boulders. And then the water. More and more water.

"It's high tide," Riel says as if this is not a great thing. "There's a dock on the other side of the inlet. It's far, but Kelsey used to do it, so it can be done."

"There's an envelope in my bag in the kitchen. Will you keep it for me? It's important."

Riel nods, then turns back to the water. "You can swim, right?"

We hear men's voices coming from the front of the house. Heading out that way is not an option. And we need to go now.

"Yeah," I say. "I can swim."

RIEL AND LEO disappear back inside as Jasper and I head down the ladder to the rocks. We kick off our shoes and toss them under the house, picking our way across the sharp stones and into the icy water. The shoreline is gooey, sucking our feet down with every step. But the dark bay in front of us is smooth. Like black glass.

"There," I whisper, pointing to a dock in the distance. It's hard to guess how far away it is. Maybe better not to know.

Trying to swim with clothes on is like trying to get through thousands of hungry, prying fish. I keep waiting for that moment when it will get easier, when my body will acclimate to the drag. But each stroke stays a struggle. Jasper is an even worse swimmer than I am. I find myself considering what I will do if he can't make it all the way.

But then I think of my mom. She had been right that day at Crater Lake. I am a decent swimmer—not half-bad endurance. And like Riel said: this swim can be done. Kelsey did it. I can too. And I will find a way to help Jasper if I need to. I will do what has to be done.

IN THE END, the dock is both closer and farther away than I think. It takes much longer to swim there, but then, suddenly, we have arrived. I follow Jasper up the slimy, algae-covered ladder and out of the water. We stand, shoeless and soaking wet in the darkness, staring back at the divide that separates us from whoever it is that is after us this time.

"You ready?" I ask, not really sure where it is I intend for us to go. But knowing that we must head somewhere.

Jasper nods, doing his best to seem confident, though I can feel that he is not. "Yeah, lead the way."

WE DON'T HAVE to walk far along the dark, quiet country road before we spot lights up ahead.

"Oh good, a gas station." Jasper smiles when the sign finally comes into view. "Maybe there'll be some nice couple with a baby who we can ask for a ride."

Luckily, when we finally step inside it's nothing like the Freshmart at the gas station where we met Lexi and Doug. This little store has five full aisles of gourmet food and a whole elaborate setup for fancy cheese, which is empty with a curtain drawn over it at this late hour. Above it, a wooden sign reads *Nibbles*. We are lucky that the store is open. It is not the kind of place that ordinarily would be at this hour.

"Do you still have the cash?" Jasper asks.

Right, money. I had totally forgotten about that little detail. I left Rachel's phone back at Riel's house, but luckily I do still have her money. I dig into my soaking-wet jeans and pull out a wet fold of twenties. I peel through, counting. At least three hundred dollars.

"Definitely enough for a cab and then the train back to Boston," I say. "Maybe we should get some dry T-shirts, too." I motion to a nearby stack of Cape Cod tees, then look down at my bare feet. "And some of those flip-flops."

I can feel the young, suntanned kid behind the counter staring at us as he fingers his summer necklace, beads on a leather cord, hoping we'll go before he has to make us comply with the *Shoes Required* sign.

"Are you sure?" Jasper asks.

"Well, I didn't count all of the money, but I think—"

"I don't mean the money," he says. Then he looks over at the kid behind the counter, clearly listening. He puts a hand on my arm, then motions me outside.

We stand alone in the dark, empty parking lot, the only sound the buzz of the cicadas.

"Are you absolutely sure you want to go back to the hospital?" Jasper goes on. "You're not obligated, you know. Leo was right: being an Outlier doesn't mean that. You still have a choice. And I think you should choose looking out for yourself."

"This *is* me choosing, Jasper," I say, and for the first time, it actually feels like the truth. And it is such a relief.

Jasper nods and exhales—exhausted, scared. Resigned. And so loyal. "Okay then. It was worth a try."

"You don't have to go with me, though," I add. "I mean it. I'm so grateful for everything you've done. But this—well, it's a huge risk. I don't want you to feel like you have to—"

"You cannot fucking be serious," he says, crossing his arms tight and glaring angrily at me. And yes, he is hurt. I can feel that, too. "After everything we've been through, you're still going to try to pull that shit?"

"What shit?" I ask, stung and stunned.

"The whole 'I'm going to let you go and that makes me a good person.'"

"Well, I don't want you to—"

"To what? Feel obligated?" he snaps. "That's such bullshit, Wylie. Stop pretending that you're looking out for me when you're really trying to protect yourself. People feel obligated to each other. That's the whole point of life. What are you afraid of?"

"Afraid?" I ask, like that's absurd.

But telling Jasper to go has become such a reflex, I've stopped considering why I'm doing it. And the truth is I'm not sure I want to know.

"That's not what—"

"Does me being here put you on the hook?" Jasper goes on without letting me finish. Which is all for the best because I have no idea what to say. "Yep, absolutely. You *will* be on the hook, Wylie. So if you don't give a shit about me, say the word and I'm gone. But don't stand there and pretend that telling me to go is some act of generosity, when it's the most selfish thing in the fucking world."

My face feels hot, and my ears are ringing. "You and I, or this, or whatever—it's a terrible idea. I'm a mess, don't you see that?"

Jasper shakes his head. "And I tried to *choke* that kid. Not because I had to either. Because he pissed me off. I got mad. And sometimes when I get mad, I snap. Just like my dad. It's not something I like about myself. I'm trying to be different. It doesn't always work." He rubs a hand over his face. "Everybody's messed up, Wylie. It's a question of degree. And intent. If you keep waiting until you're fixed to live your life, you're going to have wasted so much time."

For a second, anger still bubbles up inside me, but it lacks the necessary oxygen to catch. Jasper is right. I am trying to push him away. Not so I can avoid owing him anything. So he can't decide that me and my issues aren't worth the effort. After all, you can't be cut loose if you've never attached yourself in the first place.

But none of that actually has anything to do with how I truly feel. And I may finally be running out of time to come clean.

"Please stay," I say finally. "I'm not afraid to go back to the hospital alone. I still don't *need* you. Not in that way. But I want you to stay."

And I wait for Jasper to say something more, for him to launch into some bigger, longer discussion, in that way he has of never shutting up. But instead, he steps forward, wraps a hand around the back of my neck. And then he is kissing me.

When we finally part, I am not breathless and unmoored like I am afraid I might be. I am steady still. And I am free.

"Okay," Jasper says quietly. "Then let's go."

24

WHEN WE FINALLY GET BACK TO BOSTON, WE HAVE THE CAB LEAVE US A FEW blocks away from Boston General Hospital. It's past four fifteen a.m., cutting it way closer to our four thirty a.m. deadline with Riel than I had expected. But still in time. *If* she sticks to the plan. If Agent Klute hasn't made it so she can't.

The sidewalks inside the Boston General Hospital grounds are dead quiet, totally empty, and the trees on either side of the driveway so tall and imposing in the dark. None of it feels encouraging. But it isn't long before we're at the Dwyer Wing, near the door that I came out from at the bottom of the fire stairs. No one has stopped us. Nothing has gotten in our way.

I wonder for a stupid second whether the door might somehow already be open. But, when I tug on it, it's still locked tight. And the dread is rising so strong and fast around me, the current might sweep me away.

"What's wrong?" Jasper asks. It must show on my face.

"Nothing," I say quickly. The last thing he needs is for me to be having second thoughts. "I just want this to work."

He nods. "It will." But he is only saying that because I need him to. "I'm going to go check the time on the bank clock," Jasper says. Without our phones we have no way to know what time it is except the slowly rotating numbers on a building across the street—time, date, temperature. "I'll raise my hand at 4:28, so you know we're close. I'll come back at 4:40."

It makes sense: a window to account for a difference in that clock and whatever one Riel might be relying on. *If* she is even keeping to the plan. *If* she has figured out how to open the doors. So many ifs. And will the door even make some kind of sound so that I'll know when it unlocks? I'll have no choice but to keep trying it in case it silently opens. I watch Jasper head out to almost the middle of the street in search of a clear view of the clock, drawing an unfortunate amount of attention to himself.

And then I wait.

Finally, up goes Jasper's arm and I try the door. Still locked. I count one one thousand. And then try again. Two more tries. Nothing.

"Hey, you!" a voice calls out from the darkness behind me. A security guard maybe, at least someone official—and officially unhappy—from the sound of it. Pretty far away still—far enough that he might not even be talking to me. Except that I know he is. "That's a secure area, you can't go in there!" I tug the door again. "Hey, get away from that door!"

Definitely talking to me. Jasper has seen him too. Because he's jogging back from the street over to me.

Jasper reaches me before the guard, and just when there is finally a buzz. The sound of the lock opening. And when I tug, the door moves. I can hardly believe it.

"Holy—" Jasper whispers.

"You can't go in there!" the guard shouts.

"Come on!" I call to Jasper.

We leap through and pull the door shut. Pray that it locks behind us. Sure enough, when the guard rattles the door a second later, he's locked out like we were. Still, we have to move fast now. It won't take him long to warn the right people. Soon they will know exactly where we are.

UPSTAIRS ON THE third floor, I brace myself for another locked door. But it is open, too, and a moment later we are in. The hospital hallway is utterly still at this hour. Not a soul in sight, not a sound. Just as we had hoped. Though I wish I felt better. Like things were going as planned. Because I feel just the opposite and I'm not sure why.

I try to focus instead on the task at hand: warning the girls. Each of us is in charge of waking half of them, then we will all run down and out the fire stairs. Not everyone will get away. But all we need is enough of us to prove what has happened. After that, they will have to let everyone go. This is not the best plan. But there are no better options. There are no other options at all.

I nod at Jasper and mouth the words "good luck" before we peel off in opposite directions, toward the sleeping girls at either end of the hall. As I walk on, the quiet feels so very heavy, my dread so high in my throat that it's hard to swallow. I am worried about not getting the girls out, definitely. Worried about the possibility of running into "fake Kelsey," too. I don't want to find out what she's really up to. Definitely don't want her to know what I know, and I don't trust myself to be able to block her well enough to hide it. I hope that she got out. For my sake now, not hers.

I stop just short of the rooms and try to think strategically. Teresa will need the most help. Woken in the middle of the night, she'll definitely panic. Ramona will stay the calmest. If I can get Ramona up, she can help with the others.

When I reach Ramona's room, I slip inside the darkness and quickly pull the door shut behind me. I feel my way over to the bureau to switch on the small light beside the mirror. If I startle Ramona awake with the big overhead, she might scream. It's a relief when the room finally lights up, but only until I turn to look at the bed.

Empty. Stripped. No Ramona. No nothing.

Am I in the wrong room? I must be. Half the rooms had been empty the whole time. Maybe Ramona's room wasn't the closest to the common room like I thought. I am turning to leave when I spot something on the floor, under the edge of the bed. Small and balled up and black. I duck down to investigate. It isn't until I pick it up that I can see it's the bracelet Ramona was always snapping, twisted up into a tight knot.

Wait. Maybe they moved everyone to the other side of the hospital after the fire? I overheard that when I was running out. To the side where they brought me in the beginning. That would make total sense. Of course, it would be much better if

I even remotely believed that's where everybody was. I'm still crouched down staring at the bracelet when Ramona's door starts to open.

Shit. I drop to my stomach. And scramble to hide in the only available place: under the bed. I want it to be Jasper. But I don't think it is. He's way at the other end of the hall.

My heart pounds once I'm under the bed frame, pressed against the cold linoleum. I watch as feet appear in the doorway. Women's shoes—lizard, high-heeled. I feel like I know this person. At least, she knows me. Or thinks she does.

My heart is thumping so hard that I'm starting to feel nauseous. But I can't come out. Those shoes are still in the doorway. And they are taking way too long to leave. Finally, they move, but inside. A second later the door eases closed.

"Wylie." A woman's voice, so quiet and calm. "Come out, please."

The voice, the fancy shoes. Rachel. My mom's ring. My mom's photographs. My eyes flood with furious tears. Does Rachel work for these people—the NIH or Dr. Cornelia or the Defense Intelligence Agency? There remain countless options.

"Please, Wylie," Rachel goes on when still I do not move. "They haven't given us much time. I need to talk to you."

They. Us. Still trying to pretend that she's on my side.

"Whatever you thought you guys were doing, Wylie—whatever you were trying to do . . ." And she is sad, too, completely and totally heartbroken. Which I don't like because it doesn't fit with anything else I'm thinking. "It was—it's not going to happen now. I'm sorry. Please come out. Otherwise, I won't get a chance to explain anything before they come."

Hiding is pointless if she knows where I am. And I have never in my life wanted an explanation for something more than I do at this moment. Even one that I will not believe. Finally, I slide out from under the bed.

"Wylie, honey," Rachel says, rushing toward me with her arms outstretched.

I lean clear of her reach. "What are you doing here?" I snap. "Where is Ramona?"

"It's okay, Wylie," Rachel says, but she does not think anything is okay. Not in the least. "I am going to keep on being here. We'll get through this together."

Through what? My stomach tightens. As much as I want it to be rage that I am feeling—for my mom and whatever Rachel's lies might be—all I feel is afraid.

"Where is Ramona?" My voice is quaking now. *I* am quaking.

"Home. They are all back home. They let them go," she says, trying to sound hopeful now. "All of them."

"Let them go home?" I know better than to believe her. She does not believe it herself. I'm just not sure which part is the lie. "Why would they let them go?"

"I ended up calling that friend of your mom's from the *New York Times*. And she called that friend of mine at the Justice Department after he started dodging me. And he, in turn, finally agreed to do his job and follow up with the NIH. Apparently what they were doing here didn't exactly go through the proper channels. If you ask me, the NIH isn't even involved, and what about the CDC? If this was official, they would be here, too.

Anyway, my Justice Department contact got real vague, real fast. And then poof, two hours later they are letting everybody go."

"That's it? They haven't explained anything? What about the girls' parents?"

"From what I can tell, they are not the demanding types. Seems like they chose the right girls to pick on."

"Have you found my dad?" I ask.

"No, honey, not yet," she says, trying to keep her face so calm and still. But I can feel the tears she is holding back like they are coming out of my own eyes.

"He wouldn't leave the airport, not when he knew I needed him to come back."

She holds up her hands. "I know," she says. "Believe me. And I told them that. We'll find him, Wylie. He is going to be okay."

"He has to be," I say, my voice catching.

But do I actually think he is? Do I feel that right now? The truth is: I have absolutely no idea.

Outlier Rule #6: When your own heart is breaking, you can't read anything anymore. Least of all yourself.

"I want to go home," I say, and not even to Rachel.

"That's why I came here, Wylie. To help you," she goes on, talking to me like I am some messed-up kid she is swooping in to save. Like she is the good guy.

"Fuck you." I glare at her.

"Fuck me?" Rachel asks, startled—and hurt, I can feel that, too. But it just makes me want to see her bleed.

"Yeah, fuck you," I say. My anger has lit my mouth on fire. "For trying to pretend that you are some kind of hero. You are a *liar.* You have been lying to my family this entire time."

"What?" Rachel blinks at me. So *wounded* now. Most of all I don't like how convincing it is.

"How did you get this?" I ask, lifting my mom's ring on the chain around my neck. "And what about her photographs? They were recent."

Rachel stares at the ring for a minute and then blinks some more as tears rush into her eyes. She hangs her head, crosses her arms. Guilt, so much of it. It isn't until that moment that I realize how badly I was hoping there would be some simple explanation.

But Rachel does not offer one. She does not offer anything.

"You need to give that ring to me, Wylie," she says instead. And she is desperate. "I can't explain why right now. And I get that you think I lied to you—I did lie to you. But not for the reasons you think. It's not safe for you to have that ring."

"Safe for who? You?" Once again, I am missing the most important thing. I can feel it, just out of reach. "Did you help them kill her?"

"You can't be serious, Wylie?" Rachel shouts right back. "Listen, I understand that finding the ring must have been confusing and upsetting, and I know that you need me to explain, but—" She motions to the hospital. "This? I didn't have anything to do with this. I'm here because the police contacted me and told me they were looking for you. That they knew we had been in contact. They said they were going to go out looking for you if you didn't come in for questioning, and I told them that would be unnecessary because I thought you would be coming here sooner or later. If they'd wait that I could meet you here and arrange for—"

"You told them I'd be coming here!"

"Because otherwise they were going to find you, Wylie. I was afraid when they did you would run, which—given everything—would be understandable, and that you would end up getting hurt. That happens when people run. I wanted to help you. To keep you safe."

"Help me?" I spit out. "You are such a liar."

Rachel closes her eyes, shakes her head. Regret, sadness. And she is still hiding something, definitely.

"Listen, Wylie, we will deal with everything you're talking about. I promise," Rachel goes on. "But we need to focus on right now. We need to talk while there's still time."

Time—and I feel it then: her fear. And that sadness hanging so heavy on top of it. *Still time for what?*

The door to the room opens then. When I startle and step forward, Rachel puts a protective hand on my wrist like she's ready to stop someone from dragging me away. Her fingers feel like sandpaper.

"Don't touch me." I pull out of her grasp.

"You've got another sixty seconds," says a man through the open door, his voice gruff and deep. "And then she's got to come with us."

The door drops closed again.

"Come with who?" My panic is beginning to kick into high gear. Agent Klute is who I'm thinking. "Who was that?"

"Wylie!" It's Jasper shouting out in the hall.

I lurch past Rachel, my legs awkward and numb. The world

is far away, fractured, as I jerk open the door and lunge out. Two steps and I crash into a police officer—not Agent Klute. The regular, uniformed kind.

"Whoa!" he shouts as I stumble. He grabs me by the arm and pulls me back to my feet. Beyond him, I can see another officer on Jasper, dragging him away.

"Get your hands off him!" I scream. "He didn't do anything!!"

"Whoa!" the officer holding me says again, amused by all my silly, silly noisemaking. "Why don't we just take a breath and calm down?"

"Let him go!" I shout again, then whip around to Rachel, who is still standing in the door. "You said you're trying to help! Do something!"

"Hey, calm down now," the officer says, more sharply now. He's just a regular old Boston cop, doesn't seem wound up or to be hiding anything—just a guy doing his job. "They are escorting your friend out. That's it. Take it down a notch, or we are going to have a whole new problem."

"Jasper!" I try one last time.

Finally, he turns. And though we are far away, I can still feel something. Can't I? How much he cares about me. Or no, that's not it. I can't be sure of that. But I can feel how much I care. Jasper raises a hand in return, still looking in my direction, as the police officer pushes him ahead and out the door.

"I'm leaving," I say to Rachel, taking a step forward.

"Nope." The officer has taken his hands off me but now he steps in my path. "Afraid not."

"Nope?" I snap at him. "We're free to go. This was all a mistake. Didn't you hear?"

It's a test. I'm not even sure of whom.

"Not you," he says.

I turn to Rachel, who is hovering closer now. "What is he talking about?"

"I am going to get you home as soon as I can, Wylie. That's why I'm here. We will work this out." Rachel takes a deep breath. "They haven't gotten into details. But apparently they want to question you further. About the fire here. The best way to get you out of here is to cooperate."

"All of this because of *that* fire?" I snap. "That was only a distraction, so we could get out. Like a trash can or something. Anyway, it wasn't even me. That was Kelsey."

Though I do have a bad feeling mentioning her name. I already know it isn't Kelsey. Kind of hard to point your finger at somebody when you don't know who they are.

"I know and I believe you." Rachel frowns. "We just need to take a minute and be sure that they do, too."

25

ON RACHEL'S INSTRUCTIONS, I DON'T ASK ANY MORE QUESTIONS. BECAUSE THAT might give up information I don't intend to reveal. Actually, she suggests I don't say another word to anyone until they've transported us down to the police station where they plan to interview me. Something she says again that I could refuse to do, but she suspects that could make things worse for me.

I ride once again in the back of a police car. I tell Rachel that she can leave, that I want her to. But she insists on coming down to the police station, driving in her own car close behind the police car. I should have a lawyer, she says, whether or not I want that person to be her.

When we get to a nearby Boston precinct—which is a lot grittier than the police station in Newton or Seneca—Rachel and I wait alone in a cold little room with a small table and four cramped chairs. It feels dirty and smells like sweat.

"We should assume they're listening even now when we're alone," Rachel says, pointing to imaginary microphones in the sky. "They aren't supposed to because I'm your lawyer and this conversation is confidential. But that doesn't always stop them. They can use what they hear, even if it isn't admissible in court. And once the questioning starts, be *extremely* careful. Keep your answers to the bare minimum. You'd be shocked how the littlest thing can be held against you."

"I didn't have anything to do with that fire," I say, and I'm not even sure for whose benefit. I couldn't care less what Rachel believes. Part of me still very much wants her to leave, but I lack the energy to make her get out.

"I know." Rachel reaches forward and puts her hand over mine, smiles at me sympathetically.

"Will you just stop?" I pull my hand away. "Do you think I would ever be stupid enough to trust you again? Why are you even here?"

Rachel winces and then nods. "Every way you feel about me, everything you are thinking—it's wrong. I mean incorrect, inaccurate. But I understand why you would feel that way. I wish I could explain everything right now," she says. "But I can't. It wouldn't be—I can't."

"How fucking convenient," I say, staring straight ahead.

"We can still get you another lawyer, Wylie. But I want to get you someone good, and that could take time. For this interview, I'm afraid you're stuck with me."

Finally, there's a knock. The door opens without waiting for us to say come in and a woman steps inside. She is sturdy-looking, in her fifties maybe—older than my mom, but not old enough to be my grandmother. Her blond hair is cut into a chin-length bob, which makes her wide-jawed face look even more like a square. There is a huge guy with her, younger and much less capable-seeming in his wrinkled khakis and too-tight white button-down.

"Wylie Lang?" she asks.

Polite, but cold. Focused, though, not exactly suspicious. Or trying not to be. Like she's determined not to make her mind up about anything until she has all the facts. After that she'll bring the hammer down without hesitation.

"Yeah," I say, once it's obvious that she's actually waiting for some kind of confirmation. "That's me."

"I'm Detective Nicole Unger." She holds out a strong hand, which I shake reluctantly. "And this is my colleague, Danny Martin." He nods but does not lift his eyes. "Do you know why you're here, Wylie?"

Already it feels like a trick question. Rachel nods when I glance her way.

"You can answer that, Wylie." Rachel is right—she is better than nothing. I can already feel her calculating how and when to push the detective for an explanation.

"Because you want to ask me about the fire?" I say.

"Yes," the detective says. "We need to know about the fire. You were the last person there before it started."

"You mean back by the rooms?" I ask. "Is that where it started? Because Teresa was there, too."

"Wylie," Rachel jumps in. "Make sure there's an actual question for you to answer. Don't volunteer information."

But that's because Rachel is used to dealing with guilty people.

I don't have anything to hide. I want to get it all out in the open.

"Seriously, you should ask Teresa about all this," I go on. And I am trying to decide how and when to mention Kelsey, or whatever her real name is. Despite all her lies, I do feel a weird kind of loyalty to her. She is one of the original Outliers. Throwing her under the bus when I don't know for sure that she did anything feels wrong. "Anyway, I was back in the common room when the alarm went off."

The detective is quiet for a moment, staring past me at a blank spot on the wall, a flat expression on her face. She's pretending to consider what I've said, though she isn't really. She is waiting to ask her next question. I don't think this is going well.

"Well, we would ask Teresa, but we can't," she says. And then she waits, staring at me. This is supposed to mean something. But it doesn't. Not to me.

"Okay, I'll bite," Rachel snaps. "*Why* can't you ask her, detective? Because we're getting a little tired of the 'hide the accusation' game you're playing. We'd like to be cooperative, but if you don't get to the point soon, we're leaving. I remind you that we are still here voluntarily."

"We can't ask Teresa because she's dead, Wylie. She died in the fire."

"What?" I lean forward, heart racing. "What are you talking about?"

"Okay, hold on." Rachel holds a hand up in front of me to keep me from talking. Worried. She is a lot more worried now. "What exactly is the scope of this investigation?"

This has caught Rachel off guard. The situation is much

worse than she thought. She doubts her instinct to cooperate. But all I feel is numb. Teresa? How is that even possible?

"It's hard to say right now," the detective says. Her partner is looking on, still mute. "I will say we're doing our best to keep an open mind." Except I'm not exactly sure that's true. "We feel we have enough evidence at this point to charge your client with arson and reckless endangerment, at a minimum. Unless she can explain away some of this evidence."

"At a minimum?" Rachel snaps. "And what evidence?"

The detective's eyes stay locked on mine.

"An argument between the girls, for one. What happened between you and Teresa before the fire started, Wylie? You had a disagreement?"

"I am going to advise against answering that question, Wylie," Rachel says to me. Then she turns to the detective. "Seems like you're fishing for your evidence right now."

"We didn't argue," I answer, even though Rachel just told me not to. How can the truth possibly hurt? "Teresa was upset, and she asked me to walk her back to her room. And so we talked for a little while and then I left her room. After that, the fire must have started, I guess."

"You guess?"

I am going to have to mention Kelsey. I have no choice.

"Did you talk to Kelsey?" I ask. "Maybe she knows what happened."

"Kelsey?"

"She was another one of the girls in the hospital."

The detective consults the manila folder in front of her on the table. She pulls out a piece of paper and puts it in front of me. "This is a list of all the girls who were there," she says. "I don't see a Kelsey on that list, do you?"

Of course it's not there. Kelsey isn't her name. But how can I explain all that? Instead, I just stare down at the list of names. Whatever I say now will sound like an insane lie.

"Let's move on." The detective pulls something else out of her manila folder and slides it across the table toward me. "Do you remember seeing that?"

When I look down, it's a photograph of the baby I threw into the garbage. I pick it up with two fingers. More proof against me. None of this has been a coincidence. Of course it hasn't.

"Wylie, I advise you again not to answer that question," Rachel says, and more sharply. "They can twist things you say here in ways you can't anticipate. Don't hand them evidence."

But I still have the truth on my side. I believe that. I have to.

"Somebody left that for me," I say. Besides they must already know all of this anyway. "They used to leave dolls like that for us at my house, too, before Cassie ever—for a long time."

"Wylie," Rachel growls. "Stop talking."

"From what we've heard it sounds like you were upset to get one in the hospital," the detective says. "Were you angry that Teresa left it for you?"

"What are you talking about?" I ask. "She didn't leave it."

"Well, we found another one exactly like it in her bag. The baby definitely belonged to her."

I try not to react, though it isn't easy. Why the hell would Teresa have left that baby for me? And why would she have another one in her bag? I think back to that weird feeling I had about her being excited. Is this what she was hiding? Some connection to whoever had been sending the babies all along?

"Even if that's true, I didn't know," I say when I realize that they are still waiting for me to answer. "So how could I be angry?"

"Okay, then maybe you can explain instead why you're wearing Teresa's necklace?" she asks. I put my hand to my throat. The cross. The one that's up against my mom's ring, the one Teresa gave me for protection. I close my eyes. It had given me such a terrible feeling at the time. But I had ignored that instinct and put it on anyway because I hadn't wanted to offend her. And now it's another nail in my coffin. "Our understanding is that she never took that necklace off. It was extremely special to her. Seems unlikely she'd just give it to you. Unless maybe she was dead before the fire started, and that's when you took it off her? We'll have to wait for an autopsy to know her cause of death."

"Come on," Rachel snaps at the detective. "That's absurd. Wylie, do not—"

"They were basically holding us prisoner. I mean, that might not be important to you, but it was important to the—"

"Wylie," Rachel hisses. "Stop talking. Seriously."

When I look at her, I can feel how desperately she means this. However much of a liar she is, she is truly convinced that talking is bad for me. She may even be right. What do the lies they told us about PANDAS matter now? They've taken it all back with a well-timed "so glad we were wrong."

"We found the matches, Wylie."

"What matches?"

"Under the mattress in your room."

"Matches?" I'd think she had to be joking except for the way she keeps staring at me. "Well, I don't know how they got there."

"So they aren't yours?" the detective asks skeptically.

"No," I say. "They are not mine."

"Move on, detective," Rachel says, trying to sound relaxed, confident that we have the upper hand. But I can feel she's afraid she won't be able to drag me out of this huge hole I've jumped down into. "We've been polite and patient. We did as you asked and came here voluntarily to answer your questions. And now Wylie would like to go home."

The detective presses her lips together. But it is not a smile.

"You were involved in another fire recently, weren't you?" she asks me, ignoring Rachel. "Six weeks ago? A friend of yours died?"

"You are joking," Rachel huffs.

"A girl died in a fire in both cases," the detective says, like she doesn't understand all the fuss. "And in both situations, Wylie was right there. Like maybe it's her MO."

"That's absurd. Especially because Wylie wasn't accused of any wrongdoing in the fire in Maine. She and Cassie were both *victims*, clear and simple."

"Still, it is a coincidence. Can you explain that, Wylie?"

"Wylie, do n—"

"No," I say, because that is the whole and complete truth. "I can't explain it. There is nothing to explain."

"You were in the immediate vicinity on both occasions. You were right there when both girls died. And you seriously have no idea why that might be? Because to be clear, Wylie, Teresa wasn't just killed in the fire," the detective goes on. "Teresa *was* the fire. She was at its epicenter. Just like Cassie. At least that is my understanding. Two girls—who you were angry at—died in the exact same way. Suspicious, wouldn't you say?"

"Detective, this is ridiculous, and also unnecessarily cruel," Rachel says. Her voice is icy. And she is furious now. Furious on my behalf.

"Angry?" I ask. "I wasn't angry."

"That's not what Cassie's father says."

"Vince?" The more the detective talks, the more confused I am. "He said *I* was mad at Cassie? How would he even know? He doesn't even live here. I wasn't mad at *Cassie.*"

"But you *were* angry at Teresa then?"

"Enough!" Rachel smacks a palm down on the table. "That's it. That was the last question. We were trying to be cooperative, but you are twisting her words." She stands and motions for me to get up. "Come on, Wylie. We're leaving."

"Not tonight, I'm afraid," the detective says. "We've got witness statements, the matches, your client's history. Unless she's prepared to offer an explanation right now, that's more than enough probable cause for an arrest."

"Arrest for what?" Rachel asks.

The detective looks squarely at me. "For murder."

26

THE REST HAPPENS PRETTY MUCH EXACTLY THE WAY RACHEL SAYS IT WILL. THEY place me formally under arrest. They read me my rights, though they had already read them to me before I was questioned with Rachel.

Afterward, they transfer me to the closest juvenile detention facility. When I arrive, there is another reading of my rights, an inventory of my clothing and personal belongings, of which there is so little—what was left of Rachel's cash and my mom's wedding ring. Detached from Teresa's necklace, which was taken for evidence, the ring spins hopelessly around the empty personal-effects bin. It makes me wonder about my mom's photographs, and whether Riel really will keep them safe and sound.

By the time they have taken my clothes; searched me in more humiliating ways than I would have thought possible; finger-printed me; photographed me; and made me answer endless informational questions, I feel exactly as Rachel had warned me I would: far less than human.

My cellmate's name is Susan and she is a way nicer attempted murderer than I have any right for her to be. At least so far. By the time I meet her, I only have a few minutes before they bring me to a courthouse with others in a big van for my arraignment. It's not as stressful as it might be, because, by now, I feel nothing. I am going through the motions of basic human existence— breathing, moving, blinking—without actually being alive.

Rachel stands next to me in court. She says some things to the judge. The prosecutor—a round, bald man—says some other things. Their words are garbled and far away as though I am underwater and they are on the shore. I do hear talk about the fact that my dad cannot be located. That my mother is deceased. In the end, they deny me bail. I understand that much. I am a flight risk, they say. I have run so many times before. Finally, a fact that is hard to argue with.

When it's over, Rachel tries to hug me. I am glad when they yell at her. I don't want her touching me.

"I'm going to get you out of here, Wylie," she calls as they take me away. "I'm talking days." But she does not believe this, no matter how much she wants to.

I have not seriously considered finding a new lawyer. Not that Rachel has explained anything to my satisfaction. The only thing she has even tried to get into is why her friendship with my mom ended. She says she was representing people that my mom didn't approve of, which only makes me more suspicious. Still, I don't press for details. They no longer seem to matter. Nothing does.

AFTER BREAKFAST ON the third day, I hear my nickname for the first time—Firebug. It could be much worse. Honestly, I am lucky about the rumors: I am psychic, I lit two friends on fire. Even in here, they are freaky enough that people keep their distance.

Rachel asks me to call Gideon. *He* asked her to ask me to call. Rachel helped him clean up the house and has been checking in on him. But he is staying with friends until they find my dad. *Until.* That is a word that Rachel uses on purpose. So I am reassured.

But I am not reassured. Not in the least.

"ARE YOU OKAY?" Gideon asks after he accepts my collect call from a "Massachusetts Youth Detention Facility" on the fourth day. He sounds jittery and fragile.

"Yeah, I'm okay," I say, trying to make him feel better. Of course, I am not okay, I want to shout. I am in a "detention facility."

Rachel has hinted that Gideon is seriously freaking out. That he has been ever since I got arrested. It does not help that there is still no sign of my dad. Soon he will have been gone for a week. Rachel has said for the first time that we need to be realistic.

I see no benefit to that.

In describing Gideon, Rachel has tried to surf a more hopeful line—bad shape, but not scary. She took him to see Dr. Shepard and supposedly that helped. Sort of. Or, in other words, not much at all. Rachel was also able to confirm that none of the girls were Dr. Shepard's patients, not even Teresa. With my dad missing, and me in here, maybe it's no surprise Gideon is falling apart.

"I wanted to say . . ." Gideon's voice catches now as we talk on the phone. Is he *crying*? I have not seen Gideon cry since he was five, and that was only when he'd sliced his finger open with a broken piece of glass. He is really, seriously losing it.

"It's going to be okay, Gid," I say, though I'm not at all convinced. Also, I am kind of pissed that I have to cheer him up when I am the one locked away. Still, Gideon's need right now is real. So real it takes my breath away.

"I'm sorry," he says, pushing the words out with force.

"You don't have to be sorry, Gideon. This isn't your fault."

"But it is my fault."

"Seriously, Gid, no it is—"

"I gave them the list, Wylie!"

"What?" And for a second my brain ceases to function—the blood, the nerves, all frozen.

"I'm sorry, I was so—I'm sorry. I emailed that Cornelia guy because I was curious, and he said he agreed with me that it didn't make sense that it was only girls and that Dad must have made some kind of small error. He said he would look into it, you know. He listened to me. Dad wouldn't. And so I gave him the list and your name, too. But, I swear, I had no idea what he planned to do."

I am pressing the phone so hard to my ear, it has started to throb. The crazy thing? I want to hate him, to scream at Gideon that he is selfish and reckless. And evil. But I can't get myself to say a word. And still I don't feel a thing.

"Wylie?" Gideon says. "Are you still there? I am so sorry."

///////////////////////////////

TIME MARCHES AHEAD. I feel certain there is no way I will survive long in a place like this. And yet I keep on waking up. It's not even the Youth Detention Facility that's the problem. It's the world. A world where these terrible things keep on being true about Cassie, my mom, my dad. Gideon.

I start to have panic attacks again. Worse than ever before, two or three a day sometimes. Once I black out in the TV room. The guard on duty threatens me with solitary if I do it again. I know I could demand to see a doctor. They can't punish me for an anxiety disorder. But I don't. Because I wonder if solitary would be such a bad thing.

I've gotten letters from Ramona and Becca. Rachel asked them to write, I'm sure. She thinks it will help if I have proof the other girls really had made it out all right. The letters were mechanical, polite. Basic. I noticed what they did not say: we know you are innocent.

Riel sends a letter, too. Or rather a letter arrives that I think is from Riel. *Courage is the price that life exacts for granting peace.* That's all it says. Her name is nowhere on it.

One person I haven't heard from is Jasper. The judge issued a "no contact" order. It is a condition of his probation on the trespassing charges. The point, Rachel has said, is to make my life more miserable so I am more likely to tell them what they want to hear. So that I will confess to a crime I did not commit.

But that is something I will not do no matter how much I miss Jasper. And I do miss him. It is as simple and as complicated as that.

///////////////////////////////

BEFORE LUNCH ON the sixth day, we all head to watch TV as we do each day at that time. Or at least the TV is on, and it is in front of me as I sit on one of several long couches, each with space for six other girls. I stare at the screen, but I couldn't tell you what's ever on. Still, it seems better for me to be there with other people than alone in my room. More and more I have the overwhelming sense of something horrifying hurtling my way. And soon. I feel like there should be witnesses.

"Lang, you've got a visitor," a guard shouts.

I stare at him blankly, wonder if I am imagining things.

"Come on," he shouts, pointing me to the door. "Let's go."

Jasper? I feel a sudden wave of stupid hope. My racing heart sends blood rushing into my half-dead limbs. I jump to my feet. *Please. Please. Please.* Even though I know it can't be him. That it shouldn't be, for Jasper's sake.

"Who is it?" I ask as I make my way more quickly to the door.

The guard huffs and consults his clipboard. "Brother," he says, and my heart sinks.

I don't blame Gideon for what he did. Or I do, but I also understand. It was stupid and immature and selfish. And impulsive.

He wasn't thinking. But none of what happened is at all what he intended. Still, I don't want to actually see him. I'm not sure I have the energy to lie and let him off the hook to his face.

I consider telling the guard I am not up for visitors, but that could backfire. If I make Gideon feel worse, he'll demand that I carve out even more of my heart and hand it to him.

///////////////////////////

"NAME?" THE VISITING room guard asks when I finally make my way reluctantly down there.

"Wylie Lang," I say, still waiting for something to head me off at the pass. Instead, the guard just opens the door and waves me inside. The visiting room is a single open space with eight rectangular tables—all numbered—arranged in two rows. There are two chairs on each side. Two guards on either side of the room. It's more ordinary than I would have imagined before I was locked up in here—no plastic booths, no conversations by phone.

"Table seven, far side." He motions across the room. "You got fifteen minutes. No touching. No objects exchanged."

The room is so crowded, I don't spot Gideon until I'm on that side of the room. In a baseball hat, head low. I can't see his face, but his posture seems worse than before. So hunched. I come around from behind him and take a deep breath. Try to convince myself I can do this again. Cheer Gideon up for betraying me.

When he finally looks up at me, the world rocks hard to the side.

"Have a seat," Quentin says.

Scream. That is my first instinct. I look around, eyes wide. I want to spit at him, too. I want to slap him in the face.

"I wouldn't do that." He looks me up and down in my sad blue jumpsuit. "Any of what you're thinking."

As I lower myself onto the edge of the chair, I'm not sure I could make a sound if I tried.

"You're alive," I whisper. *Twelve not eleven bodies.* Somewhere in me I knew this, didn't I? My dad. That's what I think next. "What did you do to him?"

"Who?"

"My dad."

"Your dad?" Quentin says. "What happened to your dad?"

"He's missing," I say. "Something happened to him."

Quentin shakes his head grimly. "Well, I did warn him, didn't I? I told him there might be trouble."

"If I tell the people here who you are, they'll arrest you."

"God, you believe that, don't you?" It isn't even sarcastic. It's like he actually feels sorry for me. "Think about how much you would have to explain. And how absurd it will sound. By the time you find someone to listen, I'll be long gone. Besides, then you'll never know why I came."

"Why would they let you go?" I ask, but I'm not sure I want to know.

"'Let go' isn't exactly a fair characterization. 'Were easily misled' is more accurate. And I did have help," he says quietly, like he regrets something. "I told you North Point has significant resources."

"But why would they help you? Why would anyone?"

"I convinced them that there were things only your dad and I knew and that if they were going to make a run at winning the Outliers race, they'd need my exclusive information. That does mean I will need to show them something, or I suspect there will be nasty consequences. I'd like to avoid that, which led me here. To you."

"I would never help you," I manage through gritted teeth.

"Not even if I have information that could get you out of here?"

"Did you send that text from Jasper's phone?" Because all I can think is that this has been his end game all along.

"Text?"

"The one that told me to run. Right after we got back from Maine."

"*Run?*" And he is confused for real. "Um, no."

He didn't send it. I can read that loud and clear. Kendall maybe. Probably. He's who I have been thinking.

"You *killed* Cassie," I say, pushing myself to my feet. "I would never help you, you sick asshole."

"If you help me, I can help you get out of here. You said yourself that someone has your dad. He must need you."

Quentin believes what he's saying. He is telling the truth. His truth. Of course, his truth doesn't have anything to do with mine.

"I would rather die in here than help you."

"And what about your dad, and Gideon? You're just going to leave them out there with whoever is responsible for you being in here?" The threat is loud and clear. "There are things you don't know, Wylie."

"Like what?"

"Like who killed Teresa. And who left that baby for you. And, to be clear, it wasn't me."

"Go to hell," I whisper. But God, how I hate that he knows about that baby. How does he know that?

"I even have proof, which I could give you and you could use to exonerate yourself. Details that would make their version of events far less plausible." He takes a breath. "Provided you are willing to help me in return."

My stomach is pushing up into my throat and I feel light-headed. If Quentin knows about the baby, there is a chance he really knows something that could get me out of here. And I do need out. My dad needs me out.

"You don't know anything." A test. I need to feel his answer.

Quentin smiles. "But I do," he says, and with such awful, unavoidable certainty. Quentin stands, pushes a note card across the table to me. "Here's my number. If you change your mind about helping me, give me a call and we can make arrange-ments." He looks around the room and frowns. "But if I were you, I would hurry. Terrible things can happen in a place like this."

I AM SURPRISED to discover myself back in the TV room some time later. I walked there somehow and now I am sitting on the couch, limbs attached, heart beating. But otherwise I am completely numb. I don't remember the last thing I said to Quentin. I don't remember making it back down the hall. I am sure only of the overwhelming sense that I have lost, even if Quentin hasn't really won.

I don't know how long I sit there. Girls come and go. The TV show changes, time moves on. Eventually, I hear a distant sound at the back of the room, rattling metal, something squeaky.

"Librarian is here," one of the guards calls out. And there's an edge to his voice like he can't believe he's got to bother with this crap. "You got ten minutes to pick out some books."

Books. The idea seems so ludicrous to me. What with the world on fire and all. But the other girls head over, whooping and jostling like they are headed to an ice cream truck. It's been the same each time the volunteers have come by—a different overly kind old woman each time.

"US Weekly!" I hear someone shout, triumphant.

"You still don't got the last Harry Potter back?" someone else asks. "That is such bullshit. They can't keep it forever."

It's sad, hearing how excited they are doing something so many others their age complain about. It makes me wonder if that is how I will feel before long, excited by things I have always taken for granted. And how long it will take before I do—or say—whatever they want? Before I confess just so that they will stop asking questions. At least then I'd never have to talk to Quentin again.

I keep my eyes straight ahead when the squeaky library cart is finally coming closer and closer. I have a bad feeling that the librarian has her sights set on me, probably because I am one of the only girls who didn't get up. I brace myself for a lecture about how reading is fundamental, how it will offer me a path to redemption. I hope that I do not say something nasty in return. But I cannot be sure. I trust myself less and less with each passing hour.

"Last call for books!" the guard shouts.

Finally, the cart stops right behind me. I do not look up. But out of the corner of my eye, I watch the librarian put a paperback down on the arm of the couch next to me. And then I feel this wave of kindness. It's so strong and pure and not at all judgmental like I had expected. It catches me off guard. So much that I'm pretty sure I'll start crying if I look up at her. And so I keep my eyes down. In here, I am much better off being the girl who sets her friends on fire than being the one who cries to the volunteer librarian.

"Okay, that's it!" the guard calls.

But her cart is still there. It hasn't squeaked away. The librarian is still waiting for me. I can feel how much she wants me, needs me—in some totally irrational way—to look up and let her know that I am okay. That I will be okay. Why does this woman need that? She doesn't even know me. I try to swallow my anger back.

But maybe her caring is a sign that I need to believe myself that I will be okay. I breathe deep and try to imagine getting through this. And when I do, a little gap in time opens, a window forward.

And my instincts say that I will. That if I can just be brave enough to have faith, if I can be strong enough to have hope—that I will make it through. Like all the other terrible things that have happened, I will survive this. Whatever it takes. I can believe that. No matter how impossible it seems.

"Hey," the librarian whispers, her voice hoarse and gravelly. And now her kindness and caring are even stronger. Warm and bright around me. Like the sun. Like love. "Take this."

When I look down, she is holding out another paperback, and on top of it, a note. *I'm going to get you out of here. I promise. xoxo.*

And when I look up, it is not some friendly old librarian I see. Instead, it is my mom. Alive and well and staring down at me.

ACKNOWLEDGMENTS

To my fierce editor, Jennifer Klonsky, thank you for your brilliant editorial insight, tenacious enthusiasm, and endless kindness. Endless gratitude to my entire badass Harper team: Gina Rizzo, Elizabeth Ward, Catherine Wallace, and Elizabeth Lynch. I am so lucky to be the beneficiary of your wisdom and hard work and to get to hang out with such a fab group of women.

Deepest thanks to Suzanne Murphy and Kate Jackson for championing this series from the start and continuing to enthusiastically cheer it along.

Thanks also to the rest of the fabulous Harper marketing, publicity, and library teams: Nellie Kurtzman, Cindy Hamilton, Patty Rosati, Molly Motch, and Sabrina Abballe. Thanks also to those mad geniuses in integrated marketing: Colleen O'Connell and Margot Wood. Many thanks to the astounding art department: Barb Fitzsimmons, Alison Donalty, Alison Klapthor, and the supremely gifted Sarah Kaufman.

Thank you to the passionate and devoted Harper sales team: Andrea Pappenheimer, Kerry Moynagh, and Kathy Faber. Thanks also to Jen Wygand, Jenny Sheridan, Heather Doss, Deb Murphy, Fran Olson, Susan Yeager, Jess Malone, and Jess Abel, as well as Samantha Hagerbaumer, Andrea Rosen, and Jean McGinley.

And last, but certainly not least, thank you to all the committed people in Harper managing editorial: Josh Weiss, Bethany Reis, and proofreader Valerie Shea.

Thank you to the many bloggers dedicated to spreading the word about the books they love. And thank you, thank you, thank you to the many passionate booksellers on the front lines. We authors and readers are so grateful for your wise counsel placing books into the right hands, often at just the right moment.

Many thanks to my loyal friend and agent extraordinaire, Marly Rusoff. I am so lucky to have you captaining my ship. A special thank-you to Julie Mosow for your exceptional advice and tireless assistance. Thanks also to Michael Radulescu and Gina Iaquinta for your support. To the amazingly talented, hardworking, and miraculously resourceful Kathleen Zrelak and Lynn Goldberg—forever grateful for all you have done. Thank you also to the ever-fabulous Shari Smiley and Lizzy Kremer and a special thanks to Harriet Moore.

My gratitude to the numerous experts who have so generously lent me their time and their wisdom: Victoria Cook, Elena Evangelo, Dr. Michael Henry, Mark Merriman, Sarabinh

Levy-Brightman, Tracy Piatkowski, Dr. Rebecca Prentice, Daniel Rodriguez, Michael Stackow, and Tanya Weisman.

Endless thanks to my fantastic friends and family: Martin and Clare Prentice, Mike Blom, Leslie Berland, Catherine and David Bohigian, Cindy, Christina, and Joey Buzzeo, Jason Miller, Megan Crane and Jeff Johnson, Cara Cragan and Michael Moroney, the Cragan family, the Crane family, Joe and Naomi Daniels, Larry and Suzy Daniels, Bob Daniels and Craig Leslie, Diane and Stanley Dohm, Dan Panosian, Dave Fischer, Heather and Michael Frattone, Tania Garcia, Sonya Glazer, Nicole and David Kear, Merrie Koehlert, Hallie Levin, John McCreight and Kim Healey, Brian McCreight, Nina Mehta, the Metzger family, Jason Miller, Tara and Frank Pometti, Stephen Prentice, Motoko Rich and Mark Topping, Jon Reinish, Bronwen Stine, the Thomatos family, Deena Warner, Meg and Charles Yonts, Denise Young Farrell, and Christine Yu.

Kate Eschelbach, thank you for taking such great care of us.

To my remarkable daughters, Emerson and Harper: I am so glad that you are people who feel so much. Know that you sharing with me so many of your feelings—the good and the bad and the terrifying and the hopeful and the loving and the angry and the wise—will forever be the greatest gift I receive.

And to my husband, Tony, thank you for always being there for me—accepting and patient and understanding—to share my feelings with. Good news, bad news for you: there are *so* many more where those came from.

Find out what happens next in

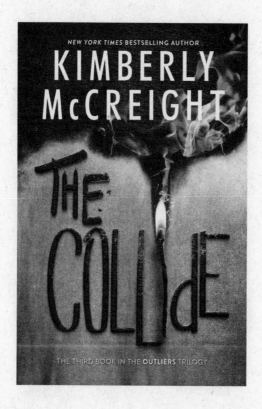

WYLIE

I STAND IN FRONT OF THE GRAY DETENTION-FACILITY DOOR, WAITING FOR IT TO buzz open. In my hand is a plastic grocery bag stuffed with the mildewed Cape Cod T-shirt and shorts I was wearing when I was arrested.

For the past two weeks, I've been in the standard-issue pajama-like shirt and pants twenty-four hours a day. So stiff, it's like they were designed so you'd never sleep again. My current outfit is the total opposite. Expensive pair of denim shorts, threadbare in just the right places, and an absurdly soft plain gray T-shirt. Without me having to ask, Rachel brought the clothes in for me to wear home. And I'm grateful for that. I've felt grateful to Rachel for a lot of things.

Like starting with getting me out on bail. It wasn't that complicated, Rachel says. Still, they went to so much trouble to get me in there, I didn't think they'd let me go just because Rachel filed some papers. But I was wrong. Rachel came through for me, once again. According to her, it wasn't just about the papers, though. It was who you called after you filed them.

And I do credit Rachel alone, not my mom. *I'm going to get you out of here. Xoxo.* That's what my mom's note said. And on the other side: *Trust Rachel. She will help you. She saved my life.*

But those were just words. It's easy to make promises and then disappear. It's sticking around to face what you've done that's the hard part.

RACHEL LOOKED SHEEPISH when she came to visit the morning after my mom had appeared like a ghost, pushing that creaky detention facility library cart. She *felt* guilty, too, I could read that loud and clear. We were in one of the small private rooms reserved for meetings with attorneys. The rooms that always smelled like onions and were freezing cold. The ones that Rachel cautioned weren't actually that private at all.

It was Rachel's guilt that erased all doubt. Not only had Rachel known my mom had come to see me in the detention facility, she had known the whole time that my mom was alive.

As I sat down across from her, I wanted so badly for her to be an Outlier, so she could feel the full force of my rage. Rachel had lied to me repeatedly. Had I felt joyful when I'd looked up and seen my mom—my actual mom, risen from the grave—staring down at me with all that love in her eyes? Sure, I guess. Okay, yes, definitely. But a day later, it was mixed up in a stew of other feelings: anger, sadness, confusion, betrayal.

But my mom wasn't there for me to take that out on her. Rachel was. And so, laying into her would have to do.

There was also no excuse for the fact that I'd missed Rachel's deception. But she was usually really hard to read; the guilt today was kind of an exception. Maybe it was so many years of saying whatever it took for her clients. The only real constant was that Rachel always told less than the whole truth. Like it was a reflex. Trying to get a fix on her true feelings was like trying to grab a bolt of lightning in your hands. It probably made her an awesome lawyer. It did not make her an easy person to trust. In my defense, I never fully had. I had just come to accept that I did not.

"First, I need to remind you, be careful what you discuss in here." Rachel motioned overhead before I could say a word, to the invisible prying eyes in our smelly "private" attorney room. "But I'm sure you're confused."

"Confused?" I snapped. "How about seriously pissed off?"

She nodded, relieved. Glad not to be keeping my mom's secret anymore, maybe. "That's fair, too."

"Explain," I shot back, leaning closer. I pressed a finger into the tabletop. "Right now."

Rachel looked away. "It was a real risk for her to come here, dangerous, you know. But she did it anyway because she wanted to be sure you believed. She knows how much you've been through, and she didn't want you to think I was making it up, or jerking you around or whatever."

Worry. For a moment, from Rachel, just a flash. But not a trace of regret. "We are lucky I know the volunteer supervisor here from the adult facility. She did me a solid, letting your special visitor volunteer."

"Right." I said, my anger seeping away despite my grip like water through cupped fingers. "So. Lucky."

"Listen, if it makes a difference, she didn't know it was going to turn out this way," Rachel said. And this much was true, I was pretty sure. "Your—" She stopped herself, eyes darting around. "*She* turned up out of nowhere at my house the night of the accident. I hadn't talked to her in what, ten years? But she thought someone was following her, and she ended up driving near my house. She was lucky I even lived there after all this time. To be honest, at first I thought she was drunk or having an episode or something. She sounded so paranoid, delusional almost. But she was just *so* freaked out. How could I risk not helping? I don't know, maybe part of it was selfish, too. We didn't end on the best terms, your mom and I. Maybe I thought this was a chance to prove that she was wrong about me."

"Wrong about what?" The question felt weirdly important.

"You know your mom. She's an avenging angel. And I gave up on noble a long time ago." Rachel shrugged. Another cold, hard truth. Rachel might not have been ashamed, but she wasn't proud of it, either. "Anyway, I didn't think it would be a big deal to ask somebody to drive your mom's car out of there. The girl in the car was the girlfriend of a client of mine. I'd hired her to clean my house, run errands. I knew she needed cash. She'd been sober for two months, trying to get her life straight. I thought it would be a win-win."

"Not so much for that girl driving," I said, deciding not to mention the vodka bottle. Maybe the girl wasn't so sober after all, but it felt wrong to expose her now.

"Yeah, not so much," Rachel said. She knew she should feel guilty but wasn't quite all the way there.

"And after the crash, my mom disappearing and pretending to be dead was, like, the only logical option?" I sounded pissed, but sadness was closing in fast. "Going to the police or something normal like that was totally out of the question?"

"You know better than anybody that trusting the police isn't always a simple proposition, Wylie. Besides, your mom was too worried about you guys," Rachel said. "Something about baby dolls? She thought they were meant as a threat to you guys, specifically—her babies."

"They weren't even for her," I said, though my mom wouldn't have known that at the time. "We kept getting them after she was gone. *I* got one in the hospital. Anyway, my mom pretended like the dolls were nothing to worry about."

"What was she supposed to say? 'Everybody freak the hell out?' Anyway, there were other things, too, apparently," she said. "Emails. Anonymous ones. They mentioned you guys specifically. After the accident, she was convinced the only way she could keep you safe was to let the people after her think they had succeeded. That she was dead."

"Great plan," I said, sounding extra snide.

"Well, it's easy to see now that everything had to do with your dad's research. But your mom had taken lots of pictures that had pissed off lots of people. It wasn't until your dad told her what happened with that assistant of his up at the camp in Maine—"

"Wait, what?" My chest clamped tight. "My dad *knew* she was alive?"

"Not until *after* the camp." Rachel avoided eye contact. "Once your mom realized that her accident—that the threats—were really about his work, she had to let him know she was alive. Your dad wasn't happy. But he understood, eventually. They decided together it was safer not to tell you and Gideon. That your mom had a better chance of helping behind the scenes if no one knew she was alive." Rachel leaned forward eagerly, but it felt forced. "And your mom's been all over the country, Wylie, working behind the scenes meeting people, enlisting help from scientists, journalists, politicians. She's been assembling a team to help. Everything has been to protect you."

"Protect me?" I swallowed over the lump in my throat, motioned to the walls of the detention facility. "How is this safe?"

"You're alive, Wylie," Rachel said. "Aren't you?"

"YO, HELLO?" THE tall guard with the long hair shouts at me. I'm still standing at the exit door. Sounds like she's been buzzing it open for a while. "You want to stay in here? Go on, go ahead!"

No, I definitely do not want to stay locked up. I startle forward, gripping my crinkly plastic bag tighter. Besides the mildewed clothes, inside are an envelope with what's left of Rachel's money (a dried and wrinkled eighty dollars) and my mother's wedding ring. Part of me wants to dig the ring out and hold it tight. Part of me wants to toss it down the nearest storm drain. My mom taking her ring off and leaving it behind had been Rachel's idea. Overkill, Rachel acknowledged now. But she had helped people disappear before. Better safe than sorry.

Finally, I step out into the July morning sun, hot already even at seven a.m., the weirdly early release time. I hold up a hand to shield my eyes from the glare as I scan the parking lot. The air is heavy and damp, weighing down my lungs. My anxiety has been relentless since I was arrested. Like a concrete slab strapped to my chest is ever so slowly crushing me to death. Dr. Shepard said this was to be expected—the stress of the detention facility, the claustrophobia.

Except, now that I'm outside, it doesn't seem better. I need to get going, and stay moving. Forward momentum always helps; it is the only good thing I learned from the horror of the camp in Maine.

It isn't until I start walking that I finally spot him, leaning against the front of the car at the far edge of the parking lot. Like he didn't want to fully commit to being there. He pushes himself up and waves, smiles way too hard.

Gideon.

Even from that distance, I can feel his guilt. The longer our dad is missing, the more Gideon blames himself. These days, guilt is what Gideon has become.

I've told him that he's holding himself responsible for way too much. The list of Outliers that Gideon gave to Dr. Cornelia might have been a shortcut to a bigger group of Outliers to round up, but I was the one who encouraged our dad to go to DC, where he was grabbed by God knows who. Somebody working for Quentin, I still assume. Though Quentin had seemed genuinely shocked when I told him about my dad the day he'd shown up in his baseball cap at the detention facility. But who else? Senator Russo? Sure, my dad was supposed to meet with him, but Rachel forced the DC police to check him out every which way. There is a mile-deep paper trail proving he was in Arizona.

And I may still be convinced Russo has done something really bad, but even I don't think that thing was taking my dad. No one was ever able to find the woman who supposedly had my dad's phone, either. Leaving the single, solitary clue about what happened to him the security video of him leaving the airport with someone, then getting into a black sedan. I haven't seen the video, but Rachel has. She says that my dad looks to be walking "normally" in the video, as in voluntarily. But then, he'd been expecting someone to come pick him up. It's not surprising that he would have gone with whoever it was.

The man, we assume a man, is only visible from the back. Shortish, with his hood up. That's all Rachel can say. Basically, he could be anyone. Quentin, even. All roads still lead back to him in my mind.

I promised Rachel that I'd tell Gideon about our mom. But now that he's there on the other side of the parking lot, I wish I had refused. Because I know just how bad it feels to find out she lied. I've been mad at Gideon a lot lately, but I would never wish that pain on him. I wouldn't wish it on anyone.

Gideon takes a couple steps toward me and waves again. I start across the parking lot to him when a white van whooshes past in front of me. So close that it sends me rocking back on my heels. I watch as the van pulls to a hard stop at the detention facility gates. A second later, they swing open and it speeds inside. That guard was right, what am I waiting for? Terrible things happen with wasted time.

"Hey," Gideon says when I finally reach him. He motions to my bag. "You need help?"

It's sweet. But sweet Gideon makes the world feel unsteady and upside down.

Even not-sweet Gideon isn't my first choice right now. I would have preferred Jasper. Then I could have finally wrapped my arms around him like I've been wanting to every day for the past two weeks. But getting out happened so fast. They told me only yesterday after Jasper had left the visitors' room that my bail had been posted. And when I tried Jasper's cell today, I got a *the customer you are trying to reach is not available* message. I've tried not to worry. Jasper probably forgot to pay the bill, I tell myself. But each time I believe it a little less.

"I'm good," I say to Gideon as I head around to the far side of our father's car. "But thanks," I add, hoping it will make him stop looking at me like the only thing that can keep him from drowning is my absolution. I'm not sure I have any more to give.

"Where to?" Gideon asks once we're in the car, trying to sound cheerful, casual. "Want to grab breakfast or something? The food must be terrible in there."

"Um, maybe later," I say. I should tell Gideon about our mom right now. Get it over with. Instead, I just look away out the window. "Let's get going. As far from here as possible."

I just can't tell him. Not yet.

GIDEON JUST GOT his license. Turns out, he is a terrible driver. Nervous and slow, but then suddenly fast. Not that I should judge. Gideon has gotten himself behind the wheel, which is more than I can say. But when he finally lurches out of the detention facility parking lot, I am thrown back against the seat, nauseous already.

"Sorry," he says, pumping hard on the brakes. "I'm still getting the hang of it."

I nod and turn again toward the widow, watching the worn-out strip malls and boarded-up fast-food restaurants pass. The area around the detention facility is an ugly, desperate place. I should feel better leaving it behind. Instead, my dread is on the rise. Like I already know that what lies ahead is worse than what lies behind.

Gideon and I drive on for another twenty minutes, exchanging harmless chitchat between long pockets of silence. How was your cellmate? Very nice. What's the food like? Very bad. Did anyone try to beat you up? No. Every time I open my mouth and don't tell him our mom is alive, I feel even worse.

I'm relieved when we're finally pulling into downtown Newton. It looks exactly as it did when I left, but feels weirdly unfamiliar. Every corner seems potentially threatening now, every street suspiciously dark. And not just because I feel anxious (though I do). But because that is the way it has become.

It isn't until we've made the next right that I realize we've turned down Cassie's street. And, up ahead, there it is: Cassie's house, with its gingerbread peaked roof and ivy-covered facade, as picture-perfect as ever. I feel the moment Gideon realizes his mistake. He may not be an Outlier, but he's not an idiot.

"Oh, um, I—crap." He slams on the brakes so hard, I have to brace myself against the dashboard to avoid bashing my face into it. "Sorry, I wasn't thinking. I can just turn around, if you—"

"No." And even I'm surprised by how forcefully it comes out. I don't really know why. "I haven't, um, been here since her funeral. I don't know . . . I kind of want to see her house."

"Want" is the wrong word. "Need" would be more accurate. Like obsessively *must*. It feels like some kind of essential truth is buried in Cassie's past, our past. Like we will only break free of this terrible loop of heartbreak and loss once we finally arrive back at the start.

"Stop up there, just for a minute?" I point toward a nearby curb.

"Seriously?" Gideon asks, gripping the steering wheel tighter, hunched over it like an old man. He feels way out of his depth with the driving, not to mention managing me. "Are you sure?"

"Yeah, I'm sure," I lie. Luckily, Gideon has no way of knowing that. "Please, just for a minute."

Finally, Gideon lurches to a stop at the side of the road. The house looks exactly the same. It's only been two months since Cassie's funeral, still I expected more decomposition. Maybe this is why I needed to stop here: to be reminded that the world rages on no matter how many of us are cut down by its wake.

No, it's not that. That sounds good, but that's not why I'm here. It's something else. Something more specific. *Cassie's house. Cassie's house. Why?*

Cassie's journal, maybe? It could be. Jasper and I never did figure out who mailed those pages to him.

"WHO CARES WHO sent them?" Jasper asked.

We were sitting across the table from each other in the detention facility visiting room. Day thirteen of my incarceration, day thirteen of Jasper faithfully coming to see me. He sat, as he always did, with his hands tucked under his legs on the hard plastic chair. So he'd remember not to try to hold my hand. He'd forgotten once and had almost been permanently banned. *No touching. No exchanging of objects. Shirt and shoes required.* There weren't many rules. But they were enforced like nobody's business.

"*I* care who sent them," I said. "It makes me nervous not to know. It should make you nervous, too."

"Nervous?" Jasper asked. I looked for an edge in his voice. *Everything always makes you nervous.* But he didn't mean it that way. Jasper wasn't about subtext. It was one of the things I loved about him.

Yeah, loved. I hadn't said it to him yet. It was more like an idea I was trying on for size. But so far it fit. Much better than I would have thought. And I kept waiting for that to make me feel stupid, like I'd been tricked or something. But instead it felt like I'd trusted my way there.

"We should at least investigate."

"It was Maia. We already decided that."

"*You* decided," I said. "*I* want confirmation."

"Wait, you're not jealous, are you?" Jasper teased. I shot him a look, and he held up his hand. "Sorry, bad joke."

And then he blushed, like actual red cheeks, which was kind of old-fashioned. But then our whole two-week-long detention facility courtship had been all chaste conversation and hands to ourselves, in twenty-six-minute, guard-supervised increments. The truth was—despite what we'd been through—Jasper and I didn't know each other *that* well. But as we unfolded slowly in front of each other, we slid more tightly into place.

Turned out, Jasper was goofy. Much more so than I realized. And so brutally, heartbreakingly sensitive underneath his many rugged layers. He talked about his dad a lot, what it meant to be afraid you were going to become something you hated. He used that fear to explain how he kind of understood my anxiety. In a way, sort of.

"I'm going to need to hear Maia say it was her who sent the journal pages before I'll believe it," I said. "Otherwise, it's going to nag at me."

Jasper's face softened. "You want me to go ask Maia?" It was a token offer.

I nodded anyway. "Yes, please."

Jasper took a breath and closed his eyes. "Okay," he said, drawing out the word. "But only because I . . ." The color rushed back into his cheeks. He waited a beat before looking up at me. "For you, I will. But only for you."

READ ALL THE BOOKS IN THE
NEW YORK TIMES BESTSELLING
OUTLIERS TRILOGY!

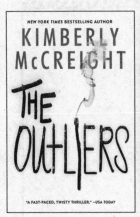

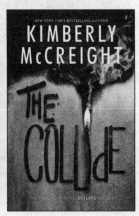

"A spellbinding thriller that keeps you guessing until the very last page."

—Sara Shepard, bestselling author of *Pretty Little Liars*

HARPER

An Imprint of HarperCollinsPublishers

www.epicreads.com

JOIN THE

Epic Reads

COMMUNITY

THE ULTIMATE YA DESTINATION

◀ **DISCOVER** ▶
your next favorite read

◀ **MEET** ▶
new authors to love

◀ **WIN** ▶
free books

◀ **SHARE** ▶
infographics, playlists, quizzes, and more

◀ **WATCH** ▶
the latest videos

www.epicreads.com